Praise for
New York Times and USA Today Bestselling Author

Diane Capri

"Full of thrills and tension, but smart and human, too."
*Lee Child, #1 World Wide Bestselling Author of Jack Reacher
Thrillers*

"[A] welcome surprise….[W]orks from the first page
to 'The End'."
Larry King

"Swift pacing and ongoing suspense are always
present…[L]ikable protagonist who uses her political
connections for a good cause…Readers should eagerly anticipate
the next [book]."
Top Pick, Romantic Times

"…offers tense legal drama with courtroom overtones, twisty
plot, and loads of Florida atmosphere. Recommended."
Library Journal

"[A] fast-paced legal thriller…energetic prose…an appealing
heroine…clever and capable supporting cast…[that will] keep
readers waiting for the next [book]."
Publishers Weekly

"Expertise shines on every page."
*Margaret Maron, Edgar, Anthony, Agatha and Macavity Award
Winning MWA Past President*

FULL METAL JACK

by *DIANE CAPRI*

Published by: AugustBooks
http://www.AugustBooks.com

ISBN: 978-1-942633-44-0

Original cover design by: Cory Clubb
Digital formatting by: Author E.M.S.

Full Metal Jack is a work of fiction. Names, characters, places, and incidents either are the product of the author's imagination or are used fictitiously, and any resemblance to actual persons, living or dead, business establishments, events, or locales is entirely coincidental.

Published in the United States of America.

Visit the author website:
http://www.DianeCapri.com

ALSO BY DIANE CAPRI

The Hunt for Jack Reacher Series
(in publication order with Lee Child source books in parentheses)

Don't Know Jack (The Killing Floor)

Jack in a Box (*novella*)

Jack and Kill (*novella*)

Get Back Jack (Bad Luck & Trouble)

Jack in the Green (*novella*)

Jack and Joe (The Enemy)

Deep Cover Jack (Persuader)

Jack the Reaper (The Hard Way)

Black Jack (Running Blind/The Visitor)

Ten Two Jack (The Midnight Line)

Jack of Spades (Past Tense)

Prepper Jack (Die Trying)

Full Metal Jack (The Affair)

The Jess Kimball Thrillers Series

Fatal Enemy (*novella*)

Fatal Distraction

Fatal Demand

Fatal Error

Fatal Fall

Fatal Edge (*novella*)

Fatal Game

Fatal Bond

Fatal Past (*novella*)

Fatal Dawn

CAST OF PRIMARY CHARACTERS

Kim L. Otto

Charles Cooper
Lincoln Perry
Eugene Hammer
Elizabeth Deveraux
Scott Greyson
Alec Murphy
Nina Cloud
Carlos Gaspar

and
Jack Reacher

Perpetually, for Lee Child, with unrelenting gratitude.

FULL METAL JACK

THE AFFAIR

by Lee Child

I was on the involuntary separation list…[He] said under the circumstances it would be the work of a moment to get me taken off again. No doubt about that…

"But your life wouldn't be worth living. You never get promoted again. You'd be terminal at major if you live to be a hundred. You'd be deployed to a storage depot in New Jersey. You can get off the separation list, but you'll never get off the shit list. That's how the army works. You know that."

I was thirty-six years old, a citizen of a country I had barely seen, and there were places to go, and there were things to do…There was company if I wanted it, and there was solitude if I didn't.

I picked the road at random, and I put one foot on the curb and one in the traffic lane, and I stuck out my thumb.

CHAPTER ONE

Friday, May 6
New York City, New York
1:15 a.m.

HE'D SLIPPED INSIDE UNNOTICED. Spoke to no one. Acknowledged nothing. He blended almost imperceptibly into the shadows inside the abandoned warehouse. Anticipation fed his smoldering rage like oxygen feeds embers before a wildfire.

He waited.

Black turtleneck shirt, black jeans and boots covered his white skin. Turned up collar on the black leather jacket hid his unshaven face. Black gloves enveloped his hands and wrists. A black wool beret covered his closely cropped brown hair.

The stale warehouse air had been warmed by the activities. He was too hot. Anger fueled his body heat, the hat retained it, and the wool itched like crazy.

Couldn't be helped.

The man in black knew too many of these people. Although he had seen none of them in years, someone might notice him.

The second-to-last thing he wanted was to be recognized.

The last thing he wanted was to fail.

His anticipation had built to a fever pitch over the years. Only with iron control had he managed the rage, always there under the surface. He'd have his revenge. He could feel it. Pak would pay. It would finally happen. Tonight.

He leaned against the steel support pole and peered into the dimly lit interior of the warehouse, ignoring the sweat trickling down inside his shirt.

The stale air was thick with the stench of sweaty humans, rancid smoke, and foul dogs. He drew a deep breath, inhaling it all. He'd missed the unmistakable smell. A unique blend signaling only one thing, buried deep in his reptilian brain, triggering his entire system to feel the thrill of the fight.

Snarling, howling, barking, cheers, and curses assaulted his ears, sending an electrical hum along every nerve in his body.

Fortunes were made and lost, all in a single night.

The potential for victory thrummed like a live wire in the cavernous space. The kind of victory few men throughout the world experienced even once in a lifetime.

The tension was palpable. Everyone could feel it. They craved it. Lived for it.

The man in black craved victory, too. Like a junkie craved heroin. Even after such a long period of abstinence, the embers of his desire smoldered.

He sometimes imagined that he'd lived a previous life. A time when dogfighting was the realm of fearless warriors. Perhaps he'd attended dog fights in the Roman Colosseum or fought wars alongside the Romans and the Britons. The same blood ran in his veins. He could feel it.

Something about the primitive nature of the sport appealed

to him. As it did to populations everywhere he'd been in the world. The magnetic pull of the sport drew bloodthirsty souls like nothing else. It was a sinkhole into which, once experienced, a man could fall deep and never emerge.

The power to suck people in was one reason why dogfighting was illegal in all fifty US states and most countries.

Another reason the sport was illegal was its popularity. If no one had wanted to participate, there'd be no need for laws against it. After all, there were no laws against dishwashing or lawn mowing or dozens of other activities no one on the planet clamored for, right? He grinned.

Dogfighting crimes were serious felonies. If caught, prison time was unavoidable. Which was why dogfighting circuits existed as far off the grid as they could get and still be found by savages like him who disrespected such misguided laws.

In cities like this one, abandoned warehouses in decrepit areas hosted the fights for one night before the circuit moved on to the next location. Authorities were bribed to look the other way if they noticed at all.

The man in black had been heavily involved in the dogfighting world during his last stint in Asia. He loved the fierce, beautiful beasts. Gallant fighters. He'd owned dogs back then. Sold them. Presented them at fights where hundreds of thousands of dollars changed hands in a single night.

When he returned to the states, his dogfighting days had ended abruptly. It was too risky for him to attend fights now.

Tonight was the first time he'd been near the arena. He hadn't realized how much he'd missed it.

He had reluctantly put his passion behind him. And moved on to other activities in the interim. More lucrative. Less risk. He had no desire to live the remainder of his life in prison.

The confinement alone would kill him.

But he'd monitored the organizers when he'd returned from Asia. He'd been waiting. For just this moment.

After two long years, the opportunity to kill his enemy had finally presented itself.

Tonight's crowd was the usual mix of dog owners and handlers, drug dealers and gang-bangers, and wannabes attracted by the illegal gambling.

From experience, he knew it was safer to assume everyone in the place was armed.

He'd brought a knife and two untraceable handguns along. One was holstered on his ankle. The second rested heavily against his torso, stuffed into his belt in the small of his back. Just in case. He didn't expect to use the guns. He wouldn't need to.

He scanned the cavernous room. If he'd been spotted, the watcher was too skilled to reveal himself.

But Pak could have been followed here. He was under constant surveillance by his own country inside its borders and every time he left it. He would have tried to sneak away from his bodyguards, and he might have managed it. He was also watched by security services in every country he visited.

Safest to assume Pak was being watched by enemies and allies at all times.

Which made the man in black's mission to kill him more difficult, but not impossible.

An hour after the qualifying fights began, he spied Pak across the smoky divide, close to the main fighting ring. Pak was easy to identify, even in the dim lighting amid the noisy crowd gathered around him.

The man in black's stomach clenched and his lip curled.

He flexed his fists inside the gloves. The obese North Korean was flat out disgusting. Always had been. Only his position and his power made him in any way palatable.

Ridding the world of Pak was a service to humanity, pure and simple.

Pak's pudgy face had reddened with heat and exertion and the stress of his wagers. He pinched a smoldering cigar between the fat fingers of one hand and grasped a glass of whiskey in the other.

The last of the amber liquid splashed out as Pak waved his arms, rooting for the dog he'd wagered would win. He'd taken heavy losses tonight and his desire to win had ramped up the tension close to his breaking point.

A slender, attractive woman dressed in a sexy silk business suit, no shirt, jacket open to her navel, was glued to Pak's side. Her name was Nina.

Tonight, Nina looked much like someone else—the love of his life the last time he'd seen her. Before Pak had kidnapped and killed her all those years ago.

Like his lover had been, Nina was way too good for Pak and everyone in the room could see that. Pak was a hideous troll. Nina was a goddess. Spectators might wonder what she wanted from him. It couldn't be helped. Pak had a weakness for beautiful women. Nina could get close enough to him when the man in black could not.

Nina gently removed the empty whiskey glass from Pak's hand with tapered fingers adorned with brightly polished fingernails flashing gold in the reflected light. She refilled the glass from a silver flask and placed the glass in Pak's sweaty palm. He downed the whiskey in two gulps. She refilled the glass again.

Watching her fawning over Pak was both exciting and revolting. The man in black's desire and revulsion flooded his body in waves, cresting and receding, like the rhythm of the sea.

He scanned the warehouse once more. Two qualifying fights battled in another dark corner. The winners would fight each other in the main ring later.

Safer to assume official and unofficial surveillance teams were stationed strategically throughout the building. He kept his distance and stayed in the shadows.

If Pak's dog won the fight he'd be a rich man.

For a very short time.

The main fight ended when Pak's one-hundred-twenty-five-pound Bully Kutta mauled the champion mixed-breed pit bull to submission.

Deafening applause and shouts of approval went up from the crowd. Nina played her part, laughing along with the rest, her total attention on Pak.

The sweaty, red-faced Pak cheered along with them. His wide grin revealed a mouth full of misshapen teeth almost more frightening than the bloody, defeated pit bull.

Pak collected fistfuls of bills from the gamblers. He dropped the whiskey glass on the ground as he filled both hands with the cash.

As more gamblers crowded Pak to pay their debts, Nina bent to retrieve the glass. The sexy woman slid behind the crowd and out of sight.

The man in black watched the show from afar and simply nodded when Nina slipped away. An overwhelming sense of accomplishment swelled his chest with every breath.

The deed was done. Pak was as good as dead. The poison he'd ingested with the whiskey would do its work.

Not immediately.

Not even tonight.

But later.

When Pak returned to his room.

After the whiskey glass and the flask had been destroyed.

When the sexy woman was long gone.

"May you die a lonely, painful death, you son of a bitch," the man in black muttered under his breath. "No one deserves that fate more than you."

He kept his gaze fixed on Pak for a few moments before he slipped farther into the shadows as the next fights began. The aromas and noises and thrills he craved enveloped him for the last time.

Only one loose end to clear up.

The woman, Nina.

But not yet.

And not here.

Ten minutes after Pak's big win, the man in black was on his way. He walked the first four blocks, scanning for threats and witnesses until he located the stolen sedan he'd parked on the street.

A piece of crap set of wheels had been rained on at least once after he'd parked it. Soot had settled on the raindrops leaving black residue on the paint.

The silver sedan looked worse than it actually was. The old beater was in good enough shape to drive a couple thousand miles at least. Enough to get him where he needed to go.

Not the kind of ride he'd normally be caught dead in.

But then, he wasn't the one he planned to bury in it.

He drove the sedan to the airport.

There he collected his personal effects and a change of

clothes from a locker. He stuffed the black outfit into three trash bags and disposed of them.

Then he moved to the rendezvous point where he met the sexy woman he'd left back at the warehouse.

Nina Cloud wasn't quite as young or attractive or sexy in the harsh overhead lighting of the terminal. She had some miles on her. She was forty, at least. Dark hair. Dark eyes. Native American. Not even the flashy gold fingernails remained to confirm potential witness accounts of her part in the murder. They'd been fake, too.

Nina offered a brown paper bag containing Pak's empty whiskey glass.

He slipped the bag into his pocket before he gave her a kiss and a stack of counterfeit fifty-dollar bills to show his appreciation. They were good counterfeits. No one would object to them.

Then he told her where to find the sedan and told her to drive herself home.

"Take your time. Do some sightseeing. You deserve a little fun," he said, pulling her close and kissing her a bit more thoroughly.

Breathlessly, she pulled away, a satisfied smile on her lips. "See you later."

"You bet," he replied as they turned and walked in opposite directions.

When he reached his gate, he looked back. Nina was already at the terminal's exit on her way to pick up the sedan. He didn't expect to see her alive again. Which was more than okay. It was perfect.

He grinned as he handed his boarding pass to the gate attendant and entered the jetway toward the plane.

CHAPTER TWO

Five Days Later
Wednesday, May 11
Washington, DC
9:15 a.m.

FBI SPECIAL AGENT KIM OTTO stepped out of the cab at the
J. Edgar Hoover FBI building and stood for a moment in the
foggy rain staring at the 935 Pennsylvania Avenue N.W.
entrance. Some said it was the most hideously ugly 2,800,000
square feet of building space in DC. Hard to argue the point.

Eight stories of damp, ugly concrete on one side, eleven
stories on the other, and three stories underground. The FBI had
been taking a media beating for the past few years. At this point,
even the building's architecture seemed untrustworthy.

A lifetime ago, simply entering FBI headquarters had filled
her with pride and excitement and a sense of belonging like no
other place on earth. Back then her chief ambition was to become
the first female director of the FBI. Back then she believed she'd
get there.

She felt none of those things today.

Kim had been working the Jack Reacher file since early November, and she'd traveled all over the country and parts of the world like a bloodhound. But she hadn't been to the Boss's office even once since she got that first 4:00 a.m. phone call.

Her assignment was off-the-books. Not undercover. Not sanctioned or monitored by the usual FBI channels. Zero supervision or accountability.

Which made it feel clandestine and lonely and extremely dangerous.

In the movies, working outside the well-trained team environment was made to seem glamorous. In real life, not so much. The work was threatening, treacherous, and too often deadly.

Kim wasn't exactly sure how she felt about walking into headquarters now, but pride and excitement were not in the mix. She was anxious, sure. Situation normal there. But what else?

She glanced at the wet scene, smelling nothing but exhaust fumes hanging on the heavy air. The famous cherry trees, a curious but welcome gift from Japan in the last century, had bloomed late this year. On the ride from National Airport, she'd seen a few wilted blossoms barely hanging on, here and there.

The National Cherry Blossom Festival had finished weeks ago, but the entire city was still flooded with tourists.

Too many people, traipsing through the puddles with their umbrellas, no reliable method for separating hostiles from friendlies. When she'd lived in Georgetown with her ex-husband, Van Nguyen, back in law school, she'd made every effort to avoid the crowds. Now, as then, the effort was futile.

An overwhelming sense of déjà vu settled on her shoulders, weighing her down whenever she thought about Van. It was strange how viscerally she reacted to him, even now. Humans seemed to absorb old wounds into our DNA somehow. We never let the anger.

She rarely allowed herself to go back there, even in her mind. She hadn't heard anything from him in years, which was the good news. She wasn't sure how she'd react if she met him on the streets of DC, out of the blue. She shivered involuntarily, all the way to her toes.

She shook off her sense of disquiet along with the rain sliding into her coat collar, squared her shoulders, grabbed her identification, and hustled toward the employee entrance. She felt like she was headed to the guillotine, but she couldn't be late. She didn't want to get fired today and she sensed she was in enough trouble already.

After she'd cleared security, Kim noticed the television mounted on the wall above the reception desk. The story that had filled the national newscasts for days was all about the mysterious poisoning of a North Korean diplomat in New York, identified by the American news media as Hana Pak.

After being hospitalized for a couple of days, the man had died. She'd heard lots of saber-rattling from the North Korean government, but he had no family and few friends. Not many who knew him or knew of him mourned Hana Pak.

She took the elevator and walked down the corridor to the Boss's office, removing her trench coat and folding the wet sides together. She draped it over her arm, knocked on the big wooden door, and entered.

She glanced out the window behind his desk.

The view wasn't that impressive. When she'd worked in a Chicago law firm, her first job after law school, her boss had been a mid-level partner. He'd had a much better office than this, with a stunning view of the city. His annual income was about ten times higher than the director of the bureau, too.

She could have surpassed her old boss by now. Sometimes she regretted getting off the glide path to a big law leadership job. Finding her soul mate. Starting a family. She'd left all of that behind a long time ago, too. Had she made the right choices?

Some days, she really wondered.

A television played Hana Pak news, which had been all over every broadcast station. The Boss was half listening while standing near the large desk, a hammer in his hand. He was hanging a framed photo of himself with the president. When she entered, he gave the nail two solid whacks and squared the picture on the wall. He placed the hammer on his desk and gestured her toward a chair.

He picked up the remote and turned off the TV.

"Strange story, isn't it?" Kim said, shaking her head. "Some North Korean diplomat who never comes to the US is in New York for two days, and someone kills him."

"Pak was a butcher who had a lot of enemies. One was finally able to kill him. No real surprise. Did the world a favor," he replied absently.

"You knew the guy?" She stood behind the chair he'd offered.

"Anyone who served in South Korea for any period of time bumped up against Pak, one way or another. Never a pleasant experience." The Boss shrugged and changed the subject. "I'm worried about you, Otto."

She sucked in a sharp breath. His simple statement seemed ominous, considering the source. She knew he had no affection for her. The feeling was mutual now, although their relationship had been much better once. Another thing that had changed.

He settled into the oversized black leather chair, his back

toward the window, and folded his hands over a slim blue folder on the desktop. He waved her to sit in one of the chairs opposite the desk and waited until she perched on it.

"You haven't begun to romanticize Reacher, have you?" he asked.

The question was bizarre, and it immediately raised her blood pressure. She arched her eyebrows, stalling. "Whatever do you mean?"

"This assignment is difficult. Not many could handle the demands. I thought you were up to it. Your record suggested that you were the best agent for the job." He paused, staring at her as if he could see all the way to her soul. "Was I wrong?"

CHAPTER THREE

Wednesday, May 11
Washington, DC
9:35 a.m.

WHAT COULD SHE say to that?

The Reacher assignment wasn't merely difficult. It was damned impossible. Had been from the start.

She'd seen more action and collateral damage in the past few weeks than in all of her life before. Her assignment was so far from difficult that the understatement was laughable.

Yet, it seemed like he wanted a response from her, so she simply said, "I appreciate your confidence."

She left out the "Sir." They were long past that level.

"I have confidence that Reacher is the best man for the job we need him to do. I'm worried that my confidence in *you* has been misplaced," he replied sternly, like a father chastising his daughter for breaking curfew. "You haven't found Reacher yet. I'm beginning to wonder if you ever will."

As if he'd believed in the team when Gaspar was her partner.

But now that Gaspar had retired, she was somehow lacking. That's what she interpreted from his tone.

Kim felt fury rising in her gut. Who was he to find her wanting? She was the one who'd been out there, in the fight, dodging bullets and worse while he sat back and watched.

He was welcome to do the job himself if he thought he could do it better. Or find someone else to use for cannon fodder.

Grace under pressure, her mother's voice repeated in her head. She didn't speak every thought that came into her head.

She nodded. "It would help if I knew what the job is that you want Reacher to do."

"Still classified and above your clearance." He frowned. "You don't need to know."

"It would help me to understand what I'm doing. Perform better," she said stubbornly.

"If you can't work under these parameters, now's the time to say so, Otto," he stated flatly.

She held her temper. The straitjacket was okay when she thought she was merely conducting a background check on a job candidate.

Now that her assignment had been upgraded to a manhunt, she wanted more intel.

Not that it mattered what she wanted.

She wasn't going to get more intel.

Take it or leave it.

And leaving it was simply not an option.

The Boss tapped the blue folder with two fingers. "The last few reports you've filed seem…misguided. Off-center."

"How so?" she asked, controlling her anger with the sheer force of will.

He frowned and leaned in, an expression resembling concern

on his face. As if he cared what happened to her. She knew damn well he didn't give a whit.

Matter-of-factly, he said, "You've gone off-mission. Reacher is not some sort of romantic hero. Not even remotely. Get that out of your head."

"You're kidding me." Her tone was barely civil, wondering where this was going and how soon she could escape.

"Make no mistake, Otto. Reacher can seem like a good man. He's not. Underneath a paper-thin suit of civility, he's a vicious killer. Particularly when provoked. And a lot of things provoke him."

She nodded. *Tell me something I don't know.*

"The army created him. Intentionally. We spent a lot of time and a lot of money training him to be exactly what he is," he lowered his chin and stared over his reading glasses. "And he's damned good at it. You've seen all his commendations, medals. You know he's an expert."

"Yeah, I understand that, even from the thin file of intel you gave me," she said, pure rage bubbling beneath the words.

She could have said there was more to Reacher than his skills as a soldier.

She'd seen Reacher's aftermath, up close and personal. She knew how he rolled.

She might have pointed out that Reacher had saved her life. More than once.

But she didn't say any of those things.

What would be the point? Arguing with the Boss solved nothing. Unless she wanted to quit now. Which she most definitely did not.

Reacher had gotten under her skin. She *wanted* to find him now. The assignment was no longer just a job. It was a point of pride for her. And if she died trying, well, everyone dies of something.

"*Do* you understand, Otto? I wonder. Because it seems like you're losing your focus." He slammed the palm of his hand onto the blue folder. The abrupt noise made her jump. "Your job is to find Reacher, when and where I send you. Period. No improvising."

She stared at him.

"If you need more resources, you ask me. I decide how you do this job. *Me*." His nostrils flared and his tone hardened as he jabbed the blue folder with his index finger to emphasize each clipped order. "You don't make up your own rules. You don't go rogue. You don't follow your whims. You definitely do not ask your own contacts to get Reacher to help you, for crap's sake!"

"I understand," she said again, hurling clipped words and a frosty tone right back at him.

This would be the time to toss her badge on the table and walk out.

But she wasn't ready to do that. And the simple fact was that he did have more resources than she could muster alone. He kept intel from her and refused backup. He had his reasons. She respected that. But she didn't see the reason for it and she didn't like it.

She didn't believe in the no-win scenario.

He withheld the tools she needed for the job. She'd find other tools. Simple as that. After she'd accomplished the mission, the rest of the chips could fall where they may.

"Let me be crystal clear." The Boss stuck out his pugnacious chin. "It's not your job to rescue Reacher's friends, or his maybe babies, or his nephew. We're not paying you to bond with his girlfriends. Or any of the rest of the crap you've been doing."

He was simply thumping his chest. Charles Cooper had been an army general and then the Deputy Director of the FBI for more years than she'd been alive. He could end her life as she knew it right here, right now.

It was a point worth keeping in mind.

"And another thing," he said coldly, "You work for me. Not Lamont Finlay. If your project needs to be run up the chain of command, I'll do it myself. Are we clear?"

CHAPTER FOUR

Wednesday, May 11
Washington, DC
9:55 a.m.

HIS COMPLAINTS WERE SO outrageous that she could barely hold her wrath. Lips pursed into a hard line, she simply nodded. For more than a full second, she considered throwing her badge at his head.

But raging and throwing tantrums was not her style.

Nor would expressing her anger have solved the core issue.

The problem was that he didn't like her going off *his* book to follow the leads *she* dug up on Reacher, sometimes getting help from Finlay or Gaspar or a third party to do it.

She wouldn't change her methods. She was the agent in charge of this mission. He was The Boss. Those facts didn't make her his toady.

So if he wanted one of his buttoned-up boys who did nothing but follow his orders, he could get someone else. And she might have tossed restraint out the window and said so.

But she could tell by the expression on his face that she didn't need to.

He already understood.

She could get the job done. And she would. And she'd do it her way.

And if she didn't make it back?

Well, too bad. He'd chosen her because she was expendable. They both knew the score.

He was just blowing off steam.

He wasn't about to destroy her.

Not yet, anyway.

She held his gaze and her tongue and waited.

After more glaring, nostrils flared, he said, "You're going to Carter's Crossing, Mississippi. The file contains all you need to know about the last case Reacher worked there before the army kicked him out."

"Kicked him out? They didn't actually do that." She cocked her head, puzzled. "He was honorably discharged. No court-martial. Not even a dishonorable. The files don't contain anything suggesting he was expelled, not for any reason. That means they didn't have enough on him to do anything, let alone kick him out."

He gave her a curt nod, barely more than a quick jerk of the chin. "There's official records available for posterity, and then there's true facts. You should know the difference."

She did know. Certain types of files were always sanitized, one way or another. And Reacher's army files were exceptionally thin. Someone had surgically removed everything remotely embarrassing. Or useful.

Which wasn't unusual for sensitive employment files. Especially when it came to decorated officers who had been allowed to slip away quietly when they should have been canned.

Reacher had been a hero. He'd collected more than his share of medals for bravery in combat.

Of course, no written record explained why he'd had to leave the army. Because senior officers would have had things to answer for. Maybe even a few high-ranking civilians, too.

Guaranteed mutual destruction if such things were ever committed to reports and the right people came looking.

But they'd *made* him leave the army.

For sure.

Otherwise, he'd still be a soldier.

He was that kind of guy. Do or die.

To him, leaving the army would have been the same as dying. He'd never have resigned voluntarily without pressure. She'd learned that and much more about Reacher over the past few weeks.

So what the Boss meant was that someone higher up persuaded Reacher it was time to go and he agreed. For reasons of his own.

"I see," she said between gritted teeth. "What's in Carter's Crossing, Mississippi?"

"An army base. Slated for closure soon. They've started drawing down personnel. Kelham won't exist much longer."

"Why?"

"Outlived its usefulness. The world has changed. We don't need all that real estate anymore. We don't need to staff it, either," he said.

"Why did Reacher go there?" Kim asked.

"Back then, it was a dead woman that called Reacher down. He was still in the 110th Special Investigative Unit, but he went in undercover."

"Why?"

"Because his CO thought a person or persons attached to the local army base might have had something to do with the murder."

"They thought Army Rangers killed a female civilian?" she shuddered, head cocked. "Were they? Responsible?"

"Final reports are a little fuzzy," he said with a scowl. "Her throat had been cut. The way Army Rangers are taught to do it. One cut. Straight and deep. Does the job fairly quickly. Rangers know that. Which meant the suggestion that a Ranger did the deed was…plausible."

"How many dead at the end of Reacher's investigation? Total," she asked. With Reacher, death and mayhem were as common as dust in the aftermath of a sandstorm.

"The final numbers aren't in the files," the Boss said.

"There's a shock," she quipped, earning a deeper scowl in response.

Reacher was probably responsible for the increased body count, one way or another. He'd likely found the killer and did what Reacher always did. Dispensed his own brand of justice.

No doubt in Reacher's mind that the guy deserved it.

Maybe the guy *had* deserved everything he got and more.

He continued, still stern, still angry, "There's trouble in Carter's Crossing again. Another dead woman. A similar cause of death to the old case. If we're lucky, Reacher may feel like he needs to fix the situation like he thought he did before. He's not one of ours anymore. We won't be able to run interference for him this time."

"Got it," she replied, because a response seemed to be expected, even as he refused to be straight with her. He never showed his hole cards.

He didn't expect Reacher to show up in Carter's Crossing simply to find out who killed a woman he didn't even know.

Reacher lived totally off-the-grid, wandering around according to his whims. He wouldn't even hear about a single murder in such a small town in the middle of the country. Her death wouldn't make the national news. It's not like someone could call him up and tell him, even if they'd wanted to.

If Reacher were that easy to find, Kim wouldn't have been given this job at all.

Which meant the Boss wasn't telling her the whole story, either. He never did. He didn't flat out lie. Nothing that obvious.

So sure. There might be another dead woman. Same method. Maybe even the same killer, although it wasn't like Reacher to have left the first scumbag alive.

But none of that was the reason the Boss thought Reacher might show up in Carter's Crossing.

Whatever his intel was on that score, he wouldn't share it with her. He never did that, either.

"So the current CO at Kelham, does he know I'm coming?" Kim asked.

"Let me be clear," the Boss said, leaning forward again. "You're already off-the-books. Stay that way. There will be authorized personnel looking into this thing. Including a guy named Major Lincoln Perry. You can work with him and liaise with the locals, too, if you want. But that's all."

"So the answer is no. You're not running interference for me at Kelham," she replied cheekily. Which earned her another glare. "So I'm using my cover story. Doing a classified background check on Reacher. Shouldn't be a problem."

"See that it isn't," the Boss said, poking the blue folder again, making her wonder what was inside it. "Your job is to be on the scene if Reacher shows up. Look for him. You know where he's likely to hang out by now. You see him, you call me. I'll deal with him myself. I don't need a dead agent to explain at the moment."

"Yes, sir," she said again, trying not to smirk.

The Boss didn't care if she died. He just didn't want to be the one on the hot seat when it happened.

Plausible deniability, they called it.

She understood the desire.

Sooner or later, if she survived, she'd be required to testify somewhere about hunting Reacher. She'd need plausible deniability, too. Many things about her Reacher assignment should be concealed from investigative spotlights.

But the last thing she intended to do was simply observe what happened in Carter's Crossing and report back to him. She'd come way too far down the road for that. If the Boss didn't understand that much, he was dumber than she gave him credit for.

"Details in the file." He picked up a padded manila envelope like all the others he'd sent her over the past few weeks and tossed it to her.

She didn't need to open it to know an encrypted cell phone and a jump drive rested inside.

"Car's waiting downstairs. Your flight to Memphis leaves in two hours."

"Memphis?"

"Closest major airport. About a ninety-minute drive from there. You'll have a vehicle."

"Got it." She stood and walked toward the door.

She stopped with her hand on the knob and turned to look at him, backlit by the big windows behind him so that she couldn't see his features clearly. Which was how he always seemed these days. Shadowed. Menacing.

"What about my new partner? Gaspar's been retired a while now. FBI field agents travel in pairs. Safer that way," she said.

"I'm still working on that," he said smoothly. "Gaspar was perfect for the job. Hard to find a replacement."

She believed him. He'd had plenty of time to replace Gaspar if he intended to do so. Gaspar had said they were both expendable. Finding another expendable agent might not be easy.

"I guess that leaves me on my own until I locate myself a partner, then," she said, stuffing the manila envelope into the pocket of her trench coat. Which pissed him off, as she'd intended.

"Just follow orders for a change, and you'll be fine," he said wearily as if tired of dealing with her. He probably was. The feeling was mutual. "There's a local sheriff. Rumor is that he's more than competent. You're not jumping out of a jet into an active volcano."

She walked through the door and left him glaring at her back.

On the way to the car, she turned up her collar against the blowing rain and hunched into her coat.

She wondered what the hell had happened in Carter's Crossing, Mississippi, fifteen years ago to get Reacher kicked out of the army and send him living so far off the grid no one could find him.

More to the point, what impending disaster might draw him back to Carter's Crossing after all this time?

CHAPTER FIVE

Wednesday, May 11
Kelham Army Base, Mississippi
11:30 a.m.

GENERAL ALEC MURPHY had a long list of tasks to complete before Friday. He kept his head down, his reading glasses on his nose, and his mind on the work at hand.

Most of the work had been done and the soldiers redeployed. The remaining base personnel were similarly occupied with final duties.

Best-case scenario was that everything would go smoothly from this point until he turned the lights out Friday morning. Which wouldn't happen. He sighed. Things rarely went smoothly with so many moving parts to be coordinated.

He'd left the most tedious work for last. Paperwork. The amount of paper the army could generate when closing a facility like Kelham would have been overwhelming to any normal civilian.

But not to Murphy.

He'd seen it all before.

In triplicate.

The work was somewhat mindless, which left him free to ponder. Damned shame he was ending his army career in a place like Kelham, and he was more than a little peeved about it.

There'd been a time when a guy like him would have been sitting at the Joint Chief's table instead of being shoved out of the way.

Murphy was a man's man. He got things done. The old-fashioned way.

Time was, his results alone would have been more than enough to satisfy the brass. These days, they all wanted to focus on the methods and motives more than results. Can't do this. Don't do that. Pure crap, that's what it was.

The army had changed, like everything else in the world. Passed him by. This man's army wasn't the army Murphy had signed up for. Not even close.

If they hadn't pushed him to retire, he'd have done it anyway. He had no desire to be a part of whatever the army was becoming.

Murphy drained his coffee mug, reviewed and signed and set aside inventory forms and transfer forms and forms for every other damned thing. His sergeant had carried them into his office by the armload and then collected them again after Murphy finished.

He shrugged. Kelham was slated for closure. Somebody had to do the grunt work. That's what soldiers were for. Always had been grunts. Always would be. No way to change the army's role in the scheme of things, and no one had the desire to change it anyway.

Which didn't mean he'd miss Kelham when he closed up shop and bugged out on Friday at dawn.

Not that it mattered how he felt about the base or this Podunk town or the rubes who lived here. He'd been a soldier more than half his life. He served where he was sent and did what he was told and he was damned good at it. Simple as that.

He wasn't leaving the army. The army had left him high and dry long ago. He just hadn't noticed until it was too late.

Again, the sergeant came in without knocking, carrying another armload, and the cup of black coffee he'd requested, and said, "General, you have a call on line three."

Murphy looked up from the mass of closure papers, "What?"

"Major Eugene Hammer on line three," the sergeant repeated.

"Who is he and what does he want?" Murphy demanded.

"I don't know, Sir. I asked. He said he outranks me and to put the call through, and that was an order," the sergeant replied as if he was more than happy to comply. He had plenty of work to do, too.

The skeleton crew still left on base was working almost around the clock to get the place closed and move on to more interesting work. Murphy, too.

The sergeant walked to the desk, picked up the completed paperwork and deposited the new batch, collected the empty coffee cup, and walked out, closing the door behind him.

Murphy looked at the blinking light on his phone, a signal that Major Hammer was still there. He'd wait until hell froze over if he had to.

"Damn straight." Murphy nodded.

Majors waited for generals. That's the way the system worked. Murphy grinned. He enjoyed that part of the army. He liked being at the top of the food chain. He'd miss the privilege of status when he retired.

He left Hammer waiting and drank the coffee while it was hot. He thumbed through the current stack of paperwork, scribbling his initials where required.

When he reached the end of the pile and swallowed the last of the coffee, he glanced at the phone. Hammer was still there.

Fifteen minutes.

That was nothing.

Murphy had waited hours for a superior officer many times.

Briefly, he considered going to lunch before he took the call. Nah. No point in jerking this guy around.

Hammer was probably calling about equipment or personnel or some such. Might as well get it handled.

Murphy picked up the handset and pushed the button. Gruffly, he stated, "General Murphy."

"Major Eugene Hammer, MP, sir. 110th Special Investigative Unit. This is a courtesy call to let you know that I'll be arriving at Kelham today at eighteen-hundred hours," Hammer said firmly, without inquiry or apology.

Which meant he was following orders. No more, no less. Straight up.

Murphy appreciated the style. Old school. Just the way he liked it.

As if Hammer's words were nothing out of the ordinary, Murphy said, "What's this about, Major?"

"I'll brief you when I arrive, Sir." Hammer paused. "It's a little sensitive."

Which meant he'd been ordered to deliver his message in person.

"You know we're closing down here Friday at oh-five-hundred. Cupboards are bare. None of the comforts of home. Might want to bring your own pillow," Murphy replied.

"Yes, Sir. I understand. Thank you, Sir." Hammer said, like a new recruit, before he hung up.

Which made Murphy both curious and suspicious.

A special investigator's arrival was strange enough at any time. Particularly when he hadn't been invited. Kelham had its own MPs.

What sensitive thing could be going on here to justify the disruption at this point?

Murphy didn't spend any more time guessing about Hammer's assignment. He had more important things to do.

CHAPTER SIX

Wednesday, May 11
Memphis, TN
3:00 p.m.

ON THE WAY TO MEMPHIS, Kim had read the contents of
the jump drive the Boss had included in the manila envelope.
The dead woman was a difficult case. The autopsy was hot off
the coroner's desk, still stamped classified, and the results were
anything but straight forward.

She'd also spent half-an-hour online during the flight
checking out the town and its public persona. Carter's Crossing
had a long and convoluted history, even in the official versions.

It was an old town near the northeastern corner of
Mississippi, close to the Alabama and Tennessee state lines. It
grew up during the nineteenth century and almost died in the
next. But for government spending, it probably would have. The
fate of Carter's Crossing seemed tied to the whims of
transportation.

Like a lot of towns in Middle America, Carter's Crossing

thrived when the railroads ruled the country. It was a stop on the route for locomotives to take on water and where the passengers could get a meal.

The town had its expansion and contraction along with the fate of the railroads until about 1950 when the Federal Government put an army base there. That worked out well for Carter's Crossing until the interstate highway system was built.

At that point, the base was too far east of I-55 and too far west of I-65 to thrive. Economies were fed by trucking and motor vehicle travel on the interstates instead of railroads. Carter's Crossing dwindled until it might have become a ghost town, like so many others.

The development of air travel changed the town's fortunes again.

Kelham Army Base had an airstrip to make it viable in the aviation age.

Until the base experienced a similar growth and decline pattern following the fortunes of the army.

Warfare had changed, and so had the need for soldiers. Kelham, like many other military bases around the country, had little to offer the modern military.

Fifteen years ago, when Reacher worked undercover on the three murders in Carter's Crossing, Kelham had already been downsized into little more than a specialized Ranger school. Which it still was.

Which meant that whatever Reacher was involved in back then didn't hit the fan enough to result in closing the base at that time.

Over the past fifteen years, the town's fortunes had improved. Industry and good jobs were lured in by tax breaks and cheap labor. A casino had opened up on the Native American reservation on the outskirts.

Jobs and tourism combined had increased the town's population from ten to sixteen thousand. Which was a respectably sized community. The town Kim grew up in hadn't been much larger.

She'd checked the maps. Tupelo, McKellar-Sipes, and Muscle Shoals regional airports were all closer to Carter's Crossing. She'd have a long drive from Memphis.

Kim assumed the Boss had chosen Memphis because it was bigger and provided more options, including nonstop flights from DC and other cities. More flights and passengers milling around made anonymity somewhat feasible, too.

When the captain announced they'd begun the initial descent, she stashed her electronics, tightened her seatbelt, and gripped both armrests, prepared, as always, for the worst.

Twenty minutes later, the plane descended through the clouds and set down on the foggy tarmac, on schedule and without mishap, which was always a miracle to her. Flying was one of her least favorite activities. She was always relieved to have her feet firmly on the ground.

As the plane taxied to the gate, her mind returned to the job at hand.

Reacher's contact back then had been the local sheriff, Elizabeth Deveraux. She was now the mayor. She was also expecting Kim to show up in her office on time tomorrow morning. Kim glanced at her watch. So far, so good.

She'd flown into Memphis before and had been stuck there a couple of times. The terminal was easily navigable and cleverly decorated with music themes. She knew exactly where to go.

After she disembarked, she rolled her travel case and laptop past an oversized guitar painted with tigers toward the rental car desk where she picked up her keys.

In the rainy parking lot, she found the Lexus SUV easily enough, stowed her bags, adjusted the seat and mirrors, and picked up US Highway 72 outside the airport toward Carter's Crossing, which was about ninety miles east.

She'd arrive long before her scheduled meeting with Mayor Deveraux. Which meant she'd have time for a nice dinner, maybe even a glass of wine or two, followed by a solid night's sleep. So far, this trip was shaping up to be better than she'd expected.

Plenty of time on the foggy route to Carter's Crossing to think about the contents of the files on that jump drive. Plenty of time once she got there to figure out how she'd approach Deveraux in the morning.

She picked up her personal cell phone and called Gaspar. The Boss would be listening to the conversation, but she didn't care. Gaspar was a man she could trust. She still thought of him as her partner in the hunt for Reacher, even though he'd retired from the FBI. He'd made it clear that he would continue to help her with the case as much as he could, and anything else he could assist her with, within reason.

He answered on the third ring. "What's happening, Suzy Wong? How's the weather in Detroit?"

She could hear the smile in his voice and it eased her anxiety, as it always did. "It was okay when I left. Spring has sprung, the birds and the bees are birthing their young, and all that. But it's warm and clammy and I'm dodging rain showers here."

"Here at Scarlett Investigations, the weather is always perfect. The work's interesting, too. You should join us," he teased, deadly serious. When she didn't reply, he asked, "How's John Lawton doing?"

"Haven't talked to him much." Kim frowned. "He's still on medical leave. Will be for a while."

Gaspar paused a moment, then picked up with the easy question. "Where are you headed?"

"Carter's Crossing, Mississippi."

"Never heard of it."

"Exactly. It's somewhere between Sweet Home Alabama and Heartbreak Hotel, I guess."

"What are you talking about?" Gaspar said, peeved now. She imagined his scowling face and grinned. It was too easy to wind him up.

"You're a music fan, Chico. You should know this. Not far east from Memphis, in which I am not walking, as enjoyable as that might be. Just west of Alabama where, today, the skies most definitely are not blue," she said, watching the dreary road ahead.

The traffic was mostly nonexistent, but every now and then, a pair of headlights broke through the gray in the westbound lanes across the median to her left.

"Let me guess. Cooper has you charging after Reacher in one of those small American towns where Reacher likes to mix things up?" He paused, and then his tone turned deadly serious. "And I take it you're alone."

"Bingo." She slowed for an eighteen-wheeler entering the foggy road ahead from a gas station on the corner. They probably had hot, black coffee for sale in there. She was tempted to stop, but she didn't feel like making an effort. So she gave the place a longing glance as she whizzed past.

Once the trucker righted the big rig on the asphalt, he began to pick up speed. She let him get several lengths ahead. The last thing she needed was to rear-end his trailer out in the middle of nowhere.

How long would it take to get a tow truck out here in the middle of nowhere, USA, she mused briefly.

"You been following the murder of that North Korean diplomat? Crazy stuff, isn't it? Reads like a spy novel." Gaspar was making conversation while he manipulated the keyboard. When she didn't reply, he said, "So besides keeping track of where you are at all times, which I'm happy to do, how can I be of assistance to you?"

She raised the corner of her lip in a quick, mirthless grin. In all the ways that mattered, Gaspar was more reliable than the Boss any day of the week. Every time she went into the field, she missed his steady presence.

Kim understood why he'd retired. He'd been shot during a mission gone bad long before she met him. He simply couldn't do the job. He was in constant pain and could barely walk around.

Putting his life on the line every day when he had five kids and a wife to consider didn't make sense.

So he'd taken a big paying job in the private sector.

Smartest thing for him to do under the circumstances.

Not so great for her.

Even with his physical limitations, no one had her back like Gaspar. Since she'd been doing this job solo, the risk factors had pushed her anxiety into the red zone and kept the needle hard against the peg.

Nothing to be done about losing her secret weapon.

So she pressed on.

She squared her shoulders and peered into the gloom. Gaspar's physical skills were weakened by his on-the-job injuries. But his background gave him the ability to think like Reacher. She'd relied on that skill to save lives more than once, including her own.

Kim didn't plan to let Gaspar go as long as he was willing to serve.

She shook off the melancholy. Because it didn't matter now.

Gaspar had retired and she was out in the middle of the fog on her own, chasing Reacher once again.

"Talk to me, Otto." Gaspar's far-away voice came through the speaker and she realized she'd left him hanging on for a while.

"Yeah. Sorry." She cleared her throat. "Okay, you can track my phone, no problem. How about this SUV?"

"Already got it. I see you inside the vehicle on the dashcam. I've located you on the map. I can probably pull up a visual of the exterior of the SUV from one of the satellites if I need more context," he reported as he worked through the issues. "The bigger problem is getting help to you if you need it. Scanning the area, there's no help anywhere near Carter's Crossing that I can see. No FBI Field Office closer than Memphis. No big towns nearby for civilian emergency services. Does the place even have a police department?"

She heard a motorcycle engine revving in the distance and glanced in the rearview mirror to see him approaching fast behind her.

The rider was leaning forward, encased in black leather from fingertips to toes. His head was completely covered by a glistening black helmet with a face shield. His entire body, and his sporty red motorcycle, were glossy and slick from the pelting rain.

She didn't envy him. He had to be cold and wet out there. She returned her full attention to the foggy road ahead, both hands firmly on the steering wheel.

"Yeah, the town's not that small, Chico," Kim replied, "I guess they do have some sort of local law enforcement. The current mayor is the former sheriff. She worked with Reacher on the last case of his army career."

Gaspar whistled, low and slow. "Reacher's last case? We never found anything about that in the army files before. Where did you get the intel? Not Cooper."

Since he'd retired, Gaspar had taken to calling the Boss by his name, Charles Cooper. Guess Gaspar figured he could do as he pleased now. She felt a little twinge of envy. Kim hadn't been free to do as she pleased in years. Hell, maybe she'd never been that free.

"The Boss gave me what I have, such as it is." She glanced into the rearview mirror again and frowned.

The motorcycle edged out around her to pass. When he had a view of the oncoming lane, he drifted back into position behind her SUV. Almost like he was hiding there or something.

"So the file's been redacted. Which means you've got much less information than you should have," Gaspar said harshly, fingers clacking keys as he talked. "I see you sent me the files. I'll take a look. Meanwhile, give me the highlights."

"Reacher was down here undercover. There's an army base in Carter's Crossing. Kelham, it's called."

The noise of the red motorcycle's engine was like an annoyingly large mosquito buzzing loud as a chainsaw too close to her ear.

"I've heard of it. Back in my army days. Kind of a down-and-out place full of misfits and castoffs, if I recall correctly. Never knew where it was, though," Gaspar replied. He sounded like he'd kicked back and crossed his ankles, which was his favorite thinking position. "What was Reacher doing there?"

The buzzing chainsaw was too loud and too annoying. She tried to ignore it.

"An army captain with a powerful daddy was suspected of some kind of involvement with the murder of three local women. Reacher was sent down to figure that out."

She wished the red speedster would just pass already and get on with going wherever he needed to be in such a damned hurry.

"I see," Gaspar said harshly. "Did Reacher figure things out? The murders, I mean?"

"Presumably. The file's unclear on that point. But I'll be asking the mayor about the specifics."

"Doesn't make sense," Gaspar said.

"What doesn't?"

"Doesn't seem like a situation that should have booted Reacher from the army. It's not easy to get rid of an officer like Reacher. Once you get to a certain level, they don't usually kick you out," Gaspar replied.

"It's all murky. You'll see when you read the files. Some of it was bad timing. The army was bloated back then." She glanced into the rearview mirror and tightened her grip on the steering wheel. "They needed to pare down. Reacher was a major and majors were too plentiful. They were looking to weed a few from the garden. He was expendable."

The big rig ahead was slowing again, but she couldn't see the cause. Maybe he was planning to turn. She slowed her speed and tried to release tension in her shoulders.

"Or unlucky. Depending on how you look at it. Can't imagine he was happy about leaving," Gaspar said.

"Hard to say. Reacher's a pragmatic guy. He was probably okay with it. It's not like they gave him a choice."

The motorcycle kept nosing out into the passing lane and then falling back, inching closer to her bumper every time. His recklessness made her nervous.

She said, "I mean, Reacher leaving the army on his own two feet was a lot better than a court-martial and incarceration at Leavenworth."

"Was that the choice they gave him?" Gaspar didn't say the options were unlikely. Because he knew deals like that had been made before.

Kim said, "Not in so many words. But reading between the lines, I'd say those were the two most likely alternatives."

She noticed the semi slowing as it approached a crossroads ahead.

Traffic on the narrow two-lane county road was supposed to stop before entering US 72. She couldn't see any reason to slow down. US 72 had the right of way.

The truck driver had no doubt traveled this way many times before. He seemed uncertain about traffic crossing the highway. He probably had a good reason.

Miles back, she'd passed a small sign pointed vaguely north along the county road toward a small town called Hopewell. But now, at this crossroads, no signs pointed to a town in any direction.

The motorcyclist seemed to notice the truck driver's behavior a bit late. The cyclist ran up almost to Kim's bumper before he backed off slightly.

If she barely tapped the brakes, the cyclist would hit the back of her Lexus.

She sucked in her breath and continued to slow without braking.

"Back off," she whispered.

The driver of the red sport bike, or whatever it was, had to know the reality.

Motorcycle hits vehicle. Motorcycle loses. Motorcycle driver, too.

Simple as that.

"What the hell did Reacher do to get kicked out of the army?" Gaspar mused as if he truly couldn't fathom such a thing. She imagined him swiping a palm over his face and shaking his head.

She tried to focus on the conversation and her driving at the same time. Her hands cramped because she gripped the steering wheel too tight.

She said, "It's possible he killed four people. Two of them army officers. And he definitely disobeyed orders. But mainly, he pissed off the wrong guys."

Gaspar chuckled without mirth. "So what else is new?"

The crossroad was closer now. The eighteen-wheeler continued to slow and Kim slowed behind him.

The big rig was carrying a lot of weight.

Which meant the tractor slowed gradually and would need to pull hard to get everything moving again on the other side of the crossroad.

Which also meant she might have a chance to pass the eighteen-wheeler after the intersection.

She edged around the boxy trailer for a better view and peered eastward into the gloom.

Which was when she had a clear sight line to the crossroad.

She could see the problem.

A small, silver sedan rolled to the intersection.

What would the little car do next?

The trucker's lack of faith in local traffic conditions paid off.

A pair of wobbly headlights crossed the first eastbound traffic lane and then, instead of going across the median to the second set of lanes, it turned west onto the eastbound fast travel lane.

Meaning the little car was heading into oncoming traffic directly toward the big rig and the vehicles driving behind it.

Kim gripped the wheel tighter and slowed her speed.

US 72 was a divided highway, which meant the confused driver of the little silver sedan, barely visible in the rainy gray gloom, was traveling in the wrong direction.

There was nowhere for the silver sedan to turn around, even if the driver realized the mistake.

Which might have been okay. Because the two eastbound traffic lanes were wide enough. If the sedan stayed in its lane. And the line of traffic following the truck stayed in line. Then, they could all pass each other safely and continue in opposite directions.

After that, the little car could find a place to turn around and cross over to the westbound lanes, where it should have been in the first place.

Their little caravan moved steadily toward the crossroads.

Kim didn't have enough clear distance to pass the semi, even if she'd been willing to take the risk that the sedan's driver wouldn't do something even crazier than driving in the wrong direction.

The sedan might stop.

Or try to make a U-turn.

Or something even less predictable.

What the hell was that driver thinking?

So Kim held onto her patience, slid back into her lane, and followed along behind the big rig, hoping the sedan would pass by them uneventfully.

She glanced at the digital clock on the dash. How long would it take?

But the motorcycle couldn't see the silver sedan from his position behind Kim. Nor could he see the crossroads. He seemed not to realize the impending danger.

As the big rig slowed, the motorcyclist revved up and pulled out around Kim's Lexus to pass.

When he got into position for an unobstructed view ahead, he must have seen the same sedan headlights traveling toward him in the eastbound roadway that Kim and the truck driver had seen.

But the motorcyclist made the opposite choice.

He didn't slow down and get behind her.

Instead, he sped past Kim like a crazy kamikaze playing a deadly game of chicken.

She sucked in a quick breath, holding it until her chest hurt and she remembered to exhale.

"Otto? Talk to me. What the hell's going on there?" Gaspar raised his voice through the speaker.

CHAPTER SEVEN

Wednesday, May 11
Carter's Crossing, Mississippi
3:30 p.m.

MAGNOLIA STREET WAS RATHER grandly named for the sketchy neighborhood. Maybe one or two of the quintessential Southern trees had sprouted here back in the day when the streets were being laid out and graded. If so, the broad leaves and fragrant blossoms were long gone, and it would take decades to grow new ones if anyone was interested in making an effort.

Which wasn't as unlikely as it would have been a decade ago. Before Big River Casino sprouted up, bringing jobs and neighborhood gentrification along with it.

The little frame rental house had been cleaned up, roofed, and painted soft yellow. The owner had added a two-car, detached garage. But that's as far as the home improvements went. The yard was nothing but dried weeds, and the driveway was a dirt rut running through from the road to the garage.

Anybody not from around Carter's Crossing might think the

spring rains would keep the dust down. They'd be wrong. As soon as the rain soaked into the thirsty ground, the yard turned dry and dusty again.

He was alone in the house. He'd been crossing off a few items on his bug-out list each day. He had a long list of loose ends to deal with before Kelham closed.

His operation here had to be shut down and all evidence appropriately disposed of. He hadn't seen Nina again since they'd parted at the airport in New York. As he'd suggested, she took a few days to drive back to Carter's Crossing. She'd texted him a few times along the way, but they hadn't talked again.

Nina had been so beautiful that night. She'd been clever with her hair and makeup as well as her wardrobe. From his position in the shadows, he'd almost let himself believe she was the woman he had loved more than any other. The afterglow had lasted a while, and he was sorry to lose her.

"Snap out of it, man. Nina has served her purpose," he said aloud, knowing he spoke the truth.

There was no place for Nina where he was going. And he certainly couldn't leave her behind. He'd made the right decision.

He reached for the silver flask. He'd refilled it with the poison he'd stolen from Kelham. He didn't expect to need the flask again. As a murder weapon, the poison was effective but clumsy. There were better ways to dispatch his enemies.

Yet, the odorless, tasteless liquid had been challenging to steal. Nothing else was as potent. A lifetime of military service had taught him the value of contingency plans.

He stored the flask at the back of the safe in the bedroom closet, just in case.

Satisfied that he'd secured the poison, he glanced at his

watch. He was running behind schedule. He needed to establish an alibi for Nina's time of death, just in case something went wrong at the scene. An ounce of prevention and all that.

The casino's poker tables should satisfy that particular requirement handily.

He had a little business to do at the tables, too.

If all went well, Lady Luck might reward him handsomely tonight. The thought lightened his mood.

There were always a few soldiers in the casino's crowds, along with tourists and locals. All he had to do was be seen at the game for an hour, give or take. Long enough for Nina's brother, the casino manager, to see him there and remember seeing him later.

The last thing he needed right now was to become a person of interest in Nina's murder. He'd been having an affair with her for a good long while. The affair had been insurance. Nothing more. But the safest thing was to assume they'd been seen together somewhere. Or that Nina had confided their relationship to her friends.

If Nina lived, sooner or later, he'd have been at risk. He wouldn't let that happen.

When she died today, he'd be above suspicion. But he'd always been a belt and suspenders guy. Extra caution had never steered him wrong.

He glanced at the open laptop on the desk. Jasper had placed a tracker on Nina's sedan.

Nina's cell phone pinged onto his laptop screen as she traveled along the county road toward US 72, exactly as he'd expected, along the fastest and the shortest route to Memphis. The route everybody in Carter's Crossing drove, especially in bad weather like this.

He slid one of the untraceable pistols and a box of ammo into the safe with the flask. He slipped the pistol with the silencer into his pocket.

"Good girl, Nina," he said as he took one last look at the laptop screen. Satisfied that his plan was in motion and proceeding as expected, he closed the laptop and stuffed it into the safe.

He pulled out two large stacks of fifty-dollar bills, closed the safe's door, and engaged the lock.

He'd bought both guns on the streets of Memphis. Neither weapon nor the bullets were in standard use by the army. Which was the reason he'd chosen them. He didn't want either traced back to him. He simply wanted them available when needed.

His truck was parked in the garage. He grabbed his jacket and slid his arms into it, stuffed the fifties into the breast pocket, and left through the back door. He used his key to turn the deadbolt and then hurried through the drizzling rain.

He stopped to punch the code on the keypad and waited while the big garage door rolled up enough for him to duck under it. He was inside the stolen truck with its big engine growling before the door reached its apex.

He reversed out of the garage and punched the remote to close the door before he backed down the driveway to the street.

His house was on the wrong side of the tracks from Carter's Crossing. Which meant it was closer to Kelham and to Big River Casino. The clock on the dashboard showed he had enough time to get settled into his poker game with at least ten witnesses before and while Nina died. Which was what mattered.

He drove north and east, away from Kelham, toward some of the richest dirt in the area, Carter's Crossing Reservation. Not because the land was fertile for crops. Not at all. The soil was too barren to nourish weeds.

The Eastern Band of Native Americans had occupied the nine acres of land east of Carter's Crossing since 1980. Before that, the land belonged to the US government. Seventeen members of Randy Cloud's family moved onto the blighted reservation at the request of the tribe to oversee the building of Big River Casino.

After the casino opened, the reservation quickly became the economic powerhouse of Carter's Crossing and the surrounding area. About a hundred members of the tribe lived out there now. The casino provided good jobs for the community. The tribe supported local schools and public works projects, too.

Randy Cloud was justly pleased with the casino and its place in Carter's Crossing. So was his sister, Nina. They'd built a thriving community from a piece of dry dirt that had never amounted to anything before.

Even Mayor Deveraux had to give them credit, while she turned a blind eye to the unsavory activities casinos invariably attracted.

He saw Big River Casino in the distance. The roomy parking lot was half empty. Two dozen vehicles of various types were scattered around, along with half a dozen buses. It was Wednesday. A workday for most folks around here.

Which was fine. He didn't need a huge audience. Just a handful of witnesses who could be counted on to remember him would be sufficient.

On weekends, the casino had a valet stand, which would have been helpful. But not today. He pulled into the lot and parked near the main entrance. He left the pistol and the silencer in the glove box, climbed out of the truck into the still dreary rain, and hustled inside.

As soon as the door opened, he was hit by a wall of stale

tobacco smoke thick enough to stop a charging buffalo. The slot machines laid out in rows near the front were beeping and clanging and playing a cacophony of animated tunes.

There were more patrons inside than he'd expected. He'd forgotten that today was Senior Day.

Every Wednesday, senior citizens were invited to gamble, given a free twenty dollars to do it with, and offered a free lunch. Management hoped they'd spend a lot more, of course. It was a business strategy employed by casinos around the country for a simple reason. It worked.

He avoided an elderly couple with matching red walkers heading toward the *Wheel of Fortune* slots. He dodged another pair of white-haired gents arguing over a triple diamond nickel slot machine. After weaving through a knot of old ladies atwitter about their knitting, he steered toward the blackjack tables and waited for an opening.

After a few minutes, a distinguished-looking older woman with a full head of coifed white hair folded her cards and left. He walked over and sat down in her seat. The other players looked him up and down and then returned their attention to their cards.

He slid ten fifties across to the dealer, hoping everyone at the table would notice and remember later. The dealer took the cash and gave him piles of chips in return. Then, the dealer nodded toward him and opened a new deck of cards.

Half an hour later, at the end of a game, a woman put her arm around his shoulders, leaned in, and kissed him on the cheek. He glanced up to see Nina Cloud standing behind him.

He blinked a couple of times to control his shock. What the hell was she doing here?

"Nice hand," she said, loud enough for his tablemates to hear, and proving she wasn't a ghost. Dammit.

He cleared his throat to steady his voice. "Thanks."

One at a time, the other players folded their cards, allowing him to win the pot. The stack of chips in front of him had grown to a satisfactory level. Winners attracted more attention than losers. Not that it mattered now. Nina was still alive. No chance he'd need an alibi for her murder this afternoon.

The guy on his right had lost enough. He cashed in his remaining chips and left.

Nina perched on the guy's seat and leaned in to flash a sexy smile. "Looks like you're doing well today."

"So far." He frowned. "I thought you were headed to Memphis? Didn't you have to pick something up before six o'clock?"

"I was. But my plans changed." She slid her hand under the table and squeezed his thigh.

The dealer broke open another deck of cards and dealt another hand.

"How come?" he asked, ignoring her hand traveling up his thigh, his mind only half occupied with the game.

He clenched his jaw to control his annoyance. She should have been on her way to Memphis. She was meant to die before she reached Memphis.

Which hadn't happened.

Which was bad enough. But she'd screwed up his schedule, too.

He frowned, working out an alternative timeline to get everything back on track.

Casually, Nina used a cocktail napkin to wipe the sweat from his brow as she explained. "I sent a friend to do it for me. Carolyn Blackhawk needed to borrow my car, anyway. She doesn't have one since she almost never drives anywhere.

You know, she's got those cataracts, so she doesn't see well. But she had to visit her sister, who's really sick. Might not make it through the night. Carolyn was really upset, but she said she was okay to drive. She'll pick the stuff up for me and go on to her sister's house. She promised she'd get there in time. I gave her my cell phone, too."

He shrugged as she blathered on. He glanced at the clock. She'd been scheduled to die ten minutes from now. He couldn't simply schedule her death again tomorrow.

His plan had been perfect. Two birds, one stone, and all that. Perfect.

Brian Jasper had been game to try the stunt because he thought he could survive. He'd seen some video online. A speeding motorcycle collided head-on with a speeding car and lived to tell about it.

Jasper was dimwitted. He was also despondent and a daredevil and more than a little reckless.

Of course, the video had been a fluke, if not a downright fake. Jasper couldn't possibly survive a head-on collision traveling sixty miles an hour.

No one else would be dumb enough to repeat the attempt.

Which meant now he had to come up with another way to kill Nina.

And he had to do it soon.

The dealer placed the cards. Bets were made. He watched the clock tick over to 4:30 p.m. and imagined he could see the scene on US 72 unfold exactly as he'd planned it.

Nina patted his thigh and removed her hand. "I've got a few things to take care of in the office. Come find me when you're finished here. We'll have dinner."

"Sounds good." He nodded. Probably better to stick around a

while and stay visible while the accident scene played out.

Sooner or later, someone would figure out that Nina Cloud should have been driving that sedan.

His anger mounted. He'd wanted to slip away and disappear. But Nina would never let that happen. She said she was in love with him. She imagined he loved her back. She wouldn't simply let him go and forget about him.

Besides, she knew about the counterfeit operation. Hell, without her, he'd never have passed all the bills. She was the one who covered his ass.

CHAPTER EIGHT

Wednesday, May 11
Outside Carter's Crossing, Mississippi
4:30 p.m.

KIM SUCKED IN A HARD BREATH. Gaspar's disembodied voice came from the phone. "Otto? Talk to me. What's the hell is going on there?"

The next few seconds passed in a simultaneous blur.

The big rig's driver applied his brakes, making an effort to slow his forward momentum to allow room for the motorcycle to pass. He let loose two short, loud blasts of his horn.

Kim braked, too, increasing the distance between the SUV and the enclosed trailer blocking her view like a wall of steel in front of her. If the eighteen-wheeler stopped, her SUV would be a bright red splotch on the back of that thing.

The noise of the motorcycle downshifting and speeding past the big double trailer roared in the fog.

Kim couldn't see what was happening as the motorcycle and the sedan hurtled toward each other unless she moved into the travel lane. The idea was foolhardy at the moment.

Which left her anxiously waiting for the cacophony and flying debris of the inevitable crash she knew was coming.

From his high-tech office, Gaspar must have found that satellite view he'd mentioned, because he said, "What the hell is that crazy dude doing?"

"Tell me. I can't see," she replied, lowering her window to hear the sounds, and falling back further from the tractor-trailer to give everyone more room to maneuver.

"He's zooming toward an oncoming car. The car could move to the shoulder of the road and let the bike pass. But if it doesn't, the bike will hit it head-on. And if they end up in the big rig's lane, that thing can't stop before running them both over." Gaspar's tone dropped an octave. "It's a small sedan. The distance between them is closing fast. It's possible the driver will survive—"

The rest of his words were consumed by the overwhelming volume of the crash.

From the noises alone, she could guess what happened.

First, the eighteen-wheeler's horn blasted the air in warning, followed by the deafening shriek of his brakes as he moved toward the right shoulder. Gravel and debris exploded behind him, pelting the Lexus.

The motorcyclist had applied his brakes hard. The bike must have lifted onto the front wheel as it skidded forward. But it was too little, too late.

Awakening to the danger, the sedan driver slammed on the brakes, and the car's wheels skidded along the wet pavement.

Both drivers had slowed, but when the sedan hit the rice-rocket head-on, the cyclist flew over the hood then the roof of the car.

He sailed through the air at least a hundred feet and landed in the middle of the road, right in front of the big rig, the trucker still desperately trying to miss him.

The sedan's front end was crumpled, and the front windshield looked like a spiderweb. The little car had been pushed off the north shoulder and down the slope. It rolled over at least twice and hit a tree.

The sedan lay on its passenger side, crumpled like a beer can.

The truck had moved farther along the south shoulder and onto the grassy apron.

The gap in front of Kim's Lexus allowed her to see the destroyed motorcycle and its rider, splayed out on the pavement.

She pulled onto the shoulder behind the truck, punched the emergency flashers, and jumped out of the SUV. At the moment, she couldn't see any oncoming traffic. She'd have grabbed a blanket, but the rental didn't have one.

Kim ran toward the cyclist. She couldn't see his head or face because of the full-face helmet. His limbs remained encased in his leathers.

She said a quick prayer when she noticed he was wearing an airbag jacket. He might still be alive. She'd known cyclists who survived worse. Rarely. But it happened. Maybe this guy would be one of the lucky ones.

The eighteen-wheeler had finally rolled to a stop. The tall, slender trucker climbed down, quickly set a few flares in the road behind her SUV and headed over to check on the sedan's driver.

Traffic was slowing in the westbound lanes, drivers gawking as they crawled past.

Kim and the trucker were moving in opposite directions, too far apart to communicate orally.

She knelt beside the cyclist, searching for space between his jacket and helmet to check his carotid pulse. A long pent up breath whooshed through her lips when she found it.

Kim's cell phone was still in her hand, the connection to Gaspar still open. "The cyclist is still alive. Pulse is weak and irregular, but present. He's breathing. Barely."

Gaspar said, "I called it in already. Help is on the way. They're sending a medivac helo from Kelham to fly the victims to Memphis."

"Kelham? The army base in Carter's Crossing?" Not exactly the way she wanted to meet anyone from Kelham, but Gaspar had done the right thing.

"They're the closest. Even though they're closing down, they still have some stuff on base. I called in a few favors. It would have taken too long to get a helo from Memphis," he said. "Local law enforcement should be on scene soon, too. I can see the oncoming traffic slowing in both directions on US 72."

She leaned closer and tried talking to the cyclist, peering through the tinted face mask. The full-face helmet wasn't the kind where she could open it to see him. "Can you hear me?"

If he heard, he gave no indication.

"Stay still. You may have spinal cord damage. We don't want to make things worse," she said as if he could hear and understand her. Maybe he could.

She scanned his body. He wasn't bleeding through his clothes. His limbs were akimbo on the pavement.

He'd suffered broken bones, for sure.

But he had a pulse, and he was breathing.

He might live.

She wouldn't risk removing his helmet or any of his clothing for fear of causing further damage. All they could do was wait. And pray.

Gaspar asked, "How's the driver of the sedan? I can't see from the satellite. Too much ground cover over there. But it looks bad."

Kim stood and turned toward the silver car and peered into the gloom. Her entire body felt clammy from the heavy mist and fog.

The trucker had tried to open the sedan driver's door, but it was jammed tight.

He'd found a rock and used it to break out the driver's side window. He shoved his head through the broken glass for a long moment, as if he was searching for something.

He didn't find it.

When he straightened, the trucker walked around the sedan looking at the ground adjacent to the shoulder. He used his arms to sweep the tall weeds away and peered toward the sedan's passenger side, which had molded to the tree trunk.

He must have found what he was looking for. He knelt. His head was camouflaged by the weeds for a bit before he stood tall again.

Gaspar said, "From his body language, I'd guess the sedan's driver didn't make it."

"Yeah. Looks like it," Kim replied. "I can't see from here. And I don't want to leave this victim here alone to go check on the other one."

The driver had made a fatal mistake. Thousands of wrong-way drivers died in similar accidents every year. They were almost always drunk or high or mentally challenged or distracted. Which made the situation sadder.

The trucker shoved his hands into his pockets and took a few long strides east on the pavement toward Kim.

As he moved closer, he seemed to grow taller and thinner. His face was gaunt. Sharp cheekbones and a thin nose were well placed above narrow lips. His ruddy brown hair was straight and thin, too.

He was a smoker. She could smell it on him. Tobacco. She hoped. He didn't deserve to get blamed for this. If he'd been smoking marijuana or taking any other drugs, he could be criminally charged. Which wouldn't be justice in his case at all.

The trucker said quietly, "She's gone. No seat belt. Flew out of the vehicle at some point. Still clutching her cell phone. Best guess is that she was talking on the phone when it happened."

Kim nodded. "You're sure she's gone?"

"Yeah. No mistaking death like that. Seen it before. Never pretty," he replied and tilted his head toward the cyclist. "How about him?"

"Still alive. Help's on the way." As soon as she'd uttered the words, she heard the helo in the distance.

"Strangest damn thing," the truck driver said, shaking his head and nodding toward the cyclist. He pulled a pack of Camels and a lighter out of his pocket and, with trembling hands, lit one, puffing steadily. "Seemed like he went right at her. On purpose."

"What? That's crazy," Kim replied, eyes wide. A shiver ran through her, which could have been caused by the dampness, but wasn't.

The trucker shrugged, taking another shaky draw from the cigarette. "He had plenty of time to slow down. To back off, like you did. He could've moved to the shoulder. Right at the end, he had room to move in front of my rig and keep right on going. I'd slowed down. He had the space."

Kim stared at him. "You're saying this was what? Suicide?"

"Stranger things have happened," the trucker shrugged again. "You've never heard of suicide by truck?"

She nodded. She knew the practice was all too common. It was kind of like suicide by cop. The victim was too scared to do the job, so he put himself in the way of a vehicle or a bullet.

It was an effective way to die. But it was a lousy thing to do to the survivors.

The cyclist was still alive, though. If suicide had been his plan, he'd screwed up.

Kim shook off the thoughts. "You have a dashcam in your rig?"

"Yeah. Sends the video straight to the company. Cops can see it soon as they ask," he replied.

Gaspar could hack the dashcam, too. He was probably doing so now.

Traffic on the westbound lanes of US 72 across the grassy median had slowed to a crawl. More vehicles were lining up behind the Lexus and the flares, too. Sirens wailed behind and ahead of the traffic, moving relentlessly toward the incident.

The helo was within sight range now, hovering overhead, scanning for a good spot to land. Visibility was barely good enough below the clouds, but dusk was fast approaching and the rain had started to drizzle again.

A few vehicles had stacked up behind the incident, but the road in front of the truck was clear. The helo set down about two hundred feet east of the big rig.

Two first responders jumped out of the helo with their equipment and hustled over to the cyclist. Kim gave them a quick report on what happened, then stepped back to let them do their jobs.

While they were working on him, another pair hurried

toward the sedan. It wouldn't take them long to realize they could do nothing for the driver. Crime scene techs would take over.

The helo's big rotors were slowing, but still roaring overhead.

Kim and the trucker stood aside. Law enforcement would need their eyewitness accounts and their contact information when they arrived on the scene.

The trucker moved the cigarette to his left hand and extended his right. "Joe Watts."

"Kim Otto," she replied, accepting the gesture.

He pulled a business card from his shirt pocket and handed it to her. "Got a card? My company will want to contact you. Take a statement about what happened. That okay with you?"

Kim nodded and handed him one of her cards.

The sirens died off as law enforcement officers came up behind the Lexus and went to work. Two more vehicles pulled up to handle traffic flow on the westbound lanes.

Shortly afterward, a uniformed officer from Carter's Crossing approached.

CHAPTER NINE

Wednesday, May 11
Outside Carter's Crossing, Mississippi
6:45 p.m.

KIM HAD WATCHED AS THE cyclist was airlifted toward Memphis. After that, the usual crash site activities consumed everyone present.

Jurisdiction over the crash site was iffy, but in small, rural communities like this, various departments worked together. Turned out the closest town was Carter's Crossing, but Mississippi State Patrol would be in charge. They probably had a Fatal Accident Crash Team to handle such situations. For now, uniformed and plainclothes personnel milled about, each one performing necessary functions.

Road flares had been set appropriately. Traffic had been rerouted at some point east and west of the scene, and traffic flow had resumed in both directions across the grassy median, using the westbound lanes. Gawkers stared at the scene as they moved slowly past, but the vehicles were moving now.

The eastbound lanes would remain closed while the scene

was processed. Kim observed the professionals at work. Photos were taken. Everything was measured and documented. Tow trucks and search warrants were on the way. The body would be removed and transported to the appropriate coroner's office for an autopsy, although the cause of death seemed abundantly clear.

But this crash wasn't her job. After she'd seen enough to know these were trained professionals at work and there was no need for her here, Kim tuned it all out.

The weather had turned dark and cold. The rain hadn't let up. She'd brought no rain gear.

She'd given her card and a statement to the appropriate officer. The trucker had done the same and returned to his cab. There was no reason for her to stay here any longer.

Kim took another quick look around, just to be sure. Across the median, the police had redirected traffic from the eastbound lanes to one of the westbound lanes. Traffic was moving again in both directions. A few motorcycles roared past, heading toward Memphis. She saw a big guy walking backward along the shoulder of the eastbound lane, thumb out, looking for a ride.

Even from this distance, there was something familiar about him, but she couldn't say exactly what it was. She watched until a pickup truck pulled over, and he stepped into the passenger seat and closed the door behind him. The truck kept going, headed toward Carter's Crossing. She couldn't see the plate on the truck. Maybe Gaspar could find a camera with eyes on the plate if she wanted to locate the driver later.

One last look around before she trudged back toward her SUV, which was still parked on the shoulder behind the big rig. She pulled the door open, slid behind the steering wheel, and pushed the start button. The engine caught and growled like a satisfied lion slept under the hood.

Before she had a chance to put the transmission in gear, knuckles rapped on her window. She glanced up to see an oversized man with an oversized mustache standing outside in the rain next to the Lexus. He was dressed in street clothes, wearing a coat with the collar turned up against the windswept rain and a wide-brimmed hat, but he held a badge in his hand.

She lowered the window.

"You're FBI Special Agent Kim Otto? I'm Sheriff Scott Greyson, Carter's Crossing. The next town east of here. People call me Chief. Mind if we talk a bit?" he said.

She could see him more clearly now. Tall and slender, he had brown hair and piercing blue eyes. About fifty, give or take five years. She guessed he'd had no trouble finding dates his entire life.

It was no surprise that he'd come over to chat. Small-town cops are always interested in strangers headed into their domain. He'd want to know who she was and why she was going to Carter's Crossing. He already had her name and her cover story from the officer who took her statement. But he'd want to judge the situation for himself. The easiest way to do that was simply to ask.

She gave him a friendly smile. "Climb in. It's too miserable to talk out there in the rain."

She raised the window while he walked around the front of the SUV and climbed into the passenger seat. His long legs covered the ground quickly. He removed his hat, opened the door, and tucked in.

He smelled of cold, damp wool. His face was lined with fatigue. No matter how experienced a law enforcement officer he was, he had not lost human compassion. She liked him for that.

Once he was settled, he handed her a business card. She offered one from her pocket in exchange.

That dance completed, he said, "So you're on the way to Carter's Crossing to complete a background check on a former army major?"

"That's right, Chief," she replied.

"Who's the subject of your inquiry?"

"Guy's name is Jack Reacher."

"When was he here?"

"About fifteen years ago, give or take."

He nodded as if he was processing new information. Which he was. She hadn't given Reacher's name to the other officer.

"Did you know him? Reacher?" she asked.

He pursed his lips and shook his head. "I wasn't in Carter's Crossing back then. Arrived about twelve years ago, when I left the military."

"You weren't in the army? My experience is that most officers at a certain level know each other at least by reputation."

"Sorry. No. Marines, actually." he said easily, clearing his throat and moving on to a new topic. "Anyway, I understand you were a witness to this accident. We'll have the dashcam footage from the truck and from your vehicle once we serve subpoenas. I know you've already given a statement, and I'll read it later. But can you give me a quick rundown?"

"Is this your jurisdiction, Chief? I thought we were outside your limits here." She was merely curious. Hunting Reacher being what it was, she wanted to be friendly with the local sheriff. It was likely she'd need his help soon enough.

"It's close, but no, not my jurisdiction. We cover the whole county—about five hundred square miles. But the county line doesn't come this far out," he replied.

"I see. That's a lot of land to cover. How big is your department?"

"Yeah, it's a lot of ground, but basically what we have is Carter's Crossing and Kelham, the army base. We've got eight of us in the department. Me and several deputies." He paused, and almost as an afterthought, added, "We've also got Big River, a casino on the reservation southwest of town. But what happens out there isn't my jurisdiction, either."

Kim cocked her head, taking the information in through her law enforcement filter and putting it into perspective. "Both Kelham and the casino have their own law enforcement personnel. So how many people do you have to serve and protect in your county?"

"We've been growing for the past decade or so. New businesses moved to town. Draws new workers. And then the casino brings in tourists. New hotels have opened up. All in all, we've got about fifteen thousand civilians now living in the county. And we get another few thousand coming and going every month," he said.

"You've got to be busy. Seems like you're short-staffed, too."

"What small municipality isn't slammed these days?" he said good-naturedly.

"Just asking, but why are you out here for this traffic accident? I know it's a fatality, but don't you have enough on your plate already?" Kim asked.

He sighed, lifted his hat, and ran a hand over his hair. "I know both of the victims. Know the truck driver, too. Joe Watts is a good guy. I don't want to see him unjustly jammed up over this. And I'll also need to deal with the families. It's better if I can give them some firsthand observations to soften the blow, usually."

"Both drivers have been identified?" She didn't ask the names of the victims. No reason to. And he shouldn't tell her anyway.

"We found her purse and ran the plate on the sedan. We're less sure about the cyclist, but we think we know who he is." He wiped the rain from his face with a quick palm. "So if you're inclined to help me out…"

"Of course. Sorry. Didn't mean to hold you up. Trying to get familiar with how things are done around here." She nodded and gave him a friendly smile. "In this case, I'm just a witness. Like you said, I gave a statement to one of the officers. Pretty straightforward."

"Uh-huh," he said, encouraging her to say more.

"The cyclist was in a hurry. He'd tried to pass me at least once before. When the truck slowed down for the crossing ahead, the cyclist pulled out to pass."

"Okay."

"My view of the collision was blocked by the big rig. But the sedan was traveling the wrong way, against traffic. The cyclist hit the sedan head-on and the sedan went off the road." She wrapped it up and put a bow on it for him. "Looks like nothing more than confusion and bad judgment is to blame. The cyclist was in a hurry. Watts told me the woman might have been talking on her cell phone at the time. Maybe she was distracted. The weather was bad. Not much more to it unless one of them was impaired. You'll need the medical examiner to make that call."

Greyson chewed on the inside of his lower lip as if he was considering something. "Joe Watts says the cyclist could have avoided the crash. Says the guy had time to move in front of the truck and get clear before he hit the sedan. That so?"

She shrugged. "I couldn't see well enough to say from back here. But Watts told me that. He thinks his dashcam video will confirm what he saw."

"Yeah. He told me that, too." Greyson nodded. "Anything else you can add?"

She shrugged. "Only that I'm shocked the cyclist is alive and the sedan driver is dead, honestly. While it was happening, I thought things were likely to go the other way."

"The cyclist isn't out of the woods yet." He stopped for a deep breath. "Coroner says they might both have survived if she hadn't hit that tree. Or if she'd been wearing her seatbelt."

Kim nodded. They didn't need the coroner to reach that conclusion.

After a few moments, he said, "Well, if you think of anything else that might be useful, I'd appreciate it if you'd let me know."

Southern charm fairly oozed from the guy. He was both handsome and nice. That seemed like a lethal combination in a small Southern town. He'd probably had women lined up his whole life. And left a trail of broken hearts longer than Main Street in Carter's Crossing.

She replied, "Of course. Glad to do what I can."

He nodded and reached for the door handle, hat in hand.

Before he left again, Kim said, "Chief?"

"Yeah?"

"I was planning to check in with you tomorrow after my meeting with the mayor," she said. Standard courtesy. Nothing more. She didn't have to do it. But she'd planned to, so there was no harm in saying so.

He arched his eyebrows all the way to his hairline. Under different circumstances, he might have asked a few more questions. But it was late, and he had more urgent matters to attend to.

After a moment, he simply nodded again. "Address is on the card. We'll talk more tomorrow. When we've both had some sleep and some coffee." With that, he stepped into the rain and set his hat firmly on his head so it wouldn't blow off.

She shrugged. He was right. This wasn't the time or the place for the longer conversation they needed to have. The Boss's file had contained summary reports on the recent murder as well as the old ones. Added to the serious injury of one of Carter's Crossing's citizens and the death of another in the accident, Sheriff Greyson had his hands full already.

She turned on her wipers and headlights and drove along the shoulder past the flares marking the end of the crime scene in front of the eighteen-wheeler. She could have continued along the now empty roadway, but one of the cops waved her through the emergency crossing.

Kim joined the line of slow-moving traffic eastward toward town, still wondering about the crash and its victims and what the hell they could have been thinking.

CHAPTER TEN

Wednesday, May 11
Carter's Crossing, Mississippi
8:05 p.m.

TWO HOURS AGO, he had cashed in his chips and made his way to the bar. The local reports from Memphis had covered the crash on US 72 west of Carter's Crossing. He'd watched the images through several rounds of breaking news alerts, each one worse than the last.

The talking heads had said the driver of the sedan was dead at the scene. Which was precisely what he'd expected to happen. Wrong driver, of course. But at least Carolyn Blackhawk was done.

The cyclist had somehow, miraculously survived. He'd been airlifted to a Memphis hospital. He was in critical condition. Which was not even remotely close to fine. That idiot Jasper should have died, too. The moron couldn't even kill himself effectively.

He had questions. Like why the hell Carolyn Blackhawk

turned too soon and ended up on the eastbound lane instead of the westbound one. Jasper had planned the stunt for the westbound lane, but he must have checked the tracker and realized the sedan was up ahead coming straight at him, the stupid kid had improvised. Disastrously.

He shook his head. Didn't matter. Whatever the explanations were, now, he had another problem.

The victims' names were withheld pending notification of the families, but he already knew who they were. Too soon, everyone else would know.

Traffic had been rerouted on US 72, which meant the seniors in the casino had been freed to climb aboard their buses. All four groups had headed back to their assisted living homes until next Wednesday when they'd make the trek again.

He'd be long gone by that time.

Once the traffic routes were opened again, the casino had filled up quickly with younger gamblers and drinkers. Cloying tobacco smoke hung suffocatingly heavy in the air. When he left here, his clothes would need to be fumigated.

The casino was abuzz now with soldiers from Kelham and Carter's Crossing residents who had finished their work shifts for the night. Everyone was looking for some fun. His senses were overwhelmed. He couldn't think straight.

Nina had joined him at the bar and they'd ordered dinner. He'd glanced at the television screen behind her from time to time. There was a game show on and local news, such as it was, crawled along the bottom of the screen.

It was too early for the baseball game. Cardinals at San Diego Padres would start later tonight. He was careful not to glance at the television too often. Nina would become suspicious if he paid too much attention.

He shrugged off his concerns. Everything would settle out. It always did.

The result was inevitable, even if things were taking longer than expected. No reason to worry.

Jasper would die tonight.

Nina had blathered on about this and that while he tried to work out a new plan for her. He was good at war games. Adjusting for contingencies on the fly was well within his skill set.

This was perhaps the most crucial war of his life. But it was by no means the most difficult.

He ticked off the elements in his head. Remove the obstacles. Gather the last of his assets. Move on.

It wasn't a complicated plan, which was fine. Simple plans were always the best. Fewer moving parts. Less to screw up.

Brian Jasper and Carolyn Blackhawk were not the obstacles. Blackhawk was already dead, and Jasper soon would be.

The real problem was Nina. She knew about Pak. She was there in New York. She knew about the counterfeiting. She'd already blabbed about the trip to New York. She'd told Bonnie Nightingale. Who else had she told?

He had to get rid of her, and soon.

He realized that Nina hadn't mentioned the crash. Which meant she hadn't heard the news yet.

She'd be devastated about Carolyn Blackhawk, partly because they'd been friends since elementary school. But mostly because Blackhawk had been driving Nina's car.

He'd seen a lot of death. He'd consoled his share of survivors. He knew what was coming.

He tuned out the words, but he watched her as her mouth ran on about nothing. Nina wasn't an overly emotional woman. But she was bound to suffer some survivor's guilt about Blackhawk, along with the inevitable horror and grief.

He shrugged.

She'd learn about the crash in the next few hours. Whatever her reaction, he didn't want to be around to experience the fallout firsthand. Better to deal with her after she'd had some time to process.

The last thing he needed was a devastated mistress to deal with now. He couldn't leave her alone for too long, though. Tomorrow, maybe.

He glanced at the clock over the bar. It was just past eight o'clock. He interrupted her flow of chit-chat.

"Aren't you supposed to work tonight?" he asked.

"Yeah. You're right. Randy's night off," she said, referencing her brother. She wiped the last crumbs of crab cakes from her mouth. The simple gesture raised his annoyance to a slow-burning rage.

Randy's night off. Of course it was.

Randy Cloud was Nina's brother. Together, they managed Big River Casino. Randy was also an asshat. Always had been. Too bad he couldn't add Randy to the casualty list. He simply didn't have the time.

His mind returned to the present when Nina leaned in to kiss him. "See you when I see you."

It was their standard farewell. He couldn't bring himself to say it. Instead, he nodded, grinned, and raised his beer in her direction. When she turned to walk away, he dropped the grin, scowled at her retreating backside, and swigged the beer.

Nina had to die because she'd killed Pak. Whether she'd known it or not at the time didn't matter. Nina was smart. She'd figure out what happened. He gave her the poison and she gave it to Pak. None of which could, under any circumstances, be discovered. Ever.

Only one man would suspect him of killing Pak. And he hadn't heard a peep out of Jack Reacher in more than fifteen years. The odds of Reacher putting things together and showing up here were less than slim and none. He wasn't worried about that in the least.

But when he added the Pak straw to the already overburdened Nina camel...well. What else could he do?

Nina had to go.

He didn't feel the least bit of grief about her.

He drained the glass, waved the bartender over, and paid the check with cash.

He stood and swallowed the last of the beer before he headed out. He'd been in the casino for hours. His image would have been captured on a dozen cameras, at least.

More than enough.

CHAPTER ELEVEN

Wednesday, May 11
Carter's Crossing, Mississippi
8:55 p.m.

HE LEFT THE CASINO BY THE FRONT door and gave the
cameras another chance to see his face, to document the time of
departure. He put his hat on and hustled out to the truck through
the drizzling rain.

The drive back to his safe house was uneventful. He parked
the truck in the garage, retrieved the gun and the silencer, and
entered the house through the back door.

He considered making a trip to the barn. "Nah. It can wait
until tomorrow," he said aloud.

He strode to the bedroom, opened the safe, and emptied his
pockets of the cash he'd won at the casino. He then closed the
safe and locked it before he stripped down and tossed his clothes
in the washer.

He took a long shower to get rid of the smoky stench,

dressed, and left the house again, this time on foot, the gun and silencer in his pocket.

He walked through the dreary darkness with his collar turned up, hat pulled low, and hands stuffed into his pockets. There were no sidewalks on this side of the railroad tracks. But the road was paved, which meant he didn't need to walk the whole way through the mud.

Soon, he'd reached the crossing point directly across from Brannan's. He left the road, walked through the tall weeds to the railroad tracks, and then crossed over to the other side.

As he moved closer, he could see maybe a dozen patrons inside Brannan's. He couldn't identify them all from this distance, but he knew they were the same guys who showed up every night during the week. No surprises. Which was exactly the way he liked it.

Three McKinneys were playing pool with another dude, waiting for the baseball game to start. The fourth guy was smaller, fitter. Luke Price. He hung around with the McKinneys because no one else would have him.

Brian Jasper had taken pity on Price, too. They'd been in boot camp together. Jasper said he owed Price for some reason. Let Price bunk out on his couch the past few months when Price said he had PTSD and he couldn't live alone. Which was another load of crap.

But boot camp was a long time ago and Price had long since worn out his welcome. With Jasper dead, Price had become irrelevant. Which meant he didn't want Price around.

Two guys from Kelham stood talking with Walt the bartender. Walt was a veteran. Army Ranger. He'd served in Afghanistan. When he came home, he bought the bar from the Brannan brothers, allowing them to retire to Arizona.

But Walt was the only McKinney worth his salt in the entire county. The other McKinneys and most of their pals were rednecks through and through. Wouldn't hurt them to take a bath now and then, either.

When he reached the sidewalk, he knocked the mud from his shoes and went inside. He stopped at the bar, acknowledged the two guys from Kelham, and collected a beer from Walt McKinney before he walked back to join Hern and Redland, huddled in a dark corner in the back, near the rear exit.

He walked around the table and sat with his back to the corner, where he could watch the room and the door and everyone coming and going and the chair across from him, the one where Jasper usually sat.

Shaking his head, Eddie Hern said, "Helluva thing about Jasper. Won't be needin' that fourth chair for a while, for damn sure."

"What about him?"

"Jasper," Tony Redland snorted. "The idiot's dead by now. Who does he think he is, Evel Knievel?"

"Stupid fool," Hern agreed. "At least he didn't try to jump the Grand Canyon."

Redland said, "It's one thing to jump a motorcycle across the tracks when the train's comin'. Train's predictable. Steady speed. Only one set of tracks. Pretty simple. Hell, anybody could do that."

Hern shook his head. "Yeah, well, it's a whole 'nother thing hittin' an oncoming car head-on driving sixty miles an hour and flying over it to land on the other side."

"Every kid has to have a hero, I guess. There's worse heroes than Evel Knievel." He swigged his beer and shook his head, as if he was hearing the story for the first time, and couldn't believe it, either.

But he'd watched Jasper practice the jump out on the county road for hours on end. He'd used an old tractor somebody had abandoned long ago. He'd adjusted his speed, doing the calculations over and over, until Jasper claimed he could practically do the stunt in his sleep. The only variable was the speed of the oncoming vehicle. He'd had to estimate that since the tractor hadn't been drivable for a couple of decades or so. Jasper had tested his calculations a few dozen times until he felt confident enough to pull it off.

Jasper was wearing protective gear for extra insurance. Full leathers and an airbag jacket and a full helmet. If he'd miscalculated somehow and come off the motorcycle, he believed he'd still be okay.

He'd planned the jump at precisely the right point on US 72, where the traffic cameras could record it all. Jasper not only wanted to do the jump but to be as famous as his hero afterward.

Jasper possibly could have done the stunt and come out fine. Worst case, he might have limped away with nothing more than broken bones.

Except things didn't work out that way. Not for Jasper.

And not for Carolyn Blackhawk.

The jump went bad.

Just about everything that could have gone wrong did go wrong.

Jasper had crashed into the car instead of flying over the hood and the roof and landing upright on the bike on the pavement on the other side of the sedan.

The car had swerved and rolled over several times, all the way off the road, down the embankment, and into a tree.

Carolyn Blackhawk flew out of the car and died.

He shook his head.

Jasper was a fool, just like Hern said.

Jasper would die tonight without waking up. Without ever knowing what happened.

But Jasper would've died soon enough, anyway. All these guys had to be dispatched before he left the country—no way around it.

He felt bad about Carolyn Blackhawk, though. He'd liked her. She was a good woman. He had nothing against her. Nothing at all.

But her death wasn't on him. Nina was the one responsible. If Nina hadn't loaned her the damned car, Carolyn would still be alive.

Nothing he could do about that now. Carolyn was dead. Jasper was hanging on by a hair unless he'd died in the past half hour.

One could hope.

And Nina was still walking around.

Which meant he had four more murders to execute before he could bug out, instead of three. Jasper, Hern, Redland, Nina.

None of these fools knew his plans, though. No reason they should. They'd find out soon enough.

Redland folded his hands around his beer and leaned forward. "We're on track. We've got the inventory at the storage joint. The trucks are rented. We want to go over the plan a couple more times, but that's easy."

Hern leaned in, too, and spoke quietly. "A few loose ends to cover yet—"

Luke Price staggered up, pulled out the extra chair where Jasper usually sat, and plopped his ass down like he owned the table. He'd been drinking for a while. The stench of stale booze wafted from his body like he'd fallen fully clothed into a vat of beer.

Redland scowled at him. "Get the hell outta here, Price. You stink."

"Whatever you boys are plotting, I want a piece of the action," Price said, his speech so slurred he was barely comprehensible.

Hern gave Price a hard stare. "We're plottin' how to kill your miserable ass. Go stand in front of the midnight train. Save us all some trouble."

"You think you can take me out, Hern? Why don't you try it." Price said, standing up so swiftly he knocked the chair over. It landed with a bang on the crusty wood floor. He swayed unsteadily on his feet from the effort.

Redland stuck his foot out and tripped Price. He plopped and splayed on his ass next to the chair. Redland gave Price a swift kick to help him along. "Get the hell outta here and leave us alone."

"Sorry." Price cackled, and drool ran down his chin. Maybe he'd noticed he was trying to fight three against one. "I'm drunk."

"No kidding," Hern sneered.

Price scrambled off the floor and righted the chair. He stuck his chin out pugnaciously. "I'll handle you tomorrow, Redland. When I sober up. Bring these two along with you."

"Yeah, sure. Whatever," Redland replied, turning his back to Price and ignoring his stumbling gait as he staggered his way toward the pool table.

After ten minutes or so, the noise level returned to normal inside Brannan's. The pool game resumed. Business as usual, like the minor altercation had never happened.

Not that it mattered. The time for quiet talking was over. The three men who had huddled at the table in the back each had things to prepare.

Hern said, "Want me to deal with Price?"

The man in the corner shook his head. "Not yet. Too obvious if something happens to him now. He's all bluster anyway. We'll meet up tomorrow at the storage joint at noon like we planned."

Redland and Hern left the bar through the back door.

He remained in the chair in the corner, blending into the shadows, waiting for the right moment. When he felt confident that he wouldn't be noticed, he slipped out the back.

He walked along the alley's deserted sidewalks, close to the buildings, careful to stay out of sight of the cameras and the glow of streetlights. He'd seen the grainy video of Pak at the dogfight in New York on an earlier newscast. Cameras were everywhere. He had to be more careful.

He turned onto Main Street and headed toward the parking lot behind the grocery store at the end of the block, where he'd left another truck earlier in the day.

A quick drive to Memphis to take care of Jasper and then back. He'd be snug in his bed before daybreak.

CHAPTER TWELVE

Wednesday, May 11
Carter's Crossing, Mississippi
9:15 p.m.

IT WAS FULL DARK AND STILL raining for the remainder of the drive. Fog had settled on the road. Even with the windshield wipers slapping time, she could see only a few feet ahead, despite the SUV's headlights.

She exited off US 72, slowed her speed, and traveled south and east. The road was dark and straight. Heavily wooded on both sides. The fog and the rain stayed with her.

After a while, the trees simply stopped, like the lumberjacks had snapped a plumb line and razed them in a straight row. Perhaps they had.

The smooth asphalt road flowed like a ribbon on a package. Open green space flanked the road on both sides, emphasizing the effect.

She followed it through a right turn to a straight street running north and south with low buildings on both sides. Main Street.

As she came closer to the town, she passed a building with a sign out front declaring it the Carter County Sheriff's Office. It was set off by itself, a large parking lot out front. Old-fashioned, but new construction, suggested it had been built within the last fifteen years, probably on the site where the old one was torn down.

A sign declared *Carter's Crossing Established 1853* and proudly pointed out that the town was listed on the National Register of Historic Places. Current population 8,628. Which meant the rest of Carter County was still sparsely settled, even after more than a hundred years.

When Reacher was here fifteen years ago, the population of the town and the whole county was only twelve hundred souls. Back then, the town had consisted of the west side and the east side, literally divided by the railroad tracks.

If Kelham had not been located east of the few rickety residences on the wrong side of the tracks, there would have been almost no business of any kind to support citizens on either side. As it was, when Reacher came through, roadside bars on the good side of the tracks provided jobs, food, and not much else to speak of.

Things were obviously different now, like Chief Greyson had said. Prosperity had come to Carter's Crossing once again.

Main Street was deserted tonight, partly because of the weather. Smooth concrete sidewalks abutted the asphalt. Red brick-faced buildings abutted one another on the sidewalks' opposite edge. Old-fashioned streetlights cast weak shadows in the gloomy rain.

She peered through the windshield. The hotel she wanted was the historic one, most likely where Reacher had stayed because it had been the only one in town back then. Toussaint's Inn, it was called. Located near the middle of Main Street on the west side.

The usual discount hotel chains had popped up on streets off the main drag, according to the signs she'd seen back on US 72. She could move to one of them if the historic place proved unsuitable.

But she figured Toussaint's had been gentrified like everything else in the town. If he showed up at all, Reacher might come back there.

On the way to Toussaint's, she'd passed a diner that was still open. After she got settled, she'd come back for food. Diners were places where the locals hung out. She might get lucky. Find someone who knew something useful about the murder. Or Kelham. Or Chief Greyson. Maybe even get some intel on Reacher.

Wishful thinking on all counts, but stranger things had happened.

When she saw the hotel, she wasn't disappointed. Her intuition had been spot-on. The building had been restored to better than its original glory. She anticipated fresh sheets and a hot shower in her future.

Toussaint's looked like it had been transplanted from the French Quarter in New Orleans. It was painted green with white trim and moldings and had iron railings on the second floor balconies. A row of floodlights in the bushes surrounding the perimeter washed the façade with a welcoming glow.

There must have been a guest parking lot somewhere, but for now, she angle parked out front. After wrestling her rolling travel case and her laptop bag out of the back, she pulled them up the sidewalk toward the entrance.

Kim took a deep breath of the damp fresh air. She shivered as a few drizzles of rain slid down her collar. She covered the short distance to the hotel, climbed six sturdy brick steps to the even wider verandah, and rolled her bag to the door.

Inside, she found a square lobby brightly lit and furnished with antiques from a bygone era. A hardwood counter polished to a high sheen rested off to the right. Mounted on the wall behind it was a matrix of pigeonholes for the old-fashioned room keys. Four high, seven wide. Twenty-eight keys for twenty-eight rooms.

All the keys were in place. Maybe there was something wrong with the rooms in this place, after all. She hoped not. It had been a long day. All she wanted was a meal followed by a hot shower and some sleep, and she didn't want to travel any further to find them.

Through the window, she saw a woman behind the counter peering through her reading glasses at a computer screen. Dark hair, parted in the middle, hung over her shoulder. Brown eyes, dark lashes, full eyebrows with a natural arch. Skin the color of caramel.

When Kim opened the door, the woman looked up and flashed a welcoming smile.

"Come in. Come in," she said, waving Kim forward. "The weather's horrible out tonight, isn't it?"

"Absolutely awful," Kim smiled. She nodded toward the pigeonholes. "Looks like you've got availability for a few nights?"

"Oh, those old keys are just for show. They don't even work anymore." She lifted her chin for a clear view above the computer screen. Her voice was softly Southern and friendly. "I'm the manager here. Janine Wood."

"Nice to meet you, Janine. I'm Kim Otto," she extended her hand and they shook.

"The tribe owns this place now," Janine said, still smiling. "When we upgraded the hotel, we installed all new systems. Plumbing, heating, electrical, fire suppression, security, the works. New door locks and keys, too."

"The tribe?" Kim asked, cocking her head.

"The Eastern Band of Native Americans. We bought the place a few years back. An elderly couple owned it before. When they died, the hotel fell into bankruptcy." She smiled and patted the wood desk with her palm. "These old hotels are a part of our heritage. We didn't want to see the old girl demolished and a modern no-tell motel installed in the center of town. So we bought it. Put some money into it. She's the star of Main Street now."

"Good to know. The place is lovely. You've done a great job with the restorations." Kim said.

Janine nodded appreciatively.

Kim's stomach growled. It had been a long time since she'd had a meal. "Sorry. I need to get some dinner. I don't have a reservation. Do you have any rooms?"

"Absolutely. How long are you staying with us?" She turned her attention to the screen again, clacking keys on the keyboard.

"I'm not sure. Depends on how things go." Kim pulled her credit card out and placed it on the counter.

"No problem. We usually have space during the week. Fill up on the weekends. Tourists like to stay here when they come to the casino," Janine said, fingers speeding over the keys, filling the room with echoing clicks. "So let's book you through to Monday, just in case. You can always check out early. No penalty for that."

"Is your kitchen still open?" Kim glanced at the big grandfather clock in the corner. It was almost ten o'clock. In a town like Carter's Crossing, the late-night dining choices were likely few and the food greasy.

"I'm afraid we don't have a dining room, and we only have room service for breakfast," Janine said, still dealing with the reservation and checking Kim's credit card and all the other tasks associated with getting her room established.

"How about that diner down the street? Any good?" Kim jerked her thumb in the right direction.

"Libby's? Closes at ten. But Libby always stays open for me. I eat dinner there every night. I was just about to head over when you came in," Janine said, picking up the keys and offering the paperwork to Kim for signature. "I can recommend the cheeseburger and fries. Best in town."

"That'd be great. I'll stash my bags in my room and go straight over." She didn't want to miss her last chance to get food tonight that didn't come out of a cellophane package.

"If you'd like company…" Janine said, her voice trailing off.

"I'd like that," Kim said, on her way up the stairs to her room. "Let me stash this stuff and wash my hands. I'll be right back."

Janine Wood might know everything there was to know about Carter's Crossing. She seemed friendly enough. She could be a valuable ally.

She grabbed the rolling travel bag in one hand and tossed the laptop case strap over her shoulder and hoofed up the stairs to the second floor.

Room Seventeen was on the street side. She swiped the key card, pushed the door open with her hip, and stepped inside. A glance was all she needed to see the room wasn't the Four Seasons, but it would be suitable for her needs.

Clean, tidy, and spacious, the room had a queen-sized bed, a loveseat across from the television, and a small desk with a chair. She couldn't have a dinner party in there, but she didn't plan to.

She left her bags, used the bathroom, and washed up, spent five seconds on the rest of her appearance, and rejoined Janine Wood downstairs.

CHAPTER THIRTEEN

Wednesday, May 11
Carter's Crossing, Mississippi
9:35 p.m.

JANINE WAS READY WHEN Kim's feet hit the ground floor.
They quick-stepped through the blowing rain with heads down
until they reached Libby's Diner. Janine pulled the door open,
allowed Kim to enter first, and then followed, pulling the door
against the wind to close it again.

Libby's Diner was a narrow building, like a box of saltines,
the short end on Main Street and the opposite end abutting the
alley. It shared walls with the buildings on each side, both of
which had been constructed in the post-Reacher era. The diner
must have stood alone and apart when Reacher was here. The
only windows overlooked Main Street.

The décor was retro to about 1960 or so, complete with an
old-fashioned payphone on the wall inside the front door.
Beyond the register and hostess station, the interior was divided
by a long straight aisle with tables on both sides. Tables for four

on the left and tables for two on the right. In the back were restrooms, one on either side of the aisle, and a swinging door that led to the kitchen.

At this hour, there was no hostess. Nor any hungry patrons. The place was almost deserted. Only one table was occupied, by a lone female deep in thought, palming an empty coffee cup and staring at a clean plate.

Kim recognized her from the Boss's files. Mayor Elizabeth Deveraux.

"Libby will be right out," Janine said, grabbing a menu and leading the way down the aisle to a table for four about halfway back.

When they approached Deveraux's table, Janine said, "Hey, Liz. How's it going?"

Deveraux blinked as if she'd been involuntarily jerked into the present. Then, like every politician everywhere, she slipped into her public persona. "As well as can be expected. You?"

"I'm good. Late dinner tonight," Janine said, nodding toward Deveraux's empty plate.

"Late dinner every night. Work comes first. Hard habit to break," Deveraux said with a smile. She turned a wide-eyed gaze toward Kim. "Welcome to Carter's Crossing. What brings you here?"

Kim shook her head. "I'm here on business for a couple of days."

Deveraux, if she knew who Kim was and why she was here, took the hint. Or maybe she was simply tired after a long day of dealing with whatever Carter's Crossing citizens tossed in her path. Either way, the conversation stopped there.

Kim might have said more, if they'd been alone, but she didn't want to get into anything in front of Janine. So she said nothing.

Janine took the hint. "I'm hungry. Let's get our order in before Libby closes up for the night. We can sit back here."

Deveraux narrowed her gaze slightly and offered a dismissive smile. "Enjoy your time in Carter's Crossing."

"Thanks." Kim nodded and followed Janine to the table she'd selected.

From force of habit, Kim chose the seat that put her back to the wall, providing a view of both the front and rear of the diner. Deveraux tossed a few bills on the table and left.

"Would you like a beer? There's only a few choices. Nothing fancy." Janine asked, handing the beer menu to Kim.

She didn't open it. "Whatever you're having."

Janine walked toward the back and disappeared into an alcove beyond the restrooms that Kim hadn't realized was there. After a few seconds, she emerged with two long-necked bottles and two frosty glasses. She placed them on the table and plopped into the chair across from Kim.

She raised the bottle and said, "Cheers."

"Cheers," Janine replied. She took a healthy swig and swallowed. "Libby'll be here in about five minutes with our food. I told her we wanted cheeseburgers and fries. Right?"

"Perfect." Kim swallowed the beer and the moment of companionable silence lasted a bit longer.

She could have steered the conversation, but she wondered whether Janine Wood had a reason for inviting herself to dinner with a total stranger. So she waited.

"I'm guessing your business in town isn't at the casino," Janine finally said. She didn't sound worried, but perhaps she was.

"Why'd you guess that?"

"Gamblers come in all shapes and sizes, but you don't look like the type to me."

Kim smiled. "Why not?"

Janine shrugged and took another swig from the bottle. "You seem like you're wrapped too tight for a gambler. Most of the gamblers we get into Toussaint's don't travel with a laptop or arrive in a rented Lexus. They don't wear suits, either. I pegged you for a federal agent of some sort. No offense."

"None taken." Kim grinned. "Why'd you think I was a federal agent? Why not just a local cop from somewhere?"

"We get a lot of feds coming through here. Because of Kelham and the casino and the railroad." Janine replied.

Kim nodded and flashed a genuine smile. "As it happens, I'm good at blackjack and I have a degree in accounting. I like math."

"Huh. I'm usually better at reading people." Janine cocked her head as if she was genuinely puzzled. Maybe she was. "So you are here for the casino, then?"

"No."

Janine's eyes widened with surprise, and then she threw back her head and laughed with gusto. After a while, she said, "You got me. Nice one."

Kim smiled and raised the long-neck again. They both drank. Then she said, "Why do you care about my reason for being in town? No offense."

Janine laughed again. Genuine mirth. "I like you, Kim Otto. You're direct. And you're quick. I'll need to stay on my game when you're around, won't I?"

Kim saw movement in the back of the diner in her peripheral vision. The swinging doors to the kitchen opened wide revealing a sturdy woman, about fifty. A blond bubble of curly hair framed her full face. Libby, presumably. Carrying two plates piled high with enormous burgers and a nest of shoestring fries. The heavenly smell wafted toward the table, preceding her arrival and making Kim's stomach growl again.

"Here you go," she said, placing the two plates in front of them.

"Libby, this is Kim Otto. She's staying at Toussaint's for a few days. I told her your cheeseburgers were the best in Mississippi," Janine said.

"Folks say that, and we sell a lot of them. Who am I to disagree?" Her vibe said she'd had a long day already and she wanted to go home. But she mustered a smile for a new customer that didn't reach her tired eyes. "Truth is, I'm not sure how much experience they have eating burgers at other places, though."

"From the smell alone, I can already tell your reputation is well deserved," Kim said truthfully.

Libby might have blushed because of the compliment. Or maybe she was just hot and tired and overworked. Hard to say.

"Glad to have you here, Kim. Come back any time. I'll let you eat while your food's hot. Save room for pie," she said as she hurried back to the kitchen.

They fell on the food like hungry wolves. Kim enjoyed every bite, resisting the urge to lick her fingers. Even as hearty as her appetite was, she couldn't finish.

"I swear, this thing is the size of half a cow." She pushed her plate away, uncomfortably full.

Janine finished every last morsel of the burger and all of the fries, too. She wiped the mayonnaise off her lips and the grease from her fingers with the napkin. "I only have time for one meal a day, and I'm always starving."

Kim hadn't seen anyone eat that much since her teenage brothers left the family farm. "Does that mean you're also going to have the pie?"

"Absolutely. You should, too. Libby's mother bakes them. The woman's eighty years old and bakes like an angel." Janine stood, collected their empty plates, and ferried them to the kitchen.

Minutes later, she returned with two pieces of peach pie a la mode about half the size of a major league home plate. "Libby's bringing the coffee."

Kim's stomach was too full to eat pie, no matter how good it was. If the weather had been better, she'd have suggested a long walk before they went back to the hotel.

After Libby brought the coffee and two plastic mugs and left again, Janine folded her arms on the table and said, "So are you going to tell me why you're here or not? Because I'm thinking it has something to do with Bonnie Nightingale's murder."

CHAPTER FOURTEEN

Thursday, April 14
6:07 a.m.
En route to Albuquerque, New Mexico

LIKE LIBBY'S CHEESEBURGERS AND FRIES, the coffee was exceptional. Libby should move her diner to a bigger town. She'd be the hottest place around, with food like that.

"Did you know Bonnie Nightingale?" Kim asked, lifting her fork to be polite.

Janine nodded. "Everyone did. Carter's Crossing is a small town. Lots of us have been living here for decades. Bonnie, too."

"Tell me what happened."

"You should ask Scott Greyson, the sheriff. He has real information. All I know is the gossip," Janine replied in a subdued tone. She continued eating the pie, but her gusto had disappeared.

"I've got an appointment with Chief Greyson tomorrow. But it might help if you'd share the gossip, too." Kim took a small bite of the pie while she waited for Janine to work out whatever issue she seemed to have with the request.

"Bonnie was a party girl. Always had been, even back when we were kids. When the guys from Kelham had leave, she liked to hang out in the bars. Nothing illegal or anything. They'd buy her drinks, and she would play pool or sing karaoke, that's all." Janine shrugged, looking down at her coffee and moving the fork around on the plate. "You know, the usual kind of thing single women do in small towns when they want some excitement, and there's none to be had."

"She was single, then? No boyfriend?"

"She was divorced about seven years back from Billy Nightingale. They were high school sweethearts, and they got married because it seemed like the logical next step after college. But they were never happy."

"What do you mean?"

"It was like watching a soap opera. He cheated on her. She kicked him out. He'd stay drunk and disappear for days, then crawl back home. You know how it goes." She stopped for a deep breath. "And one time he left after one of their big blowouts and she left, too. Went to Memphis. Got a job and a divorce. We thought she'd stay gone, but she didn't."

"Why'd she come back?"

"Billy was in the army. I mentioned that, right?" She shrugged again. "I guess when Billy died in Afghanistan, she still owned the house. So she came back."

Kim cocked her head and frowned. "She lived on the reservation?"

Janine shook her head. "She could have. That's where she grew up. Her folks lived there until they died. But she wanted to live closer to town. Her house was over on Pine Street."

"What kind of work did she do?"

"That was the crazy thing. She ran a daycare on the rez. For the casino workers' kids." Janine paused and wiped a glassy tear from the corner of her eye. "Bonnie loved those kids, too. They really miss her. I don't care what people are saying. She wouldn't have killed herself."

Kim softened her voice. "They found her body on the railroad tracks. You think it was an accident?"

She lifted her chin and scowled. "Bonnie Nightingale lived here all her life. She wouldn't have *accidentally* wandered onto the tracks when the midnight train was coming, now would she?"

"I'll admit, that doesn't seem likely. Which is why they're thinking suicide," Kim paused. "Because she must have done it deliberately."

"Well, they're wrong. Chief Greyson should know better."

"You think she was murdered?" Kim said quietly.

Janine's eyes rounded. "Isn't that why you're here?"

Kim shook her head. "The full autopsy isn't back yet. Preliminarily, it says she had so many injuries the actual cause of death requires more time and tests to figure out. Maybe the coroner will be more specific in a few days. We can take it from there."

She didn't exactly lie. But she didn't tell the whole truth either.

True, the autopsy findings were only preliminary.

Coroners had been wrong before.

Bonnie might have died because the train hit her.

Not likely.

But possible.

And no, Bonnie Nightingale's death, regardless of how it

happened, wasn't the reason Kim had been sent to Carter's Crossing.

She was here for Reacher.

Like always.

The question was, why did the Boss think Bonnie Nightingale's murder would be enough to draw Reacher back here?

And if the Boss was right, if Reacher did come, what would he do when he arrived?

Before Janine could say anything else, the diner's front door opened and the windy rain whooshed inside. Chief Greyson followed and pulled the door closed behind him. His sweeping gaze took in everything there was to see. Which wasn't much.

"Good evening, Agent Otto. Janine." He removed his hat and his wet coat and hung them on a hook near the entrance. He looked wrung out. Like the rest of his evening had been even worse than the crash on US 72.

Janine inhaled sharply as if she'd been betrayed or something. "*Agent* Otto? So you *are* a fed. I knew it."

Kim shrugged into the now uncomfortable silence. She watched Greyson.

He took long strides toward the kitchen, covering the ground in a hurry. He went through the double doors and stayed a minute before he came back to their table with a stoneware mug filled with coffee.

Greyson said, "Looks like you're done eating already. Mind if I join you anyway? Libby's bringing me a burger."

"Sure. Pull up a chair, Chief. You two probably want to talk business. I've got to get going anyway." Janine cleared her throat, pulled a fifty-dollar bill out of her pocket and dropped it on the table. A hefty tip for Libby was built into the gesture. A burger and fries, even with the beer and the pie, wouldn't cost fifty bucks. "I'll buy your dinner, Kim. You can buy next time. Your room key will open the front door of the hotel. Just wave it over the sensor to the right of the doorbell."

"Sounds like a plan," Kim replied, watching her leave.

Chief Greyson glanced at Kim and cocked his head. "Looks like you found the best hotel in town. You must have a generous boss. The feds who come through here usually stay at one of the budget places."

Kim shrugged. Anything she could say would draw the conversation into places she didn't want to go.

He scowled and leveled a flat stare toward Kim. "Did you tell Janine about the crash you witnessed?"

She shook her head. "Not my place."

He relaxed a bit. "She'll find out soon enough. Everybody in town will know before morning."

Kim felt sorry for him. It must be hard to be the top cop in a small town where he knew and cared about every soul. "I take it, you notified the sedan driver's family. How'd that go?"

"How it always goes. Worst part of the job." He ran a flat palm over his hair and shook his head. "I've known Carolyn Blackhawk all the years I've lived here. She was a good woman."

Kim asked, "What about the cyclist? How's he doing?"

"Brian Jasper. He's still critical. Probably won't survive," Greyson replied as he glanced at his watch. "Libby should have my burger done. I'll be right back."

He pushed his chair away from the table, picked up the empty dishes and the fifty-dollar bill, and carried them to the kitchen.

He returned with a plate piled high with food and an insulated pot of coffee. He poured the coffee into his cup and hers.

The freshly cooked burger and fries smelled just as good as before, making Janine's daily dinner habit completely understandable. Kim wondered how Janine worked off all those calories, eating like that every night. Kim would weigh two hundred pounds if she ate that much, even with all the running she did. Too bad.

Greyson gobbled half the burger before he spoke again. "I take it you're here about Bonnie Nightingale?"

Kim shrugged again. Gaspar's all-purpose gesture. Might as well go with that, since the rest of the town would assume the same, anyway. Fewer explanations required. "I read the preliminary autopsy report."

"So you know her throat was cut before she ended up on the train tracks," he replied. "One slice. Deep and wide. Visible bone. Which makes it my jurisdiction, not yours."

What he meant was three things.

First, since the train didn't kill Nightingale, the murder wasn't a violation of federal law. The FBI had no authority in the case unless the locals invited them in.

Second, that kind of throat wound is the way Army Rangers are taught to kill. Which suggested an Army Ranger killed Bonnie Nightingale. And, again, not a violation of federal law and the FBI had no authority there, either.

And third, what the hell was the FBI doing here when they had no jurisdiction?

Kim ignored all three meanings and nodded. "So she was dead already. Which means he tossed her into the path of the train to cover his crime. Just his bad luck that her throat remained intact enough to reveal the actual cause of death."

"Yeah. That's how I read it, too. But I'd appreciate it if you wouldn't share that theory with anyone just yet," he replied, taking another bite of the burger and stuffing fries into his mouth at the same time.

Kim didn't promise, one way or the other. "I'm meeting with Mayor Deveraux in the morning. Does she know Bonnie Nightingale was murdered?"

He nodded, still chewing. He sipped the coffee and swallowed the whole mess at once. His throat looked like a snake attempting to swallow an entire jackrabbit.

"Liz and I have discussed it. She was the sheriff here before me. We served in the Marines together. Provost Marshall's office," he said.

"How'd she take it? The murder, I mean."

He shrugged and took another bite of the burger. "We were both cops. She understands the job. I treat her like a colleague."

"You mean instead of treating her like your ex-wife?" Kim cocked her head as she revealed another piece of intel from the Boss's file.

He swallowed and grinned, showing his full set of white teeth in the process. It was the first time she'd seen him let down his guard, even a little bit. He was pretty hot when he flashed the megawatt smile, and his blue eyes sparkled like that. Hot for a small-town sheriff living in the middle of nowheresville, USA, anyway.

Still grinning, he said, "That's what I like about you Feebs. Always fully briefed. Never have to mess with bringing you up to speed."

"Right. So pretend I'm as qualified as your ex-wife and treat me like a colleague, too. Tell me what I don't know," Kim replied. Then she threw him a bone. "Even though we both realize you're not required to tell me anything."

He finished the burger and swigged more coffee while he thought about it. "Okay. For starters, your cover story is total crap. You're not here to do some deep background check on a guy who passed through fifteen years ago."

"What makes you say that?" She arched her eyebrows as if she was genuinely surprised he'd think so. Which she wasn't. The background check cover story was plausible enough. No shock that an experienced lawman like Scott Greyson would refuse to believe it, though. Cops question everything. Skepticism is like breathing to them.

"Because I run a cop shop now and I was a Marine cop before that. One government department is not much different from the next," he said, stopping for a swig of coffee. "I figure the FBI is doing what we would have done in this situation."

"What situation is that, exactly?"

"A touchy one," he paused for another swig. "A dead Native American woman. Perhaps killed by a government-owned train. Near an army base. And not too far from a casino. All under questionable circumstances. These, my friend, are the ingredients for a public relations nightmare."

She arched her eyebrows but didn't argue. "And what would all of that mean to a Marine who runs a cop shop?"

He drained his coffee mug and refilled it from the thermos, settling in for a serious talk. "We'd want to know more. We'd want our own team on the ground. And we'd send someone in to observe and report. Which is precisely what you're doing here."

"Why would you want all of that?" She cocked her head as if she was puzzled. Which she wasn't.

He folded his mug in both big palms and leaned forward. "Because the FBI thinks there's something more serious going on here. And if you're the observer, that means there's someone else working this thing, too. Someone official. Already here or on the way."

A loud crash of dishes and pots and pans sounded from the kitchen, interrupting the discussion.

"I'd better check on Libby. Make sure she's okay." Chief Greyson stood and headed toward the noise. "It's late. We'll talk more tomorrow in my office."

Kim watched him go, considering what he'd said.

He was partially right. But not about her reasons for being in Carter's Crossing. And not about the FBI's presence here, either.

When the Boss sent her here, he already knew Bonnie Nightingale's murder wasn't officially federal jurisdiction. Which meant the FBI wouldn't come in without an invitation from the locals.

So far as Kim was aware, no invitation had been issued. Chief Greyson would have known about an invitation like that, and he'd have said so. Her gut said he was that kind of guy. The straightforward kind.

Which meant Greyson was half wrong. There weren't two FBI agents on site. She wasn't likely to come across another agent while she was here.

Too bad. She could use a solid partner.

But with the army base nearby, and the manner of death suggesting a soldier had slashed the woman's throat, the army would have done exactly what Greyson had laid out. So there probably were two army investigators here.

An official army investigator at Kelham already.

And an unofficial army investigator walking around town, too.

Both were bound to have more intel than she did. About the Nightingale murder, at least. Maybe about Reacher, too.

All she had to do was find one or both of them and persuade them to tell her what he knew.

Kim glanced at the big clock on the wall over the kitchen doors and noticed it was after eleven. She was tired, but she still had work to do.

She pushed the front door open, turned her collar up, and stuffed her hands into her pockets. She glanced over her shoulder to be sure Chief Greyson wasn't watching. Whatever Libby had dropped in the kitchen seemed to have him occupied on the other side of the swinging doors. Kim could be out of sight before he realized where she was headed.

She turned and hurried outside, walking swiftly away from Toussaint's, toward the railroad tracks.

CHAPTER FIFTEEN

Wednesday, May 11
Carter's Crossing, Mississippi
11:25 p.m.

LAST CENTURY, train travel had been a lifeline, supporting businesses along its entire route. No more. This particular train now carried freight from one depot to another, where the cargo was unloaded and then moved by trucks to its final destination.

These days, no passengers disembarked. The heavy engine didn't even stop at the little towns along the tracks anymore.

Kim had checked the schedule. The train sped through Carter's Crossing once every twenty-four hours. Precisely at midnight. It never even slowed down. Just hurtled past. Came and went in about sixty seconds, depending on the number of cars the locomotive was pulling behind.

The train was impossible to ignore, but it was no longer a lifeline for the town.

One train every midnight, seven days a week, wasn't that hard to remember. Everybody around the entire county must have known the schedule.

Including the guy who threw Bonnie Nightingale onto the tracks, assuming all evidence of the murder would be obliterated by the monstrous train's impact with a fragile human body.

Bad assumption.

The file had been short on details about the crime scene. It was difficult to pinpoint the exact location the train ran over the body. The report had listed the impact point as south of the posted railroad crossing.

Kim made her way to the one-sided street that ran behind and parallel to Main Street. From the beginning of time, there were businesses on one side of that street facing a wide expanse of flat, open earth up to the railroad tracks.

On the other side of the tracks was another wide swath of weeds and dirt abutted by a dirt road and then a few decrepit homes where poorer people lived. A few had been gentrified, but most of the homes on the east side of the tracks were ramshackle structures with failing foundations. Even in the moonlight, they looked worn down or abandoned.

For decades, that one-sided street had powered the local economy in one way or another. But now, the town's prosperity was fueled by tourism and casino gambling. The old businesses were closing, one by one.

She imagined the passenger trains stopping here a century ago to let travelers stretch their legs or enjoy a meal. The one-sided street had been bustling back then. Prosperous shops and restaurants had flourished.

By the time Reacher came to town on the last case of his army career, few businesses were left. They were mostly bars, kept alive by soldiers from the base with nowhere else to go and dollars burning holes in their pockets.

Even later, after the casino was established east of town and the remaining shops and eateries folded, one by one, the soldiers took their dollars out to the gaming tables instead.

Only a couple of the old bars were still there. Soldiers still traveled the one-sided street, running their cars and trucks back and forth to Kelham. A rare few stopped in to visit the bars anymore.

The town's citizens had moved on to new homes, better jobs, and different entertainment.

Which made Kim wonder why Bonnie Nightingale had been out here on this one-sided street that night at all.

As Kim walked past, one of the bars was already closed. She glanced into the second one, which was the more decrepit of the two. A small knot of patrons gathered watching sports on a television inside. The faded sign above the door read "Brannan's."

Illumination along the street was provided by random streetlights, a many of which were not working. Neon signs inside the bars cast eerie red and green reflections on the cracked and broken sidewalk.

Kim glanced around, looking for evidence she couldn't yet recognize.

It would have been easy enough to kill Bonnie Nightingale here in the shadows between the buildings. Cutting a woman's throat doesn't take much time. A decent blade, enough force and weight, and the deed would be done in a matter of moments.

Moving Nightingale's body would have been a bigger challenge.

According to the autopsy report, she had been a petite woman. A strong soldier could have lifted her, carried her across the open dirt, and tossed her onto the tracks.

He could have made his escape and waited for the inevitable. He expected the speeding train to pulverize the body and eliminate all evidence of murder.

He could have done it all without being seen because it was midnight and no one had any reason to be watching the train.

That's what the report said.

Kim looked up and down the sidewalk, and across the road to the train tracks, confirming it could have happened that way.

Any competent Army Ranger could have committed the murder like that without breaking a sweat.

Kelham still had extremely competent Army Rangers.

Yes, killing the woman first and then disposing of the body onto the tracks would have been easy enough.

She nodded, thinking things through, looking for holes in her theory. She found none.

No wonder the army was worried.

She could imagine plausible alternative scenarios, though.

Kim considered whether Nightingale had been tossed onto the tracks while she was still alive.

He could have killed her on the spot, solving the whole issue of transporting the body.

Nightingale might have walked with him to the tracks under her own steam. Maybe they were holding hands, talking quietly the way lovers do. He could have lured her there under some pretext.

The reason she went with him didn't matter now. All he needed to do was get Nightingale to the tracks shortly before the train came through.

Either way, wherever her throat was slashed, big pools of blood would have accumulated. The stains might still be visible. She made a mental note to look for the murder site tomorrow in the daylight.

Satisfied that the killer could have done the crime and left the scene, Kim walked slowly across the dirt to the train tracks, listening for noises of all kinds.

She checked her watch. Fifteen minutes until the midnight train arrived. Plenty of time for a closer look.

Kim pulled her high-powered flashlight from her pocket and flipped it on. She climbed up the embankment, stepped over the first rail, and stood on the first tie.

The reports had been somewhat vague about the exact location of the body parts they'd located, too.

She aimed the light beam north and south, looking for any piece of trace evidence that might identify the train's point of impact with Nightingale's body.

Kim's guess that the impact probably occurred near the bars had been based on instinct at first. Nightingale's death was staged to look like a suicide.

Regardless of where he'd killed her, Kim reasoned that he'd want to avoid being seen both coming and going from the work of depositing the body on the train tracks.

He'd have wanted to be quick about the whole thing. Quick and quiet.

He'd have wanted to watch to confirm the train had done the job.

Either way, if he'd killed her elsewhere and transported the body, or if she'd walked to the tracks before he killed her, to make sure nothing went wrong, he'd have wanted to be the shortest possible distance across the open space so he could see clearly.

Which was the shadowed area directly across from Brannan's.

He'd also have needed an alibi.

If he'd left the body on the tracks and then returned to Brannan's before the midnight train sped past, other patrons in the bar would have seen him there. Talked to him. Maybe he'd even bought a few drinks and left a big tip, to be sure the bartender remembered him.

Which would have meant the point of impact had to be relatively near Brannan's to give him the time to get there and also be able to observe the train.

His alibi would have been more than sufficient for a suicide.

Unless someone figured out Nightingale wasn't killed by the speeding train.

Which she wasn't.

But it should have taken a while to figure that out if the train mutilated the body. It was simply his bad luck that the train had left the cause of death unconcealed.

Kim wondered whether he knew about the autopsy, even as Chief Greyson tried to keep a lid on that piece of intel.

As soon as Nightingale's murder became public knowledge, the killer would flee the jurisdiction. If he hadn't already. He was in the army. He might have shipped out the very next day. He might have already received his orders before he killed Nightingale.

Still standing on the railroad tie, she'd been so focused on the logistics of the Nightingale murder that she hadn't noticed the ground's faint, constant tremor at first.

The trembling transferred from the ground to the tie to her boots and then up through her body. The rails began to whine.

Kim peered into the murky distance. A single headlight

muted by the fog was still far down the tracks. The train was coming her way. Fast. She glanced at her watch. It was two minutes until midnight. The train should be right on time.

Her gaze was transfixed by the headlight, dancing like a fairy, growing larger and brighter and more terrifying by the moment.

The ground shook harder under her feet. The rails howled. The train whistle blasted two long wails that shattered the remaining silence.

The warning bells at the crossroads began to ring, and the lights flashed, and the safety arms lowered on either side.

Kim hopped off the tracks and ran toward the bars on the other side of the open dirt.

She'd waited too long.

The train was right behind her now. Outrageously massive. Insanely loud.

The engine roared past and the cars behind it followed at breakneck speed.

She kept running, fearing that she'd be sucked up in the ferocious wind current caused by the train.

When she made it safely to the sidewalk, Kim anchored her back against the building, braced her legs, breathing hard.

The train continued hurtling north, shaking the ground, impossible to stop, even if anything at all had been inclined to try.

She'd never felt so tiny and insignificant and weightless in her entire life.

The boxcars and flatbeds kept coming, flashing past.

One, five, ten. She lost count.

Until finally, she watched the back of the last one roll away.

One bit at a time, normalcy returned.

The howling wind died.

The earthquake stopped shaking the ground.

The bells and flashing lights at the crossing stopped.

The safety arms raised.

Silence filled the air once more as if peace had never been disturbed by the massive train.

Kim's body continued vibrating and the lingering sounds overwhelmed her ears.

When her ability to hear herself think returned, the first thing she did was to confirm her theory.

No one could be ambushed by that train. No chance in hell. The noise, the shaking ground, the whipping wind. All of it made ignorance of the approaching train inconceivable.

If Nightingale hadn't been dead already, she'd have had enough warning and enough time to get safely off the tracks.

Kim did it herself just moments before the train sped past. Unless she'd been incapacitated, Nightingale could have done it, too.

Which explained why the locals jumped to the conclusion that Nightingale had committed suicide.

A woman would have had to be determined and desperate to stand in front of the oncoming train to wait to be battered to death. There were easier ways to commit suicide.

Even without the evidence that her throat had been cut, Kim would have reached the same conclusion.

Bonnie Nightingale was definitely murdered.

Anybody who'd ever been anywhere near the midnight train should believe the same.

The killer had dumped the body and left before the train passed to establish an alibi.

For sure.

An old man opened one of the doors and cheers spilled out of Brannan's behind him. He held onto the door a moment to steady his feet. Then he moved clear and staggered along the sidewalk in the opposite direction.

Kim watched him until he reached the end of the block. His gait was jerky and uneven. Twice, he tripped and fell forward, but managed to stay upright. Eventually, he turned the corner out of sight.

The door to the bar had not closed completely. A televised sporting event of some sort elicited periodic whoops and jeers from a small group of spectators inside.

Kim glanced through the glass. The place was narrow and small and dark, and a hundred years of grime covered the floor. Four men huddled at the bar near the television. One might have been the bartender.

She argued with herself briefly. What were the chances that any of them had seen Bonnie Nightingale's killer? And even if they had, Chief Greyson would have already taken statements from them.

But they were old enough to have been around when Reacher was here fifteen years ago. One of them might know something.

Hell, she was already here. She might as well find out.

It was the slenderest thread of possibility.

But she was used to pulling on the least likely threads.

Hunting Reacher had proven as elusive as searching for the Loch Ness monster and ten times as dangerous.

She took a deep breath, squared her shoulders, opened the door, and stepped inside.

CHAPTER SIXTEEN

Thursday, May 12
Memphis, TN
12:05 a.m.

HE WAS TIRED AND WRUNG OUT. This wasn't a trip he'd
have chosen to make. Jasper had screwed things up royally,
leaving him no real choice in the matter.

He'd chosen the wrong vehicle, too. But there weren't many
options on that score, either.

The old pickup truck he'd found abandoned at a truck stop
was two dozen years old and rode like its shock absorbers were
made of concrete. If there were any springs left in the bench seat,
they'd long ago given up their capacity for bouncing with the
potholes.

All the way to Memphis, blowing rain pelted the truck from
every angle.

The headlights were weak and hadn't been adjusted since
Methuselah was a pup. The right headlight pointed high and the
left one low, making it difficult to see the road ahead in the rainy

darkness, even at reduced travel speeds. He'd squinted the whole way, straining his eyes and increasing his fatigue.

When he'd finally reached the turnoff, he found the hospital surprisingly busy for a weeknight.

He followed behind a trail of winking taillights. A line of vehicles turned into the main driveway and split off in several directions. He moved aside for an incoming ambulance and then followed a small SUV into the visitor parking garage.

CCTV cameras were perched here and there along the route and at the entrance. The cameras were most likely running unattended at this hour. But he didn't take the chance.

He flipped the visor down on the truck and tilted his head down. The hat worked with the visor to shield his features while he pulled a ticket from the machine, stuck the ticket in his shirt pocket, and waited for the gate arm to open.

He was expected back at Kelham before dawn. No time to rest or find coffee or anything else. He had one job here. He wanted to get in, get it done, and get on the road. The drive back to Carter's Crossing wouldn't be a walk in the park, either. But he couldn't dwell on that now.

He drove up to the seventh floor and parked the stolen pickup out of CCTV camera range. He backed into the space and rested the pickup's back bumper against the concrete wall to block the muddy license plate from view.

When he climbed down from the driver's seat, his body ached all over. He spent a few seconds stretching out the kinks in his back and loosening up his stiff muscles.

He adjusted his civilian camo. Turned his collar up, straightened his leather gloves, and pulled the hat down low on his forehead. He'd have worn sunglasses, but they'd have drawn too much attention since it was well after midnight.

He left the truck unlocked to help the next guy who tried to steal it. Then he hustled toward the down ramp where it was easier to avoid the cameras than in the stairwells or the elevators.

The air was slightly cleaner on the ramps, too. Stairwells and elevators in old garages were bound to be full of deadly germs and appalling odors.

On the ground level, he strode purposefully toward the emergency room entrance, tossing the truck's keys into a muddy ditch in the back of the building along the way.

He'd find another vehicle easily enough. There were plenty to choose from in that garage. His old bones wouldn't have survived the two-hour return trip in that heap anyway.

All he had to do was get into Jasper's private room for a few minutes alone. The rest would be easy. He fingered the syringe resting in his pocket.

He entered the hospital behind a group of people as if he'd been there a dozen times before.

The ER was crowded and chaotic and smelled like citrus. The scent was clean, even if the patients weren't. His nose wrinkled involuntarily. The guy in front of him had some of the worst body odor he'd ever encountered. He could only imagine the heavy-duty air filtration systems the hospital must have working overtime to keep the worst of humanity's stench at bay.

A line of patients waited to be checked in by an overworked desk clerk, providing identification and proof of insurance. A room full of patients were already waiting for care. Gunshot victims, sick kids, drug addicts, bar fighters, and vehicle crash victims. They were easy to classify based on appearance and blood patterns.

Enough patients and companions to keep the staff fully occupied for hours, he figured.

Which explained why Jasper had been stabilized instead of taken to surgery right away.

The overloaded ER also meant he wasn't likely to be noticed or stopped. Finally, he'd caught a break.

He skipped the line at the visitor's desk and turned left, mingling with the preoccupied crowd.

He knew exactly where he was going.

Like all hospitals, this one was clearly marked. He followed the posted signs and moved through the throngs in the hallways toward Jasper's room.

Jasper was holding in ICU for an open operating room. He'd been triaged and heavily sedated and hooked up to a dozen machines in a surgical ICU bed on the third floor.

He found the correct elevator and punched the button. The oversized elevator car lumbered to a slow stop and bounced slightly. The doors opened ever-so-slowly and closed behind him at the same snail's pace. After five seconds, the car rose to the second floor and bounced to a stop and repeated the opening-closing dance before it moved glacially up to the third floor.

He felt like he'd aged two years during the process.

He stepped out on the floor and spied a blue and white sign pointing toward the surgical ICU waiting room.

When he reached the ICU, the patient rooms were behind a closed door that required a key card for entry.

He moved into the smaller ICU waiting room and watched the door.

Hospital personnel dressed in scrubs of various colors scurried in and out, sometimes pushing a bed with a patient on it or a piece of rolling equipment and a clipboard. But more often simply walking through purposefully but empty-handed.

Like the elevator, the oversized double entry doors opened

slowly and closed even more slowly. Presumably, the idea was to give the beds enough time to roll through without interference. Which made sense.

The glacial pace of the entry system also made his plan a lot easier.

He leaned against a wall in the ICU waiting room and watched personnel, patients, and visitors come and go for a while to get the rhythm of the doors fixed in his mind.

Every time the doors opened, he could see inside. The wide hallway interior of the unit was bright and clean and mostly deserted. Rooms on the left, nurses' station on the right. From time to time, a single nurse manned the station, coming and going at irregular intervals between other duties, he assumed.

Sliding glass walls, covered with floor-to-ceiling drapes, separated the patient rooms from the hallway. To move the patients in and out, nurses folded the walls to one side along a ceiling track. They rolled the bed into place before unfolding the walls and drawing the curtains again.

Two beds sat in the interior hallway. One bed had a patient on it, waiting at the nurse's station while the orderly stopped to look at something on the computer. The other bed rested against the wall, empty.

The door slowly swung shut behind another nurse. It seemed to be operating on a timer rather than a sensor. He checked the cycle against his watch. The opening and closing process lasted a full two minutes.

He grinned. He could have moved a fully equipped six-man team through in that much time. *Piece of cake.*

On the waiting room side of the door where he was perched, the duty desk was unoccupied, too. The attendant had gone for the night.

After one more cycle of the door, he was ready to move.

He'd watched the phone posted on the wall near the door sensor, patiently waiting for his opportunity.

He didn't need to wait long.

After about ten minutes, a visitor approached, picked up the phone, and talked quietly. A young woman dressed in sneakers, jeans, and a hoodie had been crying. Barely holding it together. She said something quietly into the phone, nodded, replaced the receiver, and waited.

The door swung open in slow motion.

The visitor shuffled inside.

He paused a beat to allow her some distance and then slid through behind her as if he had every right to visit his sick relative, too.

No one seemed to notice.

No one tried to stop him.

His luck held.

The interior section of the ICU unit was almost deserted. There were no nurses at the desk at the moment. The doors to the individual rooms were closed and the curtains were drawn as if the patients had been tucked in for the night a while ago.

He knew which bed Jasper occupied. But even if he hadn't, the patient's names were posted on the wall near each entrance.

He found Jasper's room exactly where he'd expected it to be and slipped inside, making sure the heavy drapery concealed him from view.

He took a few seconds to scan the room.

Jasper was alone and heavily sedated. He was wearing a clear plastic face mask connected by tubes to a machine that pushed oxygen into his lungs with every breath. Both arms were tethered by IVs feeding him fluids, medications, and what looked like blood.

A sheet and blanket covered most of his body.

Jasper's face appeared remarkably unscathed. The helmet he'd been wearing did most of its job. The skin on his arms looked okay, too.

He approached Jasper's bed, keeping his back to the door. He pulled the big syringe from his pocket and used it to administer the lethal overdose.

He stepped back and watched Jasper's breathing for a few moments as if saying his last farewell.

The alarms on the machines hooked up to Jasper's body would sound shortly. Nurses and doctors would come running. But they'd be too late.

The injection was fatal. Every time.

He nodded once. Mission accomplished.

On his way out, he dropped the syringe into the sharps container on the wall. He was already walking through the door when the alarms began to sound. Jasper would be dead shortly.

Instead of waiting for the turtle-speed elevator, he took the stairs down three flights to the main floor.

He moved steadily forward and left the hospital through the closest exit.

In the employees' long-term parking garage, he found an SUV with the keys in the ignition and he was on his way.

"Two down, three to go," he said under his breath.

CHAPTER SEVENTEEN

Thursday, May 12
Carter's Crossing, Mississippi
1:15 a.m.

WHEN KIM'S HEELS HIT the hard floor just inside the entrance to Brannan's, the three guys at the bar turned as if they'd been choreographed in one of those late-night musicals her mother loved to watch. She expected them to hop off the stools and dance.

The effect was both comical and faintly menacing.

They were related, surely. Not brothers. Cousins, maybe. Like a kaleidoscope had fractured a single old white dude into quad images. All four were the same but slightly off-kilter, with edges not quite as sharp as if they had remained a single whole.

Faces wrinkled. Eyes scrunched to peer through the dim and hazy room. Gray eyebrows and brown eyes and various swaths of facial hair. One had a skinny mustache. Another a scraggly goatee. The other two looked like they hadn't shaved in a few days, and gray hairs dusted their faces and necks.

All four had unwashed long hair, mostly gray, gathered into ponytails low on the backs of their heads. They wore faded jeans, muddy work boots, and stained T-shirts that might have been white once. Below the short sleeve hems were thick arms covered with faded bad tattoos they'd done themselves after a night of hard drinking, like teenaged girls who pierced their ears at sleepovers.

The four men groaned in unison. Whatever they'd hoped to see when they turned to look, Kim apparently wasn't it. They turned back to the television in time to catch the batter swing and miss for the third time.

The game went to a commercial as the teams switched sides. The bartender stood and walked around the opposite end as she approached.

He was the one with the skinny mustache. His T-shirt was slightly cleaner than the others. His tattoos perhaps a bit more faded. From her new vantage point, the bottled spirts on the shelves reflected shadowed light across all four faces.

He seemed friendly enough. "What can I get you?"

"I'll take a bottle of Labatt. Got that?"

He shook his head. "We got Bud and Bud Light in bottles."

"Bud is fine," she said as if she intended to drink it.

He nodded and turned to one of the coolers. He rummaged to locate a brown longneck, picked up a napkin, and screwed off the cap. He pulled a warm glass from the shelf and plopped both down on the bar in front of her.

"Thanks…" She let her voice trail off to encourage him.

He took the hint. "Walt. McKinney. And you?"

"Kim Otto," she replied, tilting her head toward the others. "Those guys your brothers?"

"Cousins. There's lots of McKinneys around here. You'll

run into a bunch of us if you stay here long enough." He seemed open and friendly as if they were likely to meet again.

She took a pull on the beer. It was too stale and too warm, but she swallowed it without gagging. It would have been impolite to spit it out.

The game came back on and the four McKinneys turned their attention toward the television. The crawler along the bottom of the screen said the game was in extra innings. Cardinals and Padres.

The night game was broadcast from San Diego. Which, coupled with the extra innings, explained why it was still on at this late hour.

They watched while the pitcher took the mound and threw a fastball. The sound on the set was turned down, but the umpire's gestures made it clear he'd called a strike.

"I was out there when the train went through," Kim said, pointing her thumb toward the tracks. She captured the bartender's ear but not his full attention. The game magnetized his gaze.

"Uh huh. Happens every night. Midnight. Set your watch by it," he replied without looking at her. "Sorry. I got a bet on this one. He pitches a no-hitter and I win five hundred from my cousins."

"Sure. No problem."

She waited until after the second pitch. Another strike. The pitcher seemed to want a brief break. He spent some time looking around, raising his arms, digging his feet into the dirt around the mound.

"I heard a woman died on the tracks a few nights ago. Hit by the train," Kim said as if the death was a curiosity and no more.

"Yeah. Real shame. Bonnie Nightingale. Nice girl. Knowed her all my life," Walt replied, still distracted.

"You or your cousins see it happen?"

"Naw." He shook his head. "Cardinals was playin' late that night, too. We didn't see nothin' if it wasn't on TV."

The pitcher finally threw the third pitch. Another strike. The batter never risked a swing.

The four McKinneys let loose a shout of unbridled joy. Apparently they were all Cardinal fans. And there was nothing besides baseball that they were going to talk to her about tonight.

Which was okay. It was late. She could come back when they were more likely to be sober. The bartender knew Nightingale. She'd start earlier with him tomorrow to find out more.

The pitcher quickly dispatched the next two batters, retiring the side as the McKinneys cheered.

She pulled a ten-dollar bill from her pocket and tossed it on the counter.

McKinney picked up the bill. Between innings, the station broke for a quick commercial and a news update.

The local story was all about the vehicle crash she'd witnessed earlier. Nothing new to report. The national headlines were a rehash of the North Korean diplomat who had died of poisoning while meeting at the United Nations in New York.

Authorities had located a grainy video of the diplomat and a potential witness. He was standing ringside with a sultry woman wearing a blazer that barely covered her assets. The newscaster asked for help identifying the woman and said there were still no suspects in the case.

Kim watched the brief report, which illuminated nothing. Law enforcement officers would be looking for the woman. They'd find her, if she hadn't left the country already.

Walt McKinney offered her a sheepish apology. "Sorry about the beer. We mostly sell draft or cans. Easier, you know? Was there something else you wanted?"

"I was just wondering about the woman who died on the tracks. Doesn't make sense, does it? If you're outside, you know that train's coming from a couple of miles at least," Kim said. "Seems like she'd have had plenty of time to get out of the way."

"I guess you just never know what's really going on with a person," he said, shaking his head.

"Why do you say that?"

"Bonnie was in here earlier that night. I talked to her for a while. She seemed okay."

"Anything special bring her in here?"

"She came in most nights on the weekends. Lotta locals do. We've been the neighborhood place for folks around here a lotta years. Even before I bought the place from the Brannan brothers," he shrugged, keeping one eye on the television screen.

"Did you talk to her that night?"

"Sure. She sat in that seat where you're sittin'. Waitin' for Jasper to get off work, she said."

"Who's Jasper? Her boyfriend?" Kim asked.

Then the commercial ended, and so did the conversation. The next batter managed to connect with the ball, and the attention of all four McKinneys stayed glued to the set. She'd get nothing more out of them tonight.

She'd have better luck tomorrow.

When she turned toward the exit, another man emerged from the shadows. This one was younger and smaller than the McKinneys. Fitter, too. About six feet tall. Short brown hair and eyes. From the looks of him, he was connected to Kelham, one way or another.

"Where're you goin'? You're a pretty little thing," he said as softly as a lover might. His speech was slurred, perhaps by the drawl and not the booze. "Hang around. Let me buy you a drink."

"Thanks for the offer. Maybe another time," she replied evenly.

He was slightly unsteady on his feet. He'd obviously been drinking more than long enough. Something about the guy gave off a hostile vibe.

She didn't want any trouble with the locals. Not on her first night in town, anyway. But he was standing between her and the door.

So she paused to give him a chance to move aside.

He didn't.

Instead, he settled his body, squarely blocking the exit.

"One drink. Then you can go," he said as if he intended to stop her.

Politely she replied, "No. Thank you."

He didn't move out of her way.

Kim assessed the situation quickly.

She was alone.

No backup.

No one knew where she was.

One strong and wiry unarmed enemy ahead.

She was inside the bar that might have been the last place Bonnie Nightingale was seen alive.

Is this what had happened? Maybe this scum bucket tried the same routine that night. Had Nightingale refused him and ended up dead?

Kim heard laughs behind her. Four burly McKinneys back there were watching this guy's moves for entertainment during the commercial break.

Kim ran through her options.

The easy thing to do was to shoot him, but she wasn't interested in blowing her cover just yet.

She'd been confronted by drunks before. Usually they were not half as tough as they thought. She wasn't worried.

She didn't have to kill him. All she needed was to get him out of her path and leave. The McKinney asshats could have a good laugh at Romeo's expense. It would blow over and everybody would be sober in the morning. No harm done.

Romeo was bigger and stronger than she was, and maybe just as well trained from the sinewy look of him. Safer to assume that much, anyway.

Assessing Kim, he'd naturally assume she was an untrained lightweight.

Maybe he'd made the same assumption about Nightingale. Maybe he'd been right about her.

Perhaps his success with Nightingale had made him overconfident.

He cajoled, "Come on. You're lonely. You wouldn't be in a place like this if you weren't. Let me buy you a drink." As if he believed he was the sexiest man alive.

Kim wondered briefly if his technique ever worked on the women around here.

"Get out of my way," she said again, more steel in her tone this time.

Then she waited for him to make the first move.

He wouldn't have much patience. Guys like that never did.

This whole thing, whatever it was he planned to get started, would be over in a brief moment or two. He just didn't know that yet.

After a few uneventful seconds of staring her down like he expected her to change her mind and jump into his arms, his expression clouded. The smarmy smile slid off his face. He strode toward her as if he intended to grab her and force her back to the bar.

Maybe that was exactly what he'd planned because he closed the gap between them with more speed than finesse.

When he was within range, he raised his right arm away from his side, hand open to grip her bicep as he passed.

Kim held her body steady without flinching, waiting for her moment. When he swept his arm toward her, she moved swiftly aside.

The full force of his momentum whiffed his arm through the air, past the empty space her body had occupied a moment before.

Which caused him to stumble forward, briefly off stride and bewildered.

"No means no, jerk." Using his confusion and momentum against him, she elbowed the soft flesh under his raised right arm, hard. Worst case, he'd have some cracked ribs. At the very least, he'd have a hell of a bruise that would keep him out of commission for a day or two.

He yelled out and flailed his left arm around to grab his injured torso.

While he was still unsteady on his feet, she gave him a hard kick to the back of the knee and a shove in the ass to go with it.

"Ahhhh!" He screamed as he toppled, holding his leg and writhing with pain. "You bitch! I'll kill you!"

"You can try. If I'm still here when you're able to walk again," she said, not even breathing hard.

All four McKinneys were howling with laughter. Not one even shifted his weight on the bar stool or tried to come to the downed man's rescue.

She'd done a dangerous thing and she knew it.

She'd made a fool of Romeo here in front of his buddies. He'd been bested and damaged by a woman half his size. They'd ride him about it until the end of time.

Which meant he'd be doubly savage and much more cunning when he came after her again.

And then she would have to shoot him.

For now, she simply walked out. It was late and she was tired. The air was heavy and wet and smelled like the bottom of a gym locker. She turned her collar up against the wind.

Outside, a local radio motor patrol vehicle was idling parallel to the curb. Chief Greyson was sitting behind the steering wheel.

He lowered the window. "Hop in. You need a ride."

"I'd rather walk, thanks," she replied, stuffing her hands in her pockets.

He said, "And I'd rather not insist. So get in. We need to talk."

"Maybe tomorrow." She took a few steps along the sidewalk, past the alley, toward Toussaint's Hotel.

She stepped carefully because the streetlights were too dirty and spaced too far apart to illuminate much of anything. The last thing she needed was a twisted ankle or a trip and belly flop onto the pavement.

"Get in the vehicle, Otto." Greyson had put the SUV into gear and moved slowly alongside her. "Buy yourself some time. If the McKinneys think I took you into the station on an assault charge, they won't come looking for you tonight while you're sleeping."

Surely he was bluffing. But the thought of the grimy McKinneys creeping into her room at night caused a long shiver to run up her spine. If she dwelled on it for even a moment, she wouldn't sleep again until she left Carter's Crossing.

"When you put it like that…" She stepped into the street, opened the cruiser's front door, and slid into the passenger seat. They weren't going far, or fast, so she didn't bother with the seatbelt.

CHAPTER EIGHTEEN

Thursday, May 12
Carter's Crossing, Mississippi
1:55 a.m.

SHERIFF GREYSON ROLLED THE SUV slowly to the end of the block, checking the shops and alleys along the way. He turned toward Main Street where the sidewalks were slightly brighter but just as empty.

They passed one closed storefront after another, moving toward Toussaint's in the middle of the block. There were a few better-looking bars on this street, too. But mainly the shops were clothing stores of various sorts. A knitting store. Restaurants. At one end of the block was a drugstore and across the street was a grocery.

All were dark and locked up tight at this hour.

"Before you ask, no. I was not following you. I drive around town every night before I turn in. Had nothing to do with you being over here snooping around." The sheriff paused and flashed that nice grin. "I was surprised when I glanced inside at

Brannan's. I thought you'd returned to the hotel when you left Libby's Diner."

"Thanks for looking out for me, Chief. But I can take care of myself." She didn't know whether to believe he hadn't been watching her. But she appreciated the ride, so she was being nice, too.

He said, "I take it you're not interested in Luke Price's clumsy passes."

"Luke Price?" She arched her eyebrows in his direction.

"The dude back there at Brannan's. Local Lothario. Or so he believes, with some justification," Greyson said lightly. "He was Bonnie Nightingale's boyfriend for a while."

"Seriously?" Kim shuddered. "Hard to believe any woman would come within a mile of that creep. He's not exactly a smooth talker. And I'm fairly certain he hasn't bathed in a while, either."

"His appeal, such as it is, probably has more to do with his money. Rumor is he inherited a bundle from some relative, and he's willing to spend it to show a girl a good time," Greyson nodded. "Regardless, watch yourself. You've got a new enemy. The McKinney boys will ride him forever because a woman half his size took him out like that. He'll be looking for payback when he sobers up. And he won't give up until he gets it."

"Not sure how you know he made a move on me or that I took him out," she replied. "Since you said you weren't following me."

He gave her a knowing look and spelled it out. "You're an FBI agent. You've got skills. I'm the sheriff and I live in this town. Not much happens here that I don't know about. You think you're the first woman Luke Price ever made a move on who fought back?"

"I suspect I might be the first one to leave him on the floor, out cold, with fractured ribs and a helluva stomachache," she replied, serious as a heart attack.

"Maybe so." Greyson flashed her the megawatter again, crinkling his baby blues in the process. "Price definitely had it coming. I'm sorry I didn't see the fight from a better vantage point. Even worse, I didn't have a bet riding on the outcome."

"Damn straight," she nodded curtly, allowing him to smooth her ruffled feathers. Close quarters combat was not her preference. She wasn't big enough to win against a solid male opponent.

She had the skills to do the job when presented with no viable options.

The RMP finally reached Toussaint's and he parked out front in the angled slot next to her rented Lexus.

"Seriously, watch yourself," Greyson said in a somber tone. "Price is a mean drunk like I said. Truth be told, he's not all that pleasant when he's sober, either. You embarrassed him in front of his pals. He won't forgive or forget."

"No problem." She had a hundred questions she wanted to ask him, but they could wait until tomorrow. She reached for the door handle and pulled it to open the door. "I don't need Price to forgive me or to forget what happened tonight. Just the opposite. He needs to remember. If he tries anything with me again, he'll be twice as sorry."

Greyson swept a steady gaze her way but said nothing.

"Thanks for the ride."

"You're welcome," he replied. "Any time."

Kim stepped out and closed the door. The wind had passed and now the atmosphere felt like a hot steamy shower.

She hurried toward Toussaint's front door, pulling her card key from her pocket.

Behind her, she heard Chief Greyson turn off the SUV's engine. He pressed the key fob and the alarm chirped loudly.

He took half a dozen long strides and met up with her at the hotel's front steps.

"You don't need to walk me to the door, Chief," she said. "Luke Price isn't going to come after me tonight. He can't even walk right at the moment. The McKinneys won't either. The Cardinals game will keep them occupied until they're too drunk."

"You've definitely got those old rednecks pegged. Nothing will draw them away from the Cardinals." He stayed right with her up the stairs and across the wide porch to the front door. "But tomorrow, they'll be looking for something else to amuse themselves."

"I'll be careful." She waved her key card over the sensor on the right side of the door and heard the lock click open. She grabbed the door handle and pushed.

When she went inside, Chief Greyson came in behind her.

Kim focused a surprised expression in his direction.

"Don't worry. No need to demonstrate your self-defense techniques on me," he said, raising both hands palms out in response. "I live here. Third floor. In the back, where it's quieter."

"Don't you have a house somewhere?" she asked as they climbed the stairs to the upper floors.

"Wife got the house when we split. And it's just easier to live here. Janine is a friendly proprietor. I can eat most days at Libby's. I don't even need to do my own laundry. The department does most of it and the staff here does the rest," he said.

They'd reached the second-floor landing. Kim moved

toward Room Seventeen. "I'd love to hear all about it, but it's been a long day. Goodnight, Chief Greyson."

"See you tomorrow in my office as planned, Agent Otto." He kept climbing toward the third floor.

After he'd disappeared up the stairs, she used the key card to enter her room. When she opened the door, a blast of frigid air hit her in the face. Someone had cranked up the air-conditioning to what felt like sub-zero levels.

Kim closed the door behind her and hustled deeper into the room to adjust the thermostat. It wouldn't budge. She could get maintenance on it in the morning. But what would she do tonight?

A wall of drapes reminded her that the room overlooked the street, which was still deserted. She opened the window to let the cold out and allow the steamy night air inside.

She kept her coat on while she waited to warm up.

The room was equipped with a minibar. She rummaged around inside until she found a small bottle of red wine and a plastic wine glass. After she changed into red microfiber pajamas, she slipped her coat on again to stay warm. She set up her laptop and her secure hot spot on the desk.

Kim wrote a few paragraphs briefly describing the day's events and uploaded the pages to her private server. Paying her insurance premium, she called it. Someday, she'd need the reports to justify her actions. She'd long ago accepted that she wouldn't come out of the hunt for Reacher unscathed. She hoped to come out alive and still employed, though. That's what her insurance reports were for.

After she finished the secret document, she dashed off an official version of events and uploaded it for the Boss. He'd be on the phone in the morning before daylight if she didn't update him now. The report would keep him out of her way for a few hours.

Then she sipped the wine and thought about Bonnie Nightingale, Carolyn Blackhawk, and Brian Jasper. She didn't waste a moments' worth of brain cells on Luke Price or his buddies.

She considered calling her former partner to get his view of the whole situation, but she worried that he might be sleeping. Sleep was precious to Gaspar. His painful right leg didn't often allow enough peace for sleeping. He might have found a period of respite. She wouldn't awaken him when she simply needed a sounding board.

Still, the situation was more than odd.

Chief Greyson had said Jasper, the motorcyclist who had hit that sedan head-on this afternoon, wasn't likely to live through the night.

Which would mean three citizens from Carter's Crossing, all died within a week. An oddity in itself. Kim figured three citizens from this town under the age of sixty wouldn't normally die in an entire year. Statistics being what they were, the total population of this place just wasn't large enough.

She cocked her head and took another sip of the sour wine, swishing it around in her mouth in a failed attempt to improve it by infusing some air. After a few moments, she gave up and swallowed the mouthful with a wrinkled nose, still musing over the details.

These three deaths were unusual.

Each life had been extinguished too young.

Each met a violent, unpredictable end.

What were the odds of a thing like that happening in a place like this?

Slim, for sure.

She opened an official website and searched the three names. As an afterthought, she searched for Luke Price, too.

Vital statistics appeared on all four.

She scanned the pages.

Aside from sharing a Carter's Crossing mailing address, they seemed to have nothing in common. Different jobs, different ethnicities, different everything. If there was a pattern here, she couldn't see it.

She'd put Gaspar on the search in the morning. He had access to intel she couldn't hope to locate. Mostly because she was handicapped by the Boss's rules and the law. Gaspar wasn't.

Kim closed the laptop and finished the wine. It was late. She wouldn't learn anything more tonight. Time to get some sleep.

She slipped out of her coat, climbed into bed, and fell into the deep oblivion of alcohol enhanced exhaustion. The kind of sleep Gaspar never managed.

CHAPTER NINETEEN

Thursday, May 12
Carter's Crossing, Mississippi
3:35 a.m.

THE ROADS WERE QUIET AT THIS HOUR. The rain had stopped. He'd made good time driving back to Carter's Crossing. He'd only stopped once, at an all-night drive-through fast food joint for burgers and a strong black coffee to combat fatigue. The coffee helped. But not enough. He could barely hold his eyes open.

He rolled into town, driving under the speed limit, using the side streets, and backed the stolen SUV into the alley behind the grocery store. He removed the license plate and then wedged the SUV out of sight between the dumpsters.

Someone would notice it there sometime in the next few days and the vehicle would be towed. It would sit in impound for a while out in the county lot. By the time the Memphis owner claimed the vehicle, it wouldn't matter anymore. He'd be gone.

He tossed the license plate and the keys into an alley

dumpster and hustled along in the shadows through the residential areas and toward Main Street.

He glanced at his watch. He was due at Kelham soon. Which didn't give him much time for shuteye.

One thing the army had taught him well was to sleep when you can and eat when you can. He'd been well trained. Ninety minutes of sleep would suffice until he could steal another few hours later.

He felt like a warrior, returning home from a dangerous mission, triumphant and invincible. He was one of the best soldiers the army had ever trained. He had the medals and the scars to prove it.

Nothing could stop him.

Twenty-six hours from now, a few more loose ends to deal with, and he'd be free and clear.

Today's rain had softened the ground and left puddles along the alley. He'd stepped in two or three holes already. His shoes and socks were soaked. But he stayed in the alley, avoiding CCTV cameras until he reached the side street and turned right.

He saw no one wandering around Main Street and didn't expect to. All the citizens of Carter's Crossing were asleep, inside their homes, buttoned up with the air-conditioning running.

They'd had a few tornadoes since he'd been here. He'd seen the devastation the families had suffered when they slept through the tornado sirens in the middle of the night.

Hell, they slept through the midnight train night after night for their entire lives.

Nothing short of a nuclear blast on Main Street would awaken any of them, and maybe not even that.

He walked along the sidewalk, a block north of Toussaint's Hotel.

Everybody in town knew Sheriff Greyson lived there since he split with his wife and lost his house. He was even less worried about being heard by anyone inside the hotel. That thing was ancient and built like a fortress.

But the last thing he needed was to be seen by a sheriff wandering around, unable to sleep.

He had no idea whether Greyson suffered from insomnia. But an ounce of prevention was always better than a pound of cure. So he hugged the shadows close to the buildings and stayed well away from the hotel windows.

He reached Main Street and crossed quickly, looking left and right to be sure no one else was wandering around. He kept moving, headed toward the alley behind Brannan's.

He'd left his vehicle there. He intended to retrieve it and make his way back to Kelham. He didn't expect to see anyone, or to be seen.

He was almost in the clear.

The Cardinals' game had ended, so Brannan's would be closed up for the night. Even the McKinneys would be home by now and passed out, drunk.

He took another quick look over his shoulder, confirmed no one was following him, and ducked into the alley.

He didn't see the lumpy form lying on the side of the pavement until it was too late.

The guy tripped him at just the right moment when his stride was off-balance. "Where ya headed in such a hurry?"

His left foot landed wrong on the pavement and slipped into a pothole. He turned his ankle and went down, landing on his left side in the filthy gutter near the dumpster. Rage pounded in his temples.

The lighting was dim and he didn't get a good look at his attacker. But he recognized the voice.

Swearing as he struggled to climb out of the pothole on his sore ankle, he said, "What the hell is wrong with you, Price?"

"Ain't nobody ever back here. Just gettin' a li'l rest before I drive to Memphis to see Jasper." Price staggered to his feet. He groaned as he stumbled and held his side. He was still drunk. The acrid smell of stale beer saturated the air around him.

Price had been sleeping it off in the alley and the footsteps must have rattled him.

"Get out of my way. You stink."

Price replied, "You wanna be nicer to me. Jasper told me about you. Said he had somethin' to show me. Said you owed him big time, after Bonnie. He was real tore up about Bonnie. He loved that girl you know."

He felt the smoldering rage ignite and surge in an instant.

"Oh, yeah? What else did Jasper tell you?" His tone was deep and level and angry. Jasper never could keep his mouth shut. Why hadn't he remembered that?

But Price was still too drunk to read the dangerous situation he'd put himself into.

"Jasper said we was goin' to get up outta here. Head to paradise. Said he had plenty of money comin' from you." Price stuck his chin out and tried to poke a finger, but his aim fell two feet short of his target.

Jasper. Kid just couldn't keep his mouth shut. Bringing Jasper into the operation had been a mistake from the outset. Then Bonnie came along and things got even worse.

After Bonnie died, Jasper was a mess. He'd lost his focus. He'd expected his mistake to fix itself with Jasper's crazy head-on collision.

When that didn't happen, he'd gone all the way to Memphis and eliminated Jasper. Which was fine. But he was still angry about it.

But now here was Price, attempting to blackmail him. The very thought fueled his outrage to white-hot levels.

On a different night, he might have made another choice.

Infused with victory now that Jasper was dead in Memphis, annoyed because Blackhawk died and Nina was still alive, he allowed his fury to erupt.

"What else did Jasper say about me?" He didn't bother to hide his anger or keep his voice down. No one would hear. And even if they did, he'd take care of them, too. He was beyond concern for the twits in this town.

Price finally seemed to register the danger. He tried to back up, but the wall was behind him. "Nothin' else. Said he'd tell me when he got back."

Liar.

He slipped his gloved right hand into his pocket and pulled out the gun he'd bought on the street last week. He'd already fitted it with the silencer. He moved closer to Price.

He held his arm out of sight until, in one smooth, practiced arc, he raised the gun, aimed the barrel directly at Price's right leg, and shot him through the kneecap.

Price screamed. The pitch was high and piercing enough to belong to a woman. He grabbed his knee and went down, rolling in the alley's filth.

Price's screams ratcheted up a few hundred decibels and bounced off the walls in the narrow alley.

At close range, the screams seemed deafening. Like being in a walled cage with a dozen tortured vixens seeking to breed. Not that it mattered. In the distance, outside the alley, citizens might awaken and listen closer. But when they heard nothing more, they'd roll over and go back to sleep.

He moved in closer, pinned Price against the wall, and put a gloved hand firmly over his mouth.

"Shut up. Tell me what Jasper said."

Price didn't hear him or didn't care or simply couldn't make himself stop screaming.

He pointed the pistol directly at Price's forehead, and said, "Shut. Up."

Wild-eyed, Price saw the gun, realized what was coming, and gave up the struggle.

He pulled the trigger.

Instant silence.

Breathing heavily, he shoved Price's body behind the dumpster.

He tossed the gun and silencer inside.

Then he stripped the gloves from his hand and stuffed them into his pocket. He'd dispose of them elsewhere.

Problem solved.

He didn't spend even half a moment wondering if Price's screams might have been heard.

He'd be long gone before anyone came looking for the miscreant if they ever did. And there was zero evidence to tie him to the murder.

Nothing to worry about. Nothing at all.

He smiled, pleased, and kept walking around the dumpsters into the middle of the block.

He found his vehicle, started up, and drove straight to Kelham, with plenty of time to spare.

CHAPTER TWENTY

Thursday, May 12
Carter's Crossing, Mississippi
4:05 a.m.

FROM HER VANTAGE POINT ON THE TRACKS, Kim saw the train coming straight toward her through the moonless night.

The speeding engine shook the ground and the crossing lights flashed and warning bells sounded and the headlight blinded her.

A single whistle sounded long and loud and ear-splitting.

She smelled charcoal in the night air and barbeque, faintly, from the east where a few frame houses stood concealed by darkness.

Kim was rooted to the spot, panting like a terrified animal.

The ground shook and bounced, lifting her off the ground, bouncing her along with everything else, over and over again.

She raised her forearm to shield her eyes from the headlight's glare and braced against the inevitable impact.

The engine roared ever louder.

She screamed, but couldn't hear her voice in her own ears.

The overwhelming noise of the monstrously huge train drew closer, washing over her as it threatened to slam into her fragile body, tearing her into a dozen pieces.

Her arms and legs and torso would fly through the air in all directions.

Yet, she couldn't move.

She covered her ears with both hands, but still, the noise pounded like a massive explosion.

A deep gulp of air filled her chest and was stuck there, refusing to exhale. Pain seared her torso like a massive heart attack.

She squeezed her eyes closed and braced for the vicious, all-consuming impact.

The unrelenting train was so close she could almost reach out and touch it.

She wondered what would happen if she did.

Suddenly, a pair of hands as big as catcher's mitts grabbed her.

Thick, strong arms enfolded her quivering body and jerked her off the tracks.

Momentum carried them out of the path of the charging locomotive just in time.

They rolled down the embankment and into the ditch on the east side of the rails.

Her back landed hard at the bottom of the ditch, pressed against the weeds and rocks and gravel on the ground.

The big man covered her with his body, lifting his weight onto his forearms, lying in the missionary position. As if he consumed her, here and now.

He'd saved her from the speeding train. All of her limbs were still intact. She could feel every inch of her body matched by the length of his, tingling from toes to fingertips to the crown of her head.

Briefly, she tried to look into his face, but the gravel and dust swirled around and into her eyes and she closed them again as tightly as she could, feeling the grains embedded behind her eyelids.

The train sped past.

First the locomotive and then the cars, one by one, continuing for a long, long time, not slowing or stopping for even half a moment.

The ground beneath her vibrated with the rumbling wheels of the train on the tracks.

The man's body seemed to vibrate on top of her, too. But he didn't move away.

He might have said something in her ear, but the noise of the passing train obliterated every other sound.

Finally, finally, the caboose passed and kept going.

He rolled off her and left her cold and exposed at the bottom of the ditch, her body still quivering until the last vibrations of the caboose settled into the earth once again.

Her eyes popped open and she awakened from the nightmare.

Which was when she heard a terrifying sound through her open window.

Heart pounding, body still quivering, and fully awake now, adrenaline pounding through her body, safe in her bed.

She sat up to steady her rushing emotions, confused by sleep and the dream, and attempting to separate facts from fevered imaginings in the dark.

That was when she fully realized she'd heard someone screaming outside. Animal-like shrieks that had shattered the quiet night and carried through the open window.

Still shaking, Kim tossed back the soggy sheets, slid out of bed, and found her coat. She slipped her pistol into her coat pocket along with her cell phone and picked up the key card on the way out.

Briefly, she considered trying to find Sheriff Greyson on the third floor for backup. But by the time she thought of it, the door to her room had closed behind her and she was already dashing down the stairs toward the lobby.

The hotel was quiet. No one else emerged from their rooms or joined her downstairs. She ran to the front door and let herself outside.

On the sidewalk, she glanced in all directions, seeking the screamer.

Main Street was as dark and quiet and deserted as it had been when she'd arrived at the hotel several hours ago. No one lying dead or injured on the sidewalk. No vehicles on Main Street other than Chief Greyson's cruiser and her Lexus, still parked where they'd left them.

Now that she was fully awake, she struggled to wrest more details from the lingering mental fog of the terrifying nightmare.

Were the screams clear or muffled? Male or female? Close or distant?

Toussaint's Hotel was located in the middle of the block. She turned right and dashed to the south corner. She looked up and down the side street. Nothing.

She ran back the way she'd come, past the hotel, to the street north of Toussaint's. Again, no vehicles, no bodies. And no evidence that anyone had been harmed during her nightmare or otherwise. No one else had run out into the darkness carrying a gun, either.

Now she wondered whether she'd heard the screams at all.

Perhaps they'd been another figment of her overactive imagination. Like the train and the big man who'd rescued her.

Kim slid her hand into her pocket, still holding her Glock, and walked slowly back to the hotel.

She was sure she'd heard the screaming. Dead certain, once she regained consciousness, that the screaming had originated outside.

Yet...

Maybe she was losing her mind.

The nightmare had been terrifyingly real, too. But still, just a figment of her anxiety breaking through after she'd experienced the all too real midnight train.

One thing she could say about the dead woman. If Bonnie Nightingale had stepped in front of that speeding train simply to kill herself, she was braver than Kim would ever be, for damned sure.

Not that she believed the woman had done any such thing. Bonnie Nightingale had been murdered. The autopsy proved it.

But why would anyone who lived in Carter's Crossing believe the suicide idea?

Every soul in this town had witnessed that speeding train. They knew what would happen to anything left on the tracks to be destroyed by the big engine.

Perhaps there had been suicides before. Maybe that's why people around here might believe Bonnie Nightingale had taken that very horrifying way out.

But it nagged at her. Such an obvious lie. And yet people seemed to buy into the lie. It made zero sense.

Kim had reached the sidewalk in front of Toussaint's once again. She peered into the darkness along Main Street as if she might have missed something that would explain the inexplicable.

She shook her head. No one here, dead or alive.

As adrenaline drained from her body, slowing her heart rate and her breathing to normal speeds, Kim trudged up the porch steps and swiped her key card across the sensor.

She pushed the door open and entered the lobby.

Where she almost collided with Chief Greyson, standing directly in her path.

CHAPTER TWENTY-ONE

Thursday, May 12
Carter's Crossing, Mississippi
4:35 a.m.

CHIEF GREYSON STEPPED BACK, allowing her to enter and close the door. He took in her disheveled appearance, pajamas under the coat, and the curtain of black hair spread across her shoulders.

She straightened her shoulders and said, "Were you watching me again?"

"I serve as security when I'm on the premises," he explained. "There's a sensor on the door that rings in my room after hours. I heard the door open and hustled down here, expecting an intruder."

His explanation was believable enough. More than hers would have been. So she didn't offer one.

She turned and headed toward the stairs.

"What were you doing outside?" he asked, not letting her off the hook so easily.

"Taking a walk," she replied as she started up.

After the massive adrenaline rush, she felt exhausted. Maybe she could sleep another few hours. She continued her trek up the stairs.

He checked the front door to be sure it was securely locked and then took a few long strides to catch up with her before she reached the second floor.

"We don't have a lot of crime around here normally," he said. "But Bonnie Nightingale *was* murdered. Until we get that sorted out, you shouldn't go wandering around alone at all hours."

They'd arrived at her floor, and she turned toward her room. "Thanks, Chief. I'll remember that."

She could feel his gaze following her all the way to Room Seventeen. She swiped the key card and went inside without looking back.

Like a zombie in a trance, she put the "do not disturb" sign out, closed the door and flipped the deadbolt. She slid out of her coat and climbed back into bed, bringing her gun, which she tucked under the pillow within easy reach.

Within seconds, she was asleep again, unhampered by murderous trains and flying body parts and blood-curdling screams from persons and places unknown. Or big men with strong arms who said nothing.

It felt like only a few minutes had passed before a loud rap on the door was followed by Janine Wood's cheerful, "Good morning! Room service!"

Kim groaned and rolled her head to look at the clock. Seven-thirty, on the nose. Room service, as ordered.

Pushing the covers aside, she padded across the carpet through the heavily air-conditioned room. She threw back the deadbolt and opened the door.

Janine whooshed inside with the tray. "Wow! It's really cold in here. Something's wrong with your thermostat. I'll get maintenance up here right away."

"Thanks. Can you wait a while, though?" Kim replied.

"Sure." She set the tray on the desk, moving efficiently through the process. "Coffee and muffins, as promised. Libby's mother bakes the muffins for us fresh every day. They're great. Want me to pour?"

"That's okay. I'll do it. I've got a conference call and then an appointment, and I need to jump into the shower…" She let her voice trail off, hoping Janine would take the hint.

"Well, stop at the desk on your way out and let me know the coast is clear for my maintenance guys to fix things. We'll solve this meat locker situation pronto," Janine said on her way out. "I don't know how you got a wink of sleep with it so cold in here."

Kim poured a mug full of black coffee, grabbed a bite of one of the muffins, and called Gaspar. There was no way to cloak the call from the Boss's prying ears, so she didn't try. He wasn't likely to be listening in real-time anyway. By the time he discovered the conversation had happened, she'd have moved on.

Gaspar picked up on the second ring, "Good morning, Sunshine. What's happening in Our Town, USA?"

She arched her eyebrows as if he could see her and gave him a teasingly haughty tone. "You're mocking me? I'm sitting here in a frigid hotel room after three hours of sleep, and you think that's funny?"

"Sorry." He stuffed his humor, but she could hear it anyway.

"Apology accepted. Got anything for me?" She swallowed the muffin and sipped the coffee, both of which were pretty good.

She glanced outside. Main Street was slowly coming to life. The sun was shining and a few vehicles were passing by.

"Looks like the motorcyclist, Brian Jasper, died during the night," Gaspar said, bringing her attention back to the call.

"Yeah, I thought that might happen," she replied. "He was as well protected as possible, but when a human hits the pavement at a high rate of speed with that much velocity, it's never going to end well."

"Right." Gaspar cleared his throat. "But that's not the real news."

"What is?"

"They're trying to keep it quiet, but it looks like he died of a drug overdose. Fentanyl, probably. It's easy to get and way too easy to produce a deadly overdose."

"That stuff is nasty enough to kill anybody pretty quickly in a variety of ways," Kim replied.

"Yeah. But how did he manage to overdose while immobilized and monitored around the clock in an ICU bed?" Gaspar said.

"Suicide? Unintentional overdose while self-medicating?" Kim cocked her head, listing all the options that fit the facts. "Hospital error?"

"Maybe."

"But you don't think so," she said flatly.

He swallowed something. She imagined the sweet creamy coffee he loved and shuddered. Just thinking about all that sugar made her teeth hurt.

"Rather unlucky, wouldn't you say? Guy survives a head-on crash at sixty miles an hour. Neither the crash nor his survival should have happened. Gotta be long odds on both. But he did crash, and he did survive." Gaspar paused, giving her a chance to stay focused. "Then the guy is lucky enough to have me get him a medivac. He stays alive until he makes it to the ICU. They get him stabilized. He's waiting for surgery."

He paused.

She waited.

He took a deep breath and a long exhale before he finished, "And *then* he dies of hospital error within the first twelve hours he's there? They barely had time to get his name into the computers."

She nodded, finished the last of the muffin, and poured more coffee, thinking things through. "Yeah. It does seem like an extremely unusual bit of bad luck, at the very least."

Gaspar said, "I don't believe it."

"You've always been the suspicious type." She was suspicious, too. Most cops were. Suspicion was a life-saving skill in their line of work. "So you're chasing it down. Starting with the video in and around the hospital."

"Yes. But that hospital is busy. There's a lot of people moving around at all hours. Lots of video to wade through," Gaspar replied. "I'll let you know if I turn anything up."

"Thanks. For what it's worth, I think you're right," she said, and not to stroke his ego. "It's just too odd that he'd die of an overdose like that. Too many odd things happening around here. What else?"

"Two more things," Gaspar replied at the end of a really long slurp that sounded like he was licking the sugar from the cup.

CHAPTER TWENTY-TWO

Thursday, May 12
Carter's Crossing, Mississippi
8:45 a.m.

KIM HEARD HIM CLICKING KEYS on his keyboard before
he replied, "Elizabeth Deveraux. Mayor of Carter's Crossing.
You're meeting with her this morning at ten o'clock, right?"

"I ran into her last night briefly at Libby's Diner. But, yeah.
She was the sheriff here when Reacher investigated his last
case," Kim replied. "The case started out small. One dead
woman. Then it turned out to be three dead women. Probably all
murdered by the same guy. Who was most likely stationed at
Kelham at the time."

"And you're meeting with Deveraux because Cooper told
you to," Gaspar said. "But he didn't tell you why or what she's
supposed to know."

She shrugged. "You know how this works. The Boss wants
me to go in with fresh eyes. No agenda. I talk to the witness.

See if I can get her to tell me anything helpful. Sometimes they do, and most times they don't."

"Except Deveraux was more than a simple witness. She was the town sheriff's daughter. Then a Marine, Suzy Wong. Then she was the sheriff while Reacher was in town. Now she's the mayor. And she was actively investigating the last case of Reacher's army career," he said, exasperation oozing with every word as if Kim was too slow on the uptake here. "Think about it, Otto. Reacher's women are *never* willing to talk to you when you first show up. So why the hell would Cooper think Deveraux is likely to tell you anything at all? Let alone spill intel that's even remotely useful?"

"Your mindreading skills are as good as mine, Chico," she replied. "Hell, I don't even know why the Boss thinks Reacher might be hanging out around here. The murdered woman—"

"Which one?" he interrupted quietly.

"What do you mean, which one? I'm talking about the here and now." She blinked. "There's only one. Bonnie Nightingale."

"Well, that's what Reacher thought when he came to town back then, too. Remember? He found out there were more victims after he got there."

"Yeah. So?"

Gaspar paused another beat before he said, "The sedan driver in that crash you witnessed yesterday, the one who died. Carolyn Blackhawk. She was murdered, too."

Kim sat up straight and clutched the coffee cup in both hands. "What do you mean?"

"We had satellite coverage. We also had the dashcam from the big rig. I watched the videos of the crash, and events leading up to it, from way better angles than you had." He drew a deep breath and exhaled before he replied, "Long story short, it's clear now that the cyclist definitely had plenty of time to avoid that wreck."

"Which is what we thought at the scene." She stood and paced the cold floor in her bare feet. "So you're saying it's a fact. Jasper hit that sedan intentionally."

Gaspar sighed as if the intel exhausted him. He was likely running on less sleep than she was. He usually did. "There's no other reasonable explanation. Trust me. I looked half the night for a different answer. It's not there."

"So what did you find, then?"

Gaspar said, "After a few hours of analyzing everything we've got, it looks like Jasper *intended* to hit the sedan. He got a running start before he did it. I'm thinking he meant to jump over the oncoming car."

Kim stopped dead in her tracks. "What? That's crazy. Why in the hell would he do that?"

"Sorry. Hang on." Gaspar paused, covered the speaker, and mumbled to someone before he came back. "Anyway, when Jasper hit that sedan head-on like that, he had to know he could fail the attempted fly-over. And if he failed, the sedan's driver would be injured, at the very least."

Kim thought about what he'd said, which made a crazy kind of sense. Maybe. "Did Jasper know the woman?"

"Seems likely, but I haven't found a way to connect them yet. Blackhawk lived in Carter's Crossing and so did Jasper. From what I can tell, that's a pretty small town. Most people there know each other, wouldn't you say?"

She tensed. "The sheriff told me as much. No reason for him to lie."

"You mean Sheriff Scott Greyson? The one who was married to Mayor Deveraux?" Gaspar's tone suggested something nefarious, and he was probably right.

But she wanted to finish running down one rabbit hole before she headed into another.

"The very same Sheriff Greyson." Kim nodded, even though he couldn't see her. "Finish your thought about Jasper."

"Well, look. Within a few hours of Blackhawk's death, which we're pretty sure was a murder, Jasper is rather conveniently terminated. Drug overdose. In the hospital. ICU. Where he's supposed to be monitored every minute, twenty-four seven." Gaspar paused to let everything he'd said sink in. "What does that sound like to you?"

She shook her head. She didn't want to call Blackhawk's or Jasper's death murder. Not yet. "Sounds like a mess. For sure."

"It's way worse than that. Add in Bonnie Nightingale, murdered before her body was tossed onto those train tracks, and that's three homicides in less than a week. And those are just the ones we know about. You don't believe that's a coincidence any more than I do."

Her breath caught. "You're saying we've got some sort of spree killer here?"

"Three murders. Three different locations. That's a spree killer by definition and we both know it," Gaspar said. "In this case, it's a spree killer who is somehow connected to Carter's Crossing. And Kelham. And likely to Deveraux and Reacher."

"Because the Boss wouldn't have sent me to Deveraux if there was no Reacher connection to the Nightingale murder. Hold on." She took a quick breath.

She'd already bought into the spree killer theory. It did make sense. He was right.

Then the other shoe dropped right on her head. "You think *Reacher* is killing these people?"

"Possibly," Gaspar said.

She imagined him crossing his long legs and getting more comfortable in his chair. "But not likely."

"Why not?"

She replied, "For starters, Reacher doesn't usually bother with anything so complicated. If he'd wanted to kill three people, he'd have done it directly."

"You think so?"

"Definitely. And he wouldn't have tried to cover it up by pretending three homicides were something else," she said, running the scenarios in her head.

She often relied on Gaspar and gave his theories plenty of weight. Was he right? Gaspar was always her ace in the hole where Reacher was concerned. His mind worked like Reacher's. They were the same in many ways. Close in age. Similar backgrounds.

Except Gaspar wasn't a loner like Reacher was.

But she often wondered whether Gaspar could have taken the same path if his family life had been more like Reacher's lone wolf existence and less like a 1950s ideal family. A man couldn't go roaming the country and living off-the-grid with a wife and five kids at home, no matter what.

She shook her head, having reached her conclusion. "Not very likely that Reacher would do all of this, is it?"

"Okay," Gaspar said. "But your boss might not see it that way. What if Cooper thinks Reacher is the killer?"

"Then he'd know Reacher's got a damn good reason, too. A reason that makes sense. At least to him." Kim paused for a quick breath. "Reacher's a trained killer and he's good at it. But he's not a maniac. He doesn't kill for the fun of it."

"Exactly," Gaspar replied. "Assume Cooper believes

Reacher would take these three particular victims off the table. Why does he think Reacher's the one?"

"I don't know. Maybe the mayor can help me with that," she noticed the time. She'd intended to tell him about her trip to the midnight train and Brannan's and the screaming and her pre-dawn activities on Main Street, but all of that would have to wait. "I need to get going. Send me everything you've found. And keep looking, okay?"

"Copy that. I'm also sending you some help. That's the third thing I called to tell you."

The last time, he'd sent one of the most capable operatives she'd ever worked with. "What? Flint again?"

"He's already there. And I didn't exactly send him."

She wanted to get going. She hated being late. "What are you talking about?"

"Name's Major Lincoln Perry."

"Yeah, the Boss mentioned him. You know the guy?"

"I've run into him before. I told him to look you up. You can trust him." Gaspar gave her a quick rundown. "The army sent him in, undercover. Because of the autopsy report on Bonnie Nightingale. They're worried she was killed by a Ranger from Kelham. He's the outside guy."

"Okay, thanks," she replied.

"Hold your horses." Gaspar's grin was obvious in his tone, "Army also has an inside guy on the base. His name is Hulk Hammer, in case you run across him."

She almost spit out her coffee. "Seriously? Hulk Hammer? What kind of name is that?"

Gaspar laughed. "His real name is Eugene Hammer. But I guess he doesn't like the Eugene. He was a wrestler in college. Goes by Hulk."

"Oh, brother," she deadpanned and then cleared her throat. "Check out another local for me. Name's Luke Price. I met him last night in Brannan's. We didn't hit it off well."

"What do you mean?"

"He made a pass at me and I laid him out."

Gaspar chuckled. "Guess he won't try that again."

"Right." She saw the time and headed toward the bathroom for her shower. "And Gaspar?"

"Yeah?"

"Thanks for the help."

"Just stay alive, Sunshine. That's all the thanks I need."

"Your wish is my command. And if you have the time, I need to know what's going on over at Kelham."

"Such as?"

She replied, "The Boss said they're about to shut the place down. Target date is Friday the 13th. They're phasing out. If it is a Ranger we're looking for, it could help to know whatever we can about the situation out there."

"I'll look into it," Gaspar said before he hung up.

She tossed the phone onto the desk. She'd fill him in about the early morning screamer later.

In the bathroom, she closed the door, flipped on the lights, and turned the heater dial to maximum. Then she did the same for the hot water in the shower.

While she waited for everything to warm up, she brushed her chattering teeth and thought about what Mayor Elizabeth Deveraux might have to say about Reacher.

CHAPTER TWENTY-THREE

Thursday, May 12
Carter's Crossing, Mississippi
9:00 a.m.

GENERAL ALEC MURPHY, CO, had showered, shaved, dressed, and made it to his office at Kelham before his scheduled meeting with the ridiculously named Major Eugene "Hulk" Hammer. Murphy was tired. He'd only had a few hours' sleep and the dark circles under his eyes reflected it. But he outranked Hammer, so he didn't expect to get any flak about his appearance or anything else from the guy.

Murphy was seated behind his desk with his never-ending mug of black coffee.

He closed the laptop and looked up when his sergeant escorted Hammer into the room. Hammer turned sideways to walk through the door. He was almost as wide as he was tall. Not because he lacked physical stature, but because he was a huge, hulking man.

"Good morning, sir," Hammer said, offering a regulation salute to a superior officer. The oak leaves on his collar confirmed his rank, had there been any question about it. Fine lines around his eyes confirmed that he wasn't born yesterday.

"Have a seat, Hammer. No need for formality out here in the back of beyond. We're closing this place down and I'm on my way out, anyway. Haven't you heard?"

Hammer pulled one of the heavy wooden chairs away from the desk and settled his bulk into it, which was somewhat comical. He looked like he'd joined a ten-year-old's tea party. "Yes, sir. I heard you were retiring. After many years of distinguished service."

"Right," Murphy replied with more than a touch of sarcasm. "So cut to it, Major. Why are you here? Some of my guys get rowdy in town again? Mess up Brannan's?"

"Not exactly, sir."

Murphy put his pen down on the desktop, folded his hands, and stared straight into Hammer's oversized face. Everything about the guy was uncomfortably huge. He must have spent every spare moment inside a gym. "So what, exactly, is your purpose here, Major? I'm all ears."

"You know I'm with the 110th Special Investigations Unit. It's never good news when I show up on base." Hammer stared straight back. "I'm afraid we have a civilian situation. Death of a Carter's Crossing resident. A Native American named Bonnie Nightingale."

Murphy nodded easily and took a swig of the hot coffee. "I heard about her. Damn shame. Hit by the midnight train, wasn't she?"

"That's the public story, sir. That she committed suicide by train, yes." Hammer replied. "But that's not true."

"No?" Murphy cocked his head. "So what's the real story, then?"

"Looks like Nightingale was killed *before* her body was dumped in front of the train. Her throat was cut." Hammer paused. "Local sheriff thinks the homicide could have been done by one of the soldiers here at Kelham."

"That so?" Murphy said, frowning, allowing his tone to be as icy as his steely stare. "The US Army is taking orders from a civilian sheriff now, are we? A small-town sheriff who used to be a jarhead and couldn't get a job with a real department in a big city somewhere?"

"Sheriff Greyson was a Marine, yes, sir. In this case, it makes him more reliable instead of less." Hammer cleared his throat. "We're taking a look."

"And why is that?" Murphy held his temper on a short leash, but it wasn't easy. He had plenty to keep him occupied over the next few days before he retired and Kelham emptied out. He didn't have time for nonsense.

"I'm afraid the autopsy report lends some credence to the sheriff's concerns," Hammer replied.

"And let me guess. Instead of bringing it to me, to let me handle it through regular channels, some four-star sitting at a big desk in the Pentagon sent you down here to sort this thing out," he said flatly. "The army is leaving Carter's Crossing. Nobody wants a mess on our hands as we bail out of this town and leave everybody in it twisting in the wind. Do I have that right?"

"That's about the size of it, sir. PR being what it is these days, nobody wants an incident that could be avoided by a bit of handling on the front end. Shouldn't take long to figure this thing out. I've already issued an order to lock the base down until I can get to the bottom of it," Hammer said.

"What?" Murphy punched his chin forward in outrage. "Lock Kelham down? You don't have the authority to do that, soldier."

Hammer reached into his breast pocket and pulled out his orders. He passed the envelope across the desk.

Murphy removed the orders from the envelope, unfolded the document, and read the briefly stated contents. They were signed by that same four-star general at the Pentagon, the one who was way farther up the chain of command from Murphy. He then refolded the document and tossed it back.

"We've got a lot to do here to get this base closed on time, Hammer. How long is this nonsense with the Nightingale woman going to take?" Murphy demanded.

"Not long, sir. I hope. We don't have a full house of personnel here now because of the impending closure. It shouldn't take much time to get alibis from everybody on base for the time of death," Hammer said. "After that, we can lift the lockdown and let you all go about your business."

Murphy narrowed his icy blue eyes. "When, exactly, did the woman die?"

"Four days ago, sir. Sunday. May eight," Hammer replied. "Sometime before midnight."

"You know this how?"

"They found her body on the morning of Monday, May nine. Coroner says she'd been hit by the train the night before."

"And how does he know that?"

"Forensics and deduction. The train only comes through once every twenty-four hours. And the body was fairly fresh when it was discovered. Some, uh, parts were still on the tracks. If the train had run over her twice..." he paused to clear his throat again, "...well, it would have been obvious from her condition. So we've got a twenty-four-hour window we're working with."

"I take it Sheriff Greyson tracked her activities before the midnight train came through on Sunday?" Murphy asked.

"Yes, sir. Witnesses confirm she was alive until at least nine o'clock that night," Hammer replied.

"Sunday night. Between nine and midnight," Murphy said, as he thought about the timeline for a few seconds. "We've got a lot of guys living off base. Sunday is a slow day around here, too. Even slower since we've been packing up. Some of our soldiers have already been deployed elsewhere. At least half the ones we have left would have been off the base on Sunday night."

"Which means it might take me longer than I'd hoped to interview everyone. Establish alibis. Examine motives. And all that." Hammer took a deep breath, lifting his barrel chest to enormous proportions. After the exhale, he said, "I'd better get started. Do you have an office I can use? And someone to round up the personnel?"

"My sergeant will show you to your quarters and get you set up," Murphy replied, punching the intercom that rang at the sergeant's desk. "And before you have to ask, I was out at the casino Sunday night. Got there about eight and left when the tournament ended. About two in the morning. Big poker tournament. Drew a few hundred spectators. Several of our guys were out there, too."

"I see," Hammer replied. "Was Nightingale there? At the casino?"

"Could have been." Murphy shrugged and raised the coffee cup to his mouth. "They've got CCTV. They'll let you look at it. You can see for yourself."

Hammer nodded and lifted his bulk from the creaking chair. "I'll get settled and then start right in if it's okay with you."

Hammer offered another salute and left. Murphy said nothing as he watched the giant walk through the door and close it behind him.

Murphy waited a few moments before he turned to his computer to check his emails.

CHAPTER TWENTY-FOUR

Thursday, May 12
Carter's Crossing, Mississippi
10:00 a.m.

KIM HAD FINISHED HER SHOWER and dressed in a black suit. She anchored her hair in a chignon at the nape of her neck and applied a dab of makeup to cover the dark circles under her eyes. When she stepped back to examine the total effect in the mirror, she looked less like a sleepless raccoon and more like a solid FBI agent.

"Okay. That's good enough," she said aloud.

Her room was still frigid inside, but a nice warm breeze wafted through the open window overlooking Main Street. She heard cars and pedestrians bustling about outside. She wouldn't need her overcoat out there today.

There was a safe in the room, but she slung her laptop case over her shoulder. She'd lock them in the rented SUV on the way. Everything on her laptop was well encrypted. Hackers couldn't do much damage even if they tried.

On her way out, she stopped at the front desk to give Janine the all-clear for maintenance on her air-conditioning, as promised.

Kim finally stepped into the warm sunshine and locked her laptop in the rental. The heat promised to rise to oppressively humid levels later in the day, but for now, walking seemed like a better idea than driving.

She strolled north along Main Street, enjoying the quaint town at a pleasant pace. The shops were inviting, and the pedestrians she passed gave her a wave and a smile.

Except for the appalling recent death rate, Carter's Crossing seemed like a friendly American town, same as a thousand others she'd visited over the years. Not all that different, in fact, from the Michigan town where she grew up or the Wisconsin town where her extended family lived.

Three blocks north, on the opposite side of Main Street from the Toussaint Hotel, she spied her destination.

The majestic Carter County Courthouse occupied the entire city block. It was surrounded by magnificent trees and gardens. Statues, monuments, and flags were strategically placed about the grounds.

According to Kim's brief research, the brick and terra cotta courthouse building had been designed by Mississippi's beloved architect, Noah Webster Overstreet, more than a hundred years ago. The architect and the age of the building made it venerable enough to earn its place on the National Register of Historic Places.

Constructed on the site of the previous courthouse, which had burned down, this one had been hastily commissioned. Finished less than a year, its design was rather basic. A three-story center block was flanked on either side by a two-story block. The main block projected forward from the two wings.

Perhaps as an apology for the plainness of the building, the façade was adorned with windows and cornices and columns and arches galore. Clocks, an attic portico, and a full basement completed the ambitious spectacle.

Folklore had it that Elvis Presley played concerts in the large courtroom twice back in 1955, which was often used for assemblies and performances even now.

All told, the building and its grounds were the most impressive sights on the town's Main Street, to be sure. It had loads more character than the newer County Sheriff's office at the south end of Main Street.

Mayor Elizabeth Deveraux's office and Carter's Crossing Town Hall were located on the main floor of the courthouse building's south flank.

When Kim reached the courthouse, she was tempted to explore the building and the grounds for a while, but one of the big clocks rang the hour in demandingly sonorous tones. No time for sightseeing. Her appointment with Deveraux was scheduled to begin that very moment.

She climbed the front steps of the courthouse, taking the opportunity for a glance up and down Main Street in the daylight from her elevated position.

Pedestrians strolled the sidewalks, entering and emerging from the shops. Libby's Diner seemed busy in the distance as a steady stream of customers went through. Traffic on Main Street was light but steady.

The entire tableau was a slice of Americana two centuries in the making. Kim admired the preservation effort. None of the anachronisms, like the casino and the budget hotel chains and fast-food franchises, marred the Norman Rockwell illusion on Main Street.

Carter's Crossing was reminiscent of a more innocent time for the country, and for her. As a child, she'd wanted to live in such a town for the rest of her life.

She shook off the melancholy memories, turned, and hustled up the steps to the center entrance. She turned left and made her way toward the mayor's office. She pulled the heavy wooden door and stepped into the reception area.

The open floorplan inside was bright and cheerfully decorated. A nicely dressed woman greeted Kim from her seat behind a refinished desk as old as the building itself.

She took Kim's business card and headed down the corridor.

When she came back to her desk, she gestured vaguely behind her. "Mayor Deveraux is expecting you. Down the hall. You can't miss it."

"Thanks." Kim walked along a narrow corridor parallel to the exterior windows facing Main Street.

On her right, a series of closed doors were smaller offices for city workers. Halfway down the corridor was a heavy wooden door, its center brandishing the town seal, and *Mayor Elizabeth Deveraux* painted above it in bright gold letters.

Kim rapped her knuckles on the door and waited.

"Come in," the mayor called out. The kind of easy command that probably came from being a sheriff's daughter and a Marine and a sheriff herself. Mayor Deveraux was as close as it came to royalty in Carter's Crossing.

Kim pushed the heavy door open and stepped inside.

"We meet again, FBI Special Agent Kim L. Otto," Deveraux said, reading from the business card Kim had provided to her assistant out front. Deveraux's accent was local, and her voice was clear, quiet, firm. "You might have told me who you were last night. Why didn't you?"

She didn't stand up or offer to shake Kim's hand, but she gestured toward one of the chairs on the other side of her desk. An invitation. Almost, but not quite, an order.

Elizabeth Deveraux was a tall woman, maybe fifty. But she looked younger. She had a fabulous head of long, curly dark hair she'd bunched into an unruly ponytail at the back of her neck. Her makeup was minimalist but artfully applied to emphasize and conceal in equal proportion.

The total effect suggested that no matter what happened, Mayor Deveraux would stay cool, calm, and collected through it all. And maybe discover some way to find something in it to make her smile.

The moment Kim laid eyes on the mayor in her element, her gut confirmed that Deveraux and Reacher had been lovers. She'd met enough of Reacher's women now to recognize his type. Strong female, usually involved with law enforcement, definitely able to take care of herself, often the head woman in charge.

Reacher's women were all pretty, too. This one was beautiful enough to grace the cover of every major fashion magazine cover around the globe.

Kim was no psychologist, but in this instance she didn't need to be. It was apparent that Reacher's type was a gorgeous, independent woman—who didn't need him. Her assumptions were safe enough. Reacher never stuck around anywhere long enough to prove or disprove her theory.

Gaspar had agreed with Kim's assessment. His view was that the Boss had chosen Kim precisely because she, too, was Reacher's type. He said the Boss was using Kim for bait, to lure Reacher from hiding so that he could be approached.

There was more to Gaspar's idea, but Kim shook it off at the time. Over the past few weeks, she'd come to wonder whether Gaspar might be right after all.

Deveraux folded slender hands with tanned sinewy fingers and rested them on her desk. She wore no jewelry on those fingers. Which suggested she hadn't remarried after her split from Sheriff Greyson.

Deveraux didn't have a gun in a holster on her hip at the moment. But she could no doubt defend herself when the situation called for it.

"How can I help you, Agent Otto?" she asked in a slightly amused way as if she'd considered the situation and decided Kim was friendly enough.

CHAPTER TWENTY-FIVE

Thursday, May 12
Carter's Crossing, Mississippi
10:30 a.m.

KIM RELAXED A BIT. So far so good. No reason to believe she and Deveraux had to be enemies. At least, not yet. But the mayor had set a formal tone, and that suited Kim just fine. Distance, both physical and psychological, from the subjects she interviewed about Reacher was usually an asset.

"Thanks for your time, Mayor Deveraux. I'm assigned to the Special Personnel Task Force. I'm conducting a background investigation," Kim settled more deeply into her chair and her cover story. "The subject of my inquiry is being considered for a classified assignment. It's my job to fill in the blanks in his personnel file since he left the army fifteen years ago."

Deveraux cocked her head in the general direction of the army base. "A lot of guys come and go through Kelham in fifteen years. I don't even meet most of them, let alone know anything about their backgrounds."

Kim nodded. "You met this one. He was an officer."

"Okay. Fewer officers pass through here. But fifteen years is still a long time." Deveraux's cadence slowed and her eyes danced with a bit more life than before.

"It's an important job we're filling. We need to know the candidate is mentally, physically, and financially fit for it. So we're being especially thorough." It wasn't exactly a lie.

But it wasn't the whole truth, either. Not by a mile.

Deveraux nodded. Not wary yet. "What's the subject's name?"

Kim paused. This was always a tricky moment when interviewing Reacher's known associates. Things could go quickly downhill from here.

Reactions to Reacher's name had been varied and unpredictable and ranged from outrage to curiosity and all the emotions in between.

Kim took the calculated risk that Deveraux wouldn't attack her here in Carter's Crossing Town Hall. She leveled her voice and said, "The candidate is Jack Reacher. No middle name. Major Jack Reacher, when you knew him."

Deveraux's smile broadened and lit up her face all the way to her eyes. She wasn't distressed in the least. Her reaction was something closer to learning she'd won the lottery.

"Really? Reacher? I figured he'd have retired or died long ago." She shook her head slowly while thoughts of Reacher ran through her head.

"Actually, he did. Retire, I mean."

"Not surprised." Deveraux smiled again as if she remembered everything about Reacher fondly. "The army was so bloated back then. The world had changed and fighting changed with it. All branches of the military were getting rid of people left and right. Reacher said he'd be one of those that got pushed out before he wanted to go."

Kim nodded and remained silent. Whatever spell Deveraux was under at the moment was causing her to talk about Reacher. Which was something Reacher's women rarely did. Kim's plan was to ride the wave as long as it lasted.

"What can I tell you about Reacher? He was…talented. He had skills, sure. But he also had a brain. He was clever. He could work things out. Not much of a heart, though," she said, which made her laugh.

"What do you mean, he didn't have much of a heart?"

She said, "I guess that's not exactly true. His sense of justice was well-honed. I guess that shows he had a heart. Of sorts."

"What do you mean?" Kim asked again to keep her talking.

"Reacher was a military cop. I understood him because I'd been a military cop, too. He knew the law. And he knew the rules. It's not exactly that he didn't care about them. He just…didn't trust the law and the rules to get the job done, I guess." Deveraux's smile had left her lips but still brightened her eyes. She took a deep breath and exhaled slowly. "Yeah, that's as good a way to describe it as any. Reacher trusted himself above everything else. He did whatever he felt was right."

"There's a word for guys like that, Mayor Deveraux," Kim said flatly.

"Call me Liz. Everyone I like does," she replied comfortably. "And yes, there's several words for guys like that, and some of them are not so flattering, which is what you mean. Any law enforcement officer worth her salt would call Reacher a killer. Criminal. Outlaw. But anyone who really knew Reacher would say he both was and wasn't any of those things."

Kim cocked her head. "What would you call him, then?"

"It's complicated. And simple at the same time. A paradox of sorts, I guess." Deveraux grinned and shook her head easily. "I'd call him an old-fashioned vigilante. He was then, and he probably still is. In my experience, people don't change all that much. They just grow into older and more finely honed versions of themselves."

"And you were the sheriff. Sworn to uphold the law." Kim narrowed her gaze as if she was trying to figure things out. "It didn't bother you that Reacher didn't give a damn about that?"

"Not in the moment, no," Deveraux said softly. "I've been a law and order type my whole life, Agent Otto. What I know for sure is that sometimes the bad guys deserve what they get. And the law isn't always good enough. The law can't always make sure the bad guys don't do something worse the next time."

Kim nodded as her understanding dawned. She'd run into this reaction before. She knew precisely what it was. She called it The Reacher Effect. "Reacher charmed you. You think he's some kind of hero."

Deveraux's smile widened, showing perfectly whitened teeth. "I guess you could say that. He was charming enough. But it was really him, you know? Who he was. Not some sort of con."

"And you know that how?"

Deveraux's eyes crinkled when she smiled again. "Another time. I've got a television appearance in about five minutes, and I have to get outside. Carter's Crossing has been dealing with some scary sinkholes over the past few months. People here are worried about it, and I'm the mayor. So I've got to go calm them down."

"How are you going to do that? Sinkholes are acts of God, aren't they?" Kim asked.

"Mostly. In our case, the experts tell me there are some other things in play. Things we can fix." Deveraux paused as if considering something, and then she said, "Come by Libby's Diner tonight. We'll have dinner. And I'll tell you all about it. How's that?"

Without waiting for a response, Deveraux stood up and left her office. Watching her retreating back, Kim noticed again how tall she was.

Reacher was six feet, five inches tall. The top of Deveraux's head reached past his chin. Kim briefly wondered what it would be like to stand so tall and look down on everyone around you. Something she'd never know. At just under five feet, many ten-year-olds were taller than Kim.

She waited a few moments, looking around the office at the framed certificates and photos of Deveraux doing the things mayors do. Ribbon cuttings, speeches, grip-and-grins with other politicians and celebrities. A few awards littered the bookshelves, too.

Tangible proof that Deveraux was a formidable woman in many ways.

Which might have made Kim wonder what the former small-town sheriff's relationship to Reacher had been, exactly.

Except she was fairly sure she already knew. Deveraux and Reacher had been lovers. Deveraux still harbored some affection for him, after fifteen years. At dinner tonight, she'd get Deveraux to confirm her suspicions. But what more did Deveraux know about Reacher? Did she know where he was now?

Kim waited a couple of minutes and then headed outside into the warm sunshine. At the top of the stairs, she made another quick survey of Main Street. A big magnolia tree covered most of one corner of the courthouse grounds. Leaning casually against its massive trunk, watching the exit door, was Captain America.

The image of her brothers' boyhood favorite superhero flashed into her mind and she grinned. The brown-haired guy could have been the comic book character's stunt double.

He was about six feet tall. Well-worn jeans, boots, and a brown leather flight jacket over a black T-shirt. Fit and trim and squared away in the style that military men often projected.

That much of the Captain America persona was spot-on. He was military, one way or another.

Which wasn't surprising.

Military types, past, present, and future were fairly thick on the ground in Carter's Crossing. Not including Sheriff Greyson and Mayor Deveraux, she'd seen at least a dozen of them walking around town already.

But she figured this one was standing by the big tree waiting specifically for her, and she saw no reason to keep him cooling his heels.

Kim hustled down and he walked over to meet up at the bottom of the courthouse steps.

CHAPTER TWENTY-SIX

Thursday, May 12
Carter's Crossing, Mississippi
11:05 a.m.

"I'M LINCOLN PERRY," he said, pulling off his aviators to reveal startling baby blues. "You're Kim Otto, aren't you? Gaspar told me to look you up."

"That's right. He mentioned you to me, too." Kim gave him a friendly smile as she shook his hand and sized him up.

Three feet away, he looked even more like Captain America than he had from across the lawn. Clean cut. Close shaven. He smelled like Old Spice. Even the aviators reinforced his wholesome middle-America-farm-boy image.

Perry looked so much like Captain America that she imagined he must have attended costume parties dressed as the comic book hero. The mental picture broadened her grin. She almost asked him where he'd stashed his vibranium shield.

He replaced his aviators and extended his arm, palm toward Main Street, "Buy you a coffee? There's a diner four blocks down. Should be a good place to talk."

Kim inhaled the sweet fragrance of the magnolia tree's blooms. "Sounds great."

She fell into step beside him. The sun was high and hot overhead now. She found her oversized sunglasses in her pocket and slid them onto her face.

The sidewalk wasn't busy. Only a few pedestrians strolled here and there. Shops hadn't been open long, and it was too early for whatever lunch rush Carter's Crossing normally enjoyed.

"How'd you find me?" she asked as they waited at the first corner for the traffic light to change.

"Sheriff Greyson told me you had a meeting with the mayor. You had to come out eventually. And it's a nice day, so I hung around outside. No reason not to take advantage of the sunshine," he replied.

Kim gave him a side-eye from behind the sunglasses. "So last night when Sheriff Greyson told me the army had an undercover man in town, he meant you?"

He shrugged. "Can't read his mind. But as far as I know, I'm the only army undercover here. Then again, there could be others and I wouldn't know about them. That's the whole point of being undercover."

She ignored the sarcasm. "What rank are you?"

"Major."

"Should I salute?"

"Only if you want to," he replied with a smile that revealed nicely whitened teeth.

"What's your home base?"

"Varies. I was attached to the 110th Investigative Unit for a while. Now I'm 46th MP, Criminal Investigations," he said, with more than a touch of pride.

Kim nodded. Reacher had worked both units back in the day. He'd been a major, too. Twice. In fact, he was a major when he showed up in Carter's Crossing fifteen years ago. Or, as he might put it, he'd been terminal at major.

The coincidence didn't mean anything, necessarily. But she was more wary of Perry than she had been five minutes ago.

In a friendly tone, she said, "And you're not really undercover, are you? I mean, you're walking around town. I see the bulge of your gun in that holster under your arm. You're telling me who you are and why you're here. And you also told the sheriff. Who else have you shared all this intel with?"

Checking in with the locals, letting them know he was in town, was a professional courtesy. Nothing wrong with it. She'd done the same herself. She didn't expect him to argue the point.

But she wanted to know how well he could keep a secret before she considered confiding anything in him. Gaspar liked him, so that was a step in the right direction. She didn't trust the guy all the way to home base, though. Gaspar wasn't infallible.

Perry shrugged again and rested his arms easily at his sides. "What I meant was that I'm not the official army investigator of record on the Nightingale case. He's out at Kelham. We're working separately on this."

"Seems like a lot of manpower for a single civilian murder victim," Kim said.

The traffic light turned green and they crossed the intersection, resuming their pace. He walked along the curbside of the sidewalk, leaving her a safer position closer to the buildings.

She gave him points for courtesy.

"Not too much manpower yet. Because we don't know who killed her," Perry said. "Wasn't necessarily one of ours. Her throat was cut. But lots of people around here know how to do that."

"Uh, huh."

"The county is full of ex-military and hunters. Could have been anybody. Just a guess at this point," Perry said as easily as if he'd practiced the speech in front of the mirror so he could deliver it believably.

"And if you find out it was one of your guys, then what?" she asked when they reached the end of the second block. She glanced at the traffic light, which turned red just as they stopped at the corner.

A dirty old pickup truck growled halfway down the block as it accelerated toward the intersection. One of the headlights had been smashed. The whole thing was covered in dried mud as if they'd gone two-tracking in yesterday's rainstorm.

The truck had been cherry red, once upon a time. The paint was faded and scratched, and the body sported a few rough Bondo patches, suggesting more than one serious wreck during its lifetime.

The driver pulled up to the curb and slammed on the brakes. The truck's front end rolled onto the sidewalk and stopped directly in front of Kim and Perry, blocking their path.

Kim recognized the three beefy rednecks who stumbled out of the cab. Unshaven, greasy gray ponytails, furry arms, bad tattoos. One was holding a baseball bat.

McKinneys. The same ones she had seen in the bar last night after she'd watched the real midnight train.

Mentally, she dubbed the one with the baseball bat resting on his shoulder Slugger. He stood on the left, offering her a menacing stare. He bared his teeth like a rabid dog.

If his expression weren't so deadly serious, she'd have

laughed. As it was, she quickly calculated the reach of his bat. If he came at her, she'd need more room to move.

The McKinney on the right wore a black leather vest over his dirty white T-shirt. He outweighed the other two by a thirty-pound gut overhanging his belt. The stench of alcohol surrounded him like a noxious cloud. He smelled like he'd chased last night's liquid dinner with breakfast beer. He was unsteady on his feet. A hard shove at the right time could knock him out for a dozen hours.

The guy in the middle was the leader, clearly the alpha dog. He stood like an old-fashioned gunfighter, arms down but away from his sides as if he sported a belt with invisible Colts at his waist.

A lit cigarette dangled from his mouth, dangerously close to catching his wild beard on fire. Which would be worth watching.

Alpha Dog stared forward and said in a gravelly four-pack-a-day voice, "Where's Price? He didn't get home last night and we can't find him."

"You've got the wrong guy," Perry replied. "I don't know what you're talking about. Who is Price?"

"I'm not askin' you, pretty boy," Alpha Dog growled, turning his stare to focus squarely on Kim.

The drunk one ordered, "Keep quiet. We want crap from you, we'll ask."

Perry shrugged. Apparently, it was the wrong thing to do.

The drunk McKinney moved more quickly than Kim had thought possible. He pushed directly toward Perry, right arm extended with his full body weight behind it, meaning to land a solid punch.

But his balance was off and his momentum was wrong.

Perry moved aside, stuck out his foot, and tripped McKinney as he came in to deliver the blow.

His arms pinwheeled rapidly in an almost comical effort to stay upright on the sidewalk.

He might have managed it, given enough time. But Perry didn't wait. He gave McKinney a hard shove with his body weight behind it.

The drunk collapsed and fell flat on his face. Mashed his nose to a pulp.

Blood squirted everywhere half a moment after Kim jumped out of the path of the spray.

McKinney never felt the busted nose because he'd slammed his forehead on the concrete hard enough to knock himself out.

"Oh, look. Your buddy fell down," Perry said, giving the drunk a little nudge with the toe of his boot.

"What the hell is wrong with you?" Slugger snarled. He raised the baseball bat over his head and moved toward Perry with a sneer and a gleam of pure outrage in his eye.

He prepared to swing the bat with enough velocity to crack Perry's head open.

Before he had the chance, a loud pulsing "whoop" of sirens sounded on Main Street. Instinctively, Slugger turned his head toward the noise and loosened his grip on the bat.

While he was looking in the opposite direction, Kim moved in, grabbed the bat, and jerked it from his hands.

Slugger turned toward Kim, ready to brawl.

She gripped the bat with both hands, raised it to her shoulder, and swung for the fences.

The end of the bat caught Slugger right in the solar plexus. He howled and doubled over, holding his belly, moaning as if he'd been kicked by a mule.

Alpha Dog had glanced toward the siren's blast. He grabbed Slugger's arm and tilted his head toward their buddy on the ground.

"Help me get him up. We gotta go. Sheriff's comin'."

"I ain't done yet," Slugger complained, still holding his belly, red-faced and ready to brawl.

The sirens whooped again, moving closer.

"You know what Greyson said about sending us to Parchman Farm," Alpha Dog warned.

Parchman Farm was Mississippi's maximum-security prison. They believed Chief Greyson's threat was credible. Which meant the McKinneys had criminal records and violent tendencies beyond bar brawls and street fights.

Good to know.

"We're not finished with you two," Slugger growled, adding another sharp stare for good measure. Spittle ran down his beard and his eyes were wild, but after a moment of glaring, he gave up.

The two McKinneys bent to collect their drunk cousin, each one grabbing an elbow. He was heavy and still out cold. Dead weight, and a lot of it.

After some tugging and grunting, they managed to drag him to the pickup. They lifted him off the ground and flopped him into the flatbed. He didn't make a sound.

Slugger turned back to Perry and Kim, giving them each a final hard glare. "Watch yourself. We'll be back."

Kim said nothing.

"Come find me when you're ready," Perry replied. "And bring your friends. Clearly, three of you aren't enough."

Chief Greyson punched another whoop on his siren.

Slugger's nostrils flared and his breath came in ragged gasps.

"Come on," Alpha Dog called from the driver's seat. "We gotta go. Now."

Slugger didn't want to give up, but he got into the cab with his cousin. He rolled down the window and hung his head out to deliver one last warning. "Watch yourself. You won't see me coming next time."

Alpha Dog slid the transmission into drive and peeled out across Main Street and kept going.

Kim watched as Sheriff Greyson's SUV rolled through the intersection and kept his course, not following McKinney's red truck.

The light changed and Kim started forward, still holding the bat and looking for a place to leave it.

"I don't mind a good fight, but I like to know why I'm fighting. Want to tell me what all of that was about?" Perry stepped around the rapidly drying blood on the sidewalk.

"Some guy named Price, I guess," Kim replied as they crossed the street and continued toward the diner, which was at the end of the next block, past Toussaint's.

"Yeah, I got that," Perry said.

They walked in silence until they reached their destination. Kim dropped the bat into the trash can out front, then reached for the door handle, and Perry laid a hand on her arm.

"Those guys in the truck. If anybody asks, you don't know what they were talking about. You have no idea who this guy Price is," he said as if he was establishing facts instead of asking questions.

Kim shrugged and pulled the door open. "You've got blood on your shoe. You'll want to clean that off before you go inside."

CHAPTER TWENTY-SEVEN

Thursday, May 12
Carter's Crossing, Mississippi
11:25 a.m.

THE DINER WAS A LITTLE BUSIER today than it had been last night. Kim found an empty table for four in the corner and sat with her back to the wall. Perry was forced to choose his angle of exposure. So he put his back to the front window, which made him a visible target to anyone on the street but gave him an unobstructed view of the diner's entrance and the kitchen door.

Barely a minute later, Libby brought a brown plastic thermos pot of coffee and two brown plastic mugs. There was cream and sugar on the table. She looked as exhausted as she'd seemed last night.

"We can pour for ourselves," Kim said, taking the pot and the mugs. "Did you get any rest at all?"

"Not much, I'm afraid. My day shift girl's gone. No choice but to do the job myself until I find a new one. We've got a full-employment economy here, the mayor says. Hard to find people to work." She left the menus and turned back toward the kitchen.

Perry poured the coffee. He sipped while it was hot. He didn't pollute his java. Gaspar usually added so much cream and sugar that the spoon seemed to stand up in the thick liquid by itself.

"Enough about me. How long have you been in town, Otto?" Perry asked as he perused the plastic-coated menu.

"I can recommend the muffins and the cheeseburger. Pie's good, too," Kim replied, glancing at the choices.

"You've been here a while, then. Long enough to eat a couple of meals," Perry nodded and put the menu down. "Why is the FBI interested in the Bonnie Nightingale case?"

"What makes you think we're interested?" Kim replied, scanning the menu. She wasn't hungry, but she didn't know when she'd get the chance to eat again. Gaspar's rule was always to eat when you can. He'd rubbed off on her in more ways than one.

Perry said, "Because you're here. And I'm sure the FBI has plenty of other things you could be doing instead."

She glanced at him over the top of the menu. "As it happens, I'm not here about the Bonnie Nightingale case, but no matter how many times I say that, no one believes me."

He gave her a frankly appraising gaze that lasted a full minute as if he were some sort of human lie-detector.

She didn't bother to fill the silence. She chose a spinach salad for lunch and folded the menu to signal Libby that they were ready to order. Then she tried the coffee, which was just as good as it had been last night.

Perry seemed to be trying to wait her out. So she threw him a bone. "You said you were previously with the 110th Special Investigations Unit, and now you're 46th MP, Criminal Investigations."

"That's right," he replied warily. "What about you?"

"I'm assigned to the FBI Special Personnel Task Force at the moment."

"I have a vague idea what that is. When the government needs special expertise from the private sector, the SPTF finds the right butt for the chair," he said, glancing around the room as if he was looking for someone in particular. "And what's the specific assignment that brings you to Carter's Crossing?"

Kim nodded as if he were an apt pupil. "As it happens, I'm tasked to complete a thorough background check on a former member of your unit. He was a major, too. A little older than you. But maybe you knew him."

"It's a big army. But I might have. What's his name?"

Without taking her eyes off him, she said, "Jack Reacher."

He blinked. Then he moved back in the chair as if he wanted to put some distance between himself and the question.

"Do you know him?" Kim asked, deliberately asking about the present instead of the past. Reacher lived off the grid, but he'd also had contact with people for the last fifteen years. That much she knew for sure.

"I did. Back in the day. Haven't seen him in years, though." He cleared his throat. "Tell you the truth, I figured he was dead by now."

"Oh, yeah? Why is that?"

"Dunno." He shrugged. "Just that guys at a certain level or who served in the same unit tend to know each other. Vaguely, if nothing else. And you sort of hear things from time to time after they move on."

"Hear things like what?"

"Well, I heard his brother died years back. In the line of duty, they said." Perry paused as if he was searching his memory. He shook his head. "But no. I've heard nothing at all about Reacher himself. Not a word of any kind. That usually means only one thing."

"Which is?"

He gave her a level stare. "That there's nothing to say, nothing to hear."

The diner had filled to capacity with the lunch crowd. All the tables were full now, and a low hum of conversational noise had settled over the place. At least two tables were occupied by men wearing army garb.

Libby came back and took their orders. Perry wanted the cheeseburger. And the pie. She scratched a few pencil marks down on an old-fashioned green order pad and wasted no time on small talk.

"Right away," Libby said before she hustled toward the kitchen, passing their menus to another table as she moved along the aisle.

Kim asked, "So, Jack Reacher. Tell me what you'd want to know if you were in my shoes."

"I connected with him maybe once or twice. Just in passing, mostly. He was way ahead of me up the chain of command," Perry replied.

"What kind of reputation did he have back then?"

"Reacher? In the 110th, the guy is a legend, I guess. In the 46th, too. He had skills. Not just combat skills and medals and stuff like that. We all have some of that stuff. Reacher was also sharp." Perry tapped two fingers to his temple. "He had brains, you know?"

Then he finished his coffee and poured another mug full from the pot. He topped off hers, too. He seemed like he had more to say, so she waited, giving him a chance to figure out how he wanted to deliver the news, whatever it was.

After another moment, Perry said, "Reacher could really figure things out. When he caught a case, he never gave up until he got to the bottom of it. It didn't usually take very long. The bad guy paid for his crimes. Every time. No matter what. That was Reacher's way."

"I see," she said, attempting to draw him out.

Perry grinned as if he'd thought of something else. Something amusing. "He had what we called Reacher's Rules. People talked about them. Made jokes, you know? Some of them were kinda funny, I guess, in retrospect."

"What kind of rules?"

He cocked his head as if making an effort to recall. He grinned. "One was, after a fistfight, the best cure for a sore hand is to wrap it around a cold beer."

Kim smiled. "Sounds like he had a sense of humor."

"Yeah, he did." Perry grinned, too. "But some of it was stuff he'd figured out along the way and passed to the guys junior to him, and they passed it down to guys like me. Helped us solve some cases."

"Such as?"

"Like, he said if a guy had money outside his salary, it would show up somewhere. Find it, and you'd know if the guy was dirty."

Kim nodded. "That's a pretty standard truth, isn't it?"

"Yeah. Reacher wasn't much for fancy stuff. He made solid use of the basics, mostly," Perry replied.

Kim cocked her head, considering. "You said Reacher never gave up until the bad guy was caught and dealt with, right?"

His eyes narrowed. "Yeah. So?"

"So, is there anybody here in town that Reacher might still be interested in?"

"A civilian, you mean?"

"Maybe. Or somebody out at Kelham?" Kim asked.

Libby came back with the food and a fresh pot of coffee and placed everything on the table before she hustled off again.

He waited until she'd left to answer the question. "Could be. Reacher's been gone a while. But there's people still around who might have been sideways with him, one way or another."

"Is there some easy way to check that out?" Kim asked.

"Maybe. I'll make a call." Perry fell on the cheeseburger as if he hadn't eaten in a month.

Kim moved the spinach salad around with her fork, thinking about what he'd said.

He finished the food in half a dozen big bites and way less than six minutes, just like Gaspar. He was always hungry and never left so much as a morsel on his plate. She wondered if eating fast was a necessary army skill, too.

When he'd finished, and while she played with her salad, he said, "Something to keep in mind. One thing I recall about Reacher very, very clearly."

She glanced across the table to look him in the eye. "Which is what?"

CHAPTER TWENTY-EIGHT

Thursday, May 12
Carter's Crossing, Mississippi
11:30 a.m.

IGNORING MAJOR HAMMER'S lockdown orders, he left
Kelham. At an old gas station, he found a truck he could steal
and drove ten miles on unpaved country roads to the abandoned
barn he had rented months ago.

The barn stood alone at the end of a dusty two-track in the
middle of an empty field west of Carter's Crossing. The farmer
who'd owned the barn and the acreage that surrounded it had
died ten years before. His heirs were not interested in farming.
Which meant no maintenance of the property or the barn in the
intervening years.

The flat plank siding had been painted red once when the
farm was prosperous. The paint was long gone now. The
damaged and warped timber had weathered to a silver gray.

Gaps and missing boards allowed ventilation, which was
okay because otherwise, last summer's heat and humidity would

have been stifling inside. But the open spaces also let the cold, wind, and rain infiltrate, which wasn't okay because of its potential to damage the equipment.

He was hours behind schedule.

Most of his preparations were in place, but the trip to New York to deal with Pak had thrown his schedule off-kilter. The Bonnie Nightingale mess had not helped, either. And then there was Jasper. Add Nina calling to tell him she was pregnant, and he'd maxed out his patience.

All told, he was running seriously behind schedule. And that was before Major Hammer showed up at Kelham. Situation normal, all fouled up.

He sped along the dirt driveway, throwing dust up behind the truck until he reached the open front door of the barn. He braked beside the three trucks that were already there. Redmond and Hern had arrived separately. Nina was here already, too. They were inside, working.

He slammed the transmission into park and climbed out.

Spring heat engulfed him instantly in the sultry Mississippi morning. His shirt stuck to his chest with sweat. Humidity had to be close to one hundred percent. The air was almost too heavy to inhale. He couldn't wait to leave the oppressive weather behind.

He had intended to get here first, to set up his final preparations. Now he'd need to come back again to accomplish the things he needed privacy to complete. He grunted with annoyance. One more thing to slow him down.

He stepped into the cooler interior and heard the generator running in the back. But they need electricity to run the printers and the washing machines and the rest of the equipment. This place was completely off-the-grid. No electrical power lines within ten miles in every direction. Hence, the generator. He nodded approval.

Counterfeiting twenty- and fifty-dollar bills was relatively easy. He'd learned the techniques when he was posted to Peru a few years ago, which some called the counterfeiting capital of the world. Nina's position at the casino helped to pass the counterfeits, which made the trickiest part of the operation simpler, too.

Inside the barn, Nina was standing near Redmond, watching the printer finish the fake currency, and then stacking it to one side.

Hern was in the other room where they had been packing up in preparation for departure. Four crates were ready to go. There were two more to fill.

Redmond, Hern, Nina, and he were each slated to take one crate. The other two were for Jasper and Bonnie. Both were dead. But the supplies had been acquired, and there was no reason to crate less simply because Jasper and Bonnie wouldn't need their share.

That's what he'd told Redmond and Hern last night at Brannan's. No need to say anything to Nina.

He walked over and slid his arm around her. She tilted her face for a kiss. She looked as slender and beautiful as ever. If she hadn't claimed she was pregnant, he'd never have guessed. Her body revealed no evidence of preparation for motherhood. Not that it mattered. Nina had become a liability, regardless of the pregnancy, if it existed.

"You're running late, aren't you?" Nina asked after the kiss. "Problems?"

He swept his palm across his sweaty face and stepped back to watch the printing for a few moments. "The army has sent a guy to investigate Bonnie Nightingale's death. They think she was killed."

Nina looked startled. Her eyes opened wide and her lips formed a little "O" just before her palm flew up to cover her mouth. Tears gathered in her eyes.

"Bonnie killed herself, didn't she?" Redmond asked. "Walked in front of the train, I heard."

"Major Hammer says not. He says the autopsy found her throat had been cut before she was hit by the train." He draped his arm around Nina's waist to catch her if she fainted. "Pentagon's worried that a Ranger might've done it. Someone from Kelham."

"Well, that's a problem right there," Redman said. "Didn't some guys ship out the next day after Bonnie died? How do we know it wasn't one of them?"

"They don't know anything yet. They don't know if the killer was active or retired or not even military. Could've been a vet. Or a hunter. Lots of possibilities at this point," he paused to inhale and exhale deeply. "They just don't want Kelham to get a black eye that'll interfere with closing it down. You know how the army is about schedules. We're set to close just before dawn. Last man out will turn off the lights. End of an era and all that. Pentagon doesn't want anything getting in the way."

Nina was crying now. He held her awkwardly and allowed her to bury her tears in his neck while he tried to conceal impatience with her theatrics. If she hadn't opened her mouth and spilled the beans to Bonnie about the trip to New York, he wouldn't have needed to slit her throat.

Bonnie's death was on Nina.

But there was no point in making an issue of it. He didn't have the time.

"Where's Hern?"

Redmond tilted his head in the right direction and said, "He's in the other room packaging up the new bills. We got the hearse from a dealer in St. Louis and repainted it. We should be able to get all of the bills inside the coffins. We'll be ready to ship them out as planned."

Nina had managed to pull herself together, although she was still sniffling into a wet tissue. He patted her shoulder. "Why don't you go home and get some rest. I know the news about Bonnie is a shock. It was a shock to me, too. But there's nothing we can do about her now. We're running out of time. We have to keep going."

"I can't believe this. My closest friends in the world. Carolyn…and Bonnie." Nina sniffled and dabbed and her eyes widened again. "I guess Bonnie died first, didn't she?"

He nodded. "Yeah."

"Do you think Jasper might have killed Bonnie? Where is he? Maybe that Major Hammer should talk to him, too. I never liked Jasper. I told Bonnie not to go out with him, but she wouldn't listen to me…" Her voice trailed off into more sniffles and tears.

Time was short and marching relentlessly forward, and he was rapidly losing his patience. He tried to keep his anger under control. "Nina, just go home. You're too upset. Don't talk to anyone. Don't tell anyone about Bonnie. The last thing you want is to be involved in a murder investigation. Trust me on this."

"Right, but—" Nina began.

"Nina! Stop!" he shouted angrily.

She startled and then stared at him, shocked.

He gentled his tone. "That's enough. Don't upset yourself further. Go home. I'll come by later after I'm finished here. We can talk then. Right now, I have a lot to do and not much time to get everything done."

"I have to work—" she argued.

He calmed his tone and tried to persuade instead of issuing orders, or shooting her on the spot, which was what he itched to do. "I'll call your brother. I'll tell him you're not feeling well. He can handle the casino without you today."

"Come on, Nina. I'll walk you out." Redmond grasped her bicep and coaxed her toward her truck.

He shook his head as he watched her stumble forward. He hoped she was calm enough to drive home. She climbed into her truck, started it up, and turned it around. He watched as the truck moved slowly toward the road.

Redmond came back inside. "She's pretty shaken up. You think we can trust her to keep her mouth shut until we bug out?"

He shrugged. "Hell if I know. What do you think?"

"Hard to say. She had Bonnie to confide in before. Now, she's got no one except us. Not sure that's enough," Redmond replied and paused a few beats. "Anyway, this is the last batch of fifties. We're out of paper, and we can't get more. Our supplier is tapped out."

"Okay."

Redmond said, "When we're done here, I'll destroy the printers and what's left of the supplies."

"Good. I'll go check on Hern," he said, turning toward the packing room where the hearse was parked.

He was a dozen steps away when Redmond said, "Hell of a thing about Bonnie, though. You think Jasper killed her? That why he was so hell-bent on doing that crazy stunt yesterday? Was he feeling guilty?"

"Hell, I don't know anymore. I guess we'll have to ask him."

He shook his head and ran a weary hand over his close-cropped hair.

Redmond cocked his head and shoved both hands into his back pockets. "You haven't heard, then?"

"Heard what?"

"Jasper died last night in the hospital. Too banged up from that crash yesterday, I guess. He didn't make it," Redmond said quietly, scuffing the toe of his boot on the dusty floor.

"Ah, crap," he whispered, swallowing hard before he turned and walked away, satisfied that everything was falling into place despite the screwups.

CHAPTER TWENTY-NINE

Thursday, May 12
Carter's Crossing, Mississippi
11:45 a.m.

"I'M DYING TO KNOW. What's the one thing you recall so clearly about Reacher?" Kim prompted Perry after a short silence.

"One thing? Hard to name just one…" He seemed to consider the question seriously before a big grin split his face when he figured out the answer like he'd just saved the universe or something. "Reacher wasn't afraid of anything. Partly because he was so huge. Not many guys could best him in any kind of fight, and most never even tried."

Kim deadpanned. "Which explains why he wasn't afraid."

Perry cocked his head and raised his eyebrows. She waited while he figured it out. "You mean because he always won any kind of fight he got into? Yeah, I guess that's partly true."

"What's the untrue part?"

"I mean, sure, he expected to win," Perry said slowly. "But it was also like he accepted that there would come a time when he would lose. And that was okay, too. Like he could handle defeat, should it happen."

"So he was a fatalist?" she asked with a grin.

Perry shrugged. "Like I said, I didn't know the guy that well. I'm just telling you what I heard. What got passed around about him."

"What else got passed around about him?" She chewed a forkful of spinach while he talked.

"He was weird about owning stuff. He said don't own a car. Or a house. Or rent an apartment. You could be traced," Perry cocked his head and squinted as if attempting to see his memory better. "I took it that he was a guy who didn't want to be found, so he'd worked out the best way to be invisible. Thinking it over, maybe I'm wrong about him. Maybe he's not dead after all. Maybe he's just not findable."

Kim said nothing while she ate several bites of her salad and considered what he'd revealed.

A few minutes later, Libby picked up the dishes and brought Perry's pie. She changed out the empty coffee pot for a full one and scurried toward the kitchen for more food. The lunch service was in full swing now and she was running herself ragged.

Perry poured more coffee for both of them and tasted his pie. "You were right. This is really good."

"I'm told her mother does the baking," Kim replied, tilting her head toward Libby.

He took another bite of the pie. "Well, she's really good at baking."

Kim said nothing.

"Now it's my turn to ask the questions. What do you know about Bonnie Nightingale?" Perry said while giving the pie the attention it deserved. "Could have been an accident, couldn't it?"

"Definitely not," Kim replied.

"Ignoring the autopsy report, I mean. You shouldn't even have those results, and I'm not clear on why you saw them. Regardless, we're keeping that quiet for the moment," he offered a meaningful look.

She nodded.

He continued, "Because without the autopsy report, it could have been accidental death or suicide. Either would have made sense."

"Not at all." Kim shook her head. "Doesn't make any kind of sense. Not in the least."

"Why not? We need some breathing room here to investigate without spooking her killer. If the autopsy wasn't in the mix, either option works with these facts," Perry said with an annoyed frown.

"Accidental death is not possible. You're wasting your breath with that." Kim shook her head, emphatically. "She didn't commit suicide, either. I have no idea why anyone around here would say that."

"But people are saying it. Because, like I said, it's plausible." Perry cocked his head.

"According to Janine. She's the desk clerk at Toussaint's Hotel. She claims people are saying it was suicide. Janine seems to know everything about everyone around here," Kim replied. "You'll want to talk to her. See what you think of her reporting skills."

"Okay. I'll bite." He scraped the filling off the pie plate as if he wanted to lick every last crumb. "Why don't you think Nightingale killed herself?"

The vivid images from Kim's dream flashed to mind, and a

shudder ran through her body from toes to scalp. Once again, she felt the rumbling of the earth and heard the wailing of the wind. The warning bells and lights flooded her senses. The train rushed toward her until she realized she was trembling again.

She shook off the terrifying flashback and sipped coffee to cover her lingering uneasy reaction. "No way either theory makes sense. Not for anyone who lives here. Or knows the first thing about that midnight train."

Perry cocked his head. "Why's that?"

"Have you seen that train? Stood near the tracks at midnight while it passes?" The visceral rush from her nightmare was pulsing through her body, setting every nerve ending afire.

Perry said, "I'm planning to do that tonight. Want to come with?"

Get a grip. Kim squared her shoulders and gave herself a mental shake. "Bonnie Nightingale had lived in Carter's Crossing most of her life. People who live here know everything about that train. They know how fast it comes up on you and how hard it slams anything and everything unlucky enough to be sitting on the tracks when it passes. And they know how that velocity and volume destroys everything the train touches. How it would batter a human body."

She shivered again. The nightmare had been so vivid, so fresh. She couldn't shake it.

Softly, Perry said, "So if you lived here, and if you knew all of that, and if you wanted to kill yourself, and if you had anyone you cared about who was still alive…you wouldn't want to leave them with that mess to clean up."

Kim didn't reply. The uneasiness she'd felt when she'd awakened last night adhered to her as if she'd been slathered with it.

Not only the nightmare had her spooked.

The terrified screams she'd heard afterward through her open window added its own horror.

Kim shook herself off, cleared her throat twice, and then sipped the coffee to wet her vocal cords to strengthen her tone. "If I were you, I'd want to know how that suicide theory got started and who spread it around. Even if relying on it helps to buy you some time."

Perry arched his eyebrows. "I plan to leave the rumor out there as long as I can. But why should I spend any time investigating a false lead like that?"

Kim replied, "Because whoever started that story already knew Bonnie Nightingale never stepped in front of that train either accidentally or on purpose. He knows exactly how she got there. And he knows why she got herself killed, too."

She glanced up just as the diner's front door opened, and Sheriff Greyson came inside. He glanced around, taking in the crowded tables before he made a beeline toward them.

He approached the table casually, removing his hat on the way. He glanced at the empty dishes on the table. "Perry. Otto. Looks like you're about done here."

He pulled one of the empty chairs and sat with his back to the kitchen. He rested his forearms on the table and leaned in, speaking quietly. "I've got a situation."

"What kind of situation?" Perry asked.

Greyson gave him a solid stare. "The kind I don't want to talk about here. Too many people around. If you're both done, I'd like you to come with me."

"We haven't paid for our lunch yet," Perry replied.

He didn't seem particularly cooperative, which was unusual for a military cop, and Kim wondered why.

232 | DIANE CAPRI

"Happy to help, Chief." Kim pulled two twenties from her pocket and tossed them on the table. She pushed her chair back and stood.

Chief Greyson flashed an irritated look toward Perry and led the way to the door. Out on the sidewalk, Greyson moved toward his SUV and Kim followed. Before they reached the vehicle, Perry caught up.

Chief Greyson gave him a sneer. "Didn't want to miss anything huh, Major?"

Perry scowled and climbed into the back of the car. "Where are we going?"

"To the morgue." Chief Greyson started the engine and backed away from the curb. He pointed the SUV northward.

"I'm surprised this town has a morgue and a pathologist on staff," Perry replied, clearly interested now. "You have that much violent crime in this county? Enough autopsies required to warrant the expense?"

"Not exactly. We've got a part-time coroner, which is all we need." Chief Greyson inhaled deeply and exhaled slowly. "Most people die here of old age or an obvious farming accident or even a car crash. Maybe a bar fight goes bad every dozen years or so. Lately, we've had more bodies to process than we're used to."

"And we're on our way to the morgue because now you've got another one," Kim said from the passenger seat.

CHAPTER THIRTY

Thursday, May 12
Carter's Crossing, Mississippi
1:15 p.m.

CHIEF GREYSON DROVE ALONG Main Street, past Toussaint's Hotel, beyond the point where the McKinneys had stopped to fight. He passed the courthouse and approached a white plantation-style building, which might have been a home once upon a time.

The façade, complete with columns and a two-story covered porch, was set back from the street. On each side of the double entry door were six tall and narrow windows accented by black shutters, making the windows seem even taller and narrower than they were.

Surrounding the building were deep green lawns, expertly trimmed and bordered by flower beds overflowing with blossoms.

The sign out front said Baker's Funeral Home. On the right

side, a covered drive was attached. An empty hearse waited on the driveway.

Chief Greyson turned onto a side street and drove around to an equally empty parking lot in the back.

"Why are we here, Chief?" Perry asked again. He'd asked basically the same question twice before and received the same stony silence in response.

"Let's take a look first. See what the coroner has to say. Then we'll talk," Greyson replied. He parked the cruiser and they stepped out into the steamy midday heat.

Greyson led the way to the back entrance. He pressed a bell and waited, feet wide apart, hands on his belt until a middle-aged woman came to the other side.

She peered from behind the glass, giving each of them a thorough once-over. Kim wondered whether they'd had break-ins and that's why she was so cautious.

Finally, she turned a deadbolt and opened the door.

"Chief Greyson. Come on in," she said as if welcoming a guest for dinner.

"Thanks, Mabel. We'll just go down to see Donnie if it's okay with you," Greyson replied, continuing through the door.

"Sure," she said, although Greyson didn't give her a chance to object or stick around to hear her gripes. She seemed like a woman who would have a litany of complaints ready for all occasions. No doubt he'd heard them all before.

Greyson led the way, followed by Kim and Perry to a door under the stairs. Greyson opened it, ducked to avoid the transom, and headed down. Kim cleared the low ceiling easily, of course. Perry also had to duck.

At the bottom of the stairs, the basement opened up into one huge room with a standard eight-foot ceiling. Kim wondered if the basement had been added long after the plantation days when most homes would have had nothing larger than a root cellar under the house.

She caught a whiff of disinfectant, formaldehyde and the unmistakable odor of decaying human flesh. She wrinkled her nose.

The space was cool and quiet. Bright overhead fluorescents washed green hues over everything down to the shiny clean beige tile covered floor. The walls were lined with stainless steel supply cabinets, their doors closed and locked.

One end of the cavernous room was set up like a smaller version of every morgue Kim had ever seen. Two stainless steel wheeled mortuary tables stood in the middle. A drain in the floor tiles between them served both. A sprayer was attached to the ceiling above each table.

Blindingly bright lights that could be switched on and off as needed during procedures hung on stainless steel cables. Mounted on the wall closest to the tables were large stainless steel sinks. Bottles of chemicals lined open shelves above the basins.

At the moment, one of the tables was occupied by a naked corpse.

Kim's view of the body was blocked by Chief Greyson's back.

An older man dressed in surgical scrubs, wearing a plastic face mask, was across the table and bent over the body. He glanced up briefly and then returned his attention to his work.

Chief Greyson made the introductions. "This is Major Perry and Agent Otto." No one offered to shake hands. "Dr. Dennis Baker. He's the mortician here. He's a pathologist. Also our local coroner."

As they reached the table, Kim had a clear and unobstructed view of the body. He hadn't been on the table long. She pressed her lips and steeled her gut to avoid retching. The odor was overpowering.

Price had been photographed, undressed, and partially cleaned up. Dr. Baker hadn't started cutting for the autopsy yet, so the body was still intact.

Kim's shallow breathing paused. She recognized the corpse right away. She'd last seen him prone on the floor at Brannan's. He didn't look a lot different now from when she'd left him there. Except he'd been alive and breathing and not full of bullet holes then.

"Luke Price," she said quietly. "What happened to you?"

Perry's eyebrows arched all the way to his hairline. "This is Luke Price? The guy those charming rednecks were looking for earlier?"

Chief Greyson frowned. "What rednecks?"

Kim replied, "McKinneys. Same ones who were at Brannan's last night. They came around hours ago asking about Price. Said he didn't make it home last night, and they couldn't find him today."

"He's been right here. Hasn't moved a muscle since Chief Greyson brought him in." Dr. Baker deadpanned.

Greyson scowled. "You figured out the cause of death, Dennis?"

Dr. Baker shrugged. "Not a big challenge. Shoot a guy in the head, he's usually gonna die."

"Did you recover the bullets?" Perry asked the sheriff.

"Still looking," Greyson replied. "We found him behind a dumpster full of garbage. It'll take a while to sort through everything else in there to locate any evidence that might be useful."

"I'm no firearms expert, but it looks like small-caliber bullets to me." Dr. Baker said, manipulating the body as he pointed out the holes, one at a time, "One in the kneecap. One in the head. Small, splintery entrance wounds and big messy exit wounds."

"Characteristic of a small-caliber, soft-nosed bullet. A twenty-two?" Perry said.

Dr. Baker nodded. "I'd vote for a twenty-two. With a silencer, most likely."

"A silencer. Why?" Perry asked.

"The bullets were slow coming out of the barrel. Lotta folks sleeping around town where you found him. Without a silencer, someone might have heard the shots," Dr. Baker replied. "He would've made a helluva racket, too. Somebody shot me like that, I wouldn't go quietly. Would you?"

Kim silently agreed. That's what a soft nose bullet does. It goes in and flattens out and becomes a blob of lead about the size of a quarter. Makes for a big exit hole. And a twenty-two made sense for a silencer.

Plus, she hadn't heard any gunshots in the night. Without a silencer, she would have heard them through the open window.

"Why shoot him in the kneecap, though?" Perry mused aloud. "I mean if the shooter was going to hit him in the head anyway. The kneecap shot seems unnecessary, doesn't it?"

Dr. Baker shrugged. "All I can tell you is that the two gunshot wounds were inflicted with the same weapon and fairly quickly. There wasn't enough time between shots to get anything much out of the guy. Which rules out shooting his knee to torture him for intel."

"Intel?" Kim asked, raising her eyebrows. "What would Price know about anything that would be worth killing him for?"

Chief Greyson cleared his throat and cut off her questions. "Anything else we need to know right now, Dennis?"

"Nothing yet," Dr. Baker said as he lowered his plastic face shield and returned to his work.

Kim continued to look at Price's body. The shot through his kneecap would have caused excruciating pain. She grimaced just thinking about how much a shattered kneecap would have hurt.

On the other hand, the shot through the head was quick and fast and painless. He'd have died almost instantly from that one.

So the order was first the knee and then the headshot. It suggested that Price was coming at the shooter when the killer disabled him with the first shot to the knee.

She cleared her throat and asked, "Chief Greyson, where'd you say you found the body?"

"Behind a dumpster in the alley between Main Street and Brannan's. About half a block from Toussaint's," Chief Greyson replied. "I haven't had a chance to ask over at Brannan's, but it happened after closing time. He was likely headed home and crossed the wrong guy along the way."

"Any idea on exact time of death?" she asked Dr. Baker.

The doctor looked up and met her gaze. "Not yet. But if he was in Brannan's until closing time, a safe guess would be after two o'clock in the morning. Maybe even later. But before six in the morning. Too much traffic in that area after daylight."

"Why later than two a.m.?" Perry asked.

Kim nodded. "Because the Cardinals game was broadcast from San Diego last night and it ran into extra innings. So if they wanted to see the end of the game, they'd have been at Brannan's until after two."

Dr. Baker gave her an approving nod and returned to his task.

Greyson said, "Let me know if you find anything else worth mentioning, Dennis. We're headed to my office."

Dr. Baker nodded but didn't reply.

On the way up the basement stairs, Kim said, "Let's make a stop on the way back. I'd like to get a look at the murder scene."

"Crime scene techs are still out there right now. We'll go later. The three of us first need to have a sit down with the mayor," Greyson replied.

They'd reached the parking lot. He pushed the remote to unlock his SUV and climbed inside.

Kim reclaimed the front passenger seat.

"What's the mayor got to do with anything?" Perry asked from the backseat.

Greyson started the engine and rolled out of the lot onto the side street. "She's meeting us at the station. You can ask her yourself."

Perry joked, "I imagine the first thing she'll want to know is whether Otto owns a twenty-two caliber pistol with a silencer."

"What? Why would you say that?" Kim asked, craning her neck around to glare at him over the seat.

"Those McKinneys will want to know, too. They already suspect you of foul play where Price is concerned," Perry continued. The more he talked, the more reasonable his accusations became.

"Oh, for cripe's sake." Kim glanced toward Sheriff Greyson and shook her head. "Just to be clear, no, I don't own a .22. And I didn't kill Luke Price. And if I had, do you think I'd be sitting around waiting to be arrested?"

Greyson lifted his eyebrows. Gruffly, he said, "For the record, and to cover my butt, where had you slipped out to when I met you in the lobby at Toussaint's before dawn this morning?"

"Seriously?" Kim demanded. "Why would I kill Luke Price?"

"Luke Price was a nasty piece of work. You laid him out at Brannan's a few hours before in front of his pals. Embarrassed the guy. Wounded his ego." Greyson shrugged. "Maybe he came around looking for payback."

"That's ridiculous," Kim said flatly.

"We're still gonna need to test your service weapon. Check the ballistics. Just to rule you out, so the killer's defense attorney doesn't crucify me when the time comes. The .22 is just a guess. Could be wrong," Greyson replied.

Perry chuckled in the backseat.

"We'll need to test your sidearm, too, Major," Greyson said, looking into the rearview to see Perry's reaction.

The rest of the short trip continued in stony silence. When they reached the Carter County Sheriff's Office parking lot, Greyson parked in a spot reserved for the county's top cop.

Two minutes later, they walked into the station. Greyson called a deputy over to take their weapons for ballistics testing. Not that they were happy about it, but to avoid unnecessary problems, Kim and Perry handed over their pistols. There was no chance either one of them had shot and killed Luke Price, and they all knew it.

They followed Greyson toward the conference room where Mayor Elizabeth Deveraux waited. Greyson reached to open the door.

Before she walked inside, Kim said, "Ballistics will prove my gun didn't shoot Price. I'll expect your apology."

Perry grinned. "Me, too. What she said."

CHAPTER THIRTY-ONE

Thursday, May 12
Carter's Crossing, Mississippi
2:30 p.m.

"MAN, IT'S HOT IN HERE," Hern said. He'd removed his shirt. Sweat glistened in his hair and slicked his torso. "I won't miss working in this heat."

An equally sweaty Redmond replied, "That's for damn sure."

The temperature inside the decrepit old barn had become stifling hours ago. The sun was high and breezes nonexistent. There were no trees to shade the metal roof, which seemed to cook the moisture from the air itself.

They had no air-conditioning. Not even a fan. The generator wasn't big enough to power the equipment and cool the air at the same time.

He wouldn't miss the wretched conditions in this place or Redmond and Hern. Not even a little bit.

"Glad the Mississippi summer heat isn't here yet." He said

as he wiped perspiration from his face and neck with a grimy bandanna and slipped it back into his pocket. He had pulled a bottle of water from the cooler and stood back to survey the area one last time.

"You got that right." Redmond drained the last of the water from his bottle and tossed it into the pit. "But it's damn close enough. Let's get this done and get the hell out of here."

He'd watched as Redmond finished running the remaining paper through the printers about an hour ago. He was close to the point of no return. Should he cut his losses now? Or could he afford to follow the plan and wait?

He noticed that Redmond's knife dangled from his belt, as it always did. Hern carried his weapons everywhere, too. Standard procedure for army personnel.

Which was when he acknowledged that either Redmond or Hern could have killed Bonnie Nightingale. Both were trained Rangers. They both had means and opportunity on Sunday night.

As far as he knew, neither had a motive to kill her. But that meant nothing, really. Either one might have done the job. Neither one had an alibi. That's all Major Hammer needed to know.

He'd put the last of the counterfeits into three duffle bags and stashed them in the cab of the truck. Nina would take them off his hands at the casino tomorrow and give him genuine bills in return.

Hern had packed the coffins with the last of the real cash and nailed the lids shut.

They had muscled the coffins into the hearse, which Hern had parked inside the barn.

Two coffins full of greenbacks should be enough to carry him until he could access the money he'd stashed offshore when he arrived at his new home.

Absently, he felt the hearse's key fob resting in his pocket, securely nestled against his leg.

They were ready to go. Only one thing left to do here. Destroy the evidence.

The plan was to leave the fully-prepped hearse parked in the barn. He'd drive it to the helo pad at Kelham where the coffins filled with cash would be loaded in due course.

The three of them would be the last men out of Kelham on the final day. Hern had been chosen because he was a pilot. He'd fly the helo to the private airstrip where they'd move to the Gulfstream and head out of the country.

He'd worked on the plan for weeks, going over and over it with Redmond and Hern. The plan was solid. Nothing could go wrong.

But now he'd been forced to improvise.

Major Hammer had arrived to investigate Bonnie Nightingale's murder. Only a matter of time before Hammer uncovered the truth. Not only about how and why Bonnie died, either. It wouldn't take Hammer long to get around to Jasper's murder, too.

Which would lead him to the counterfeiting operation. Inevitably.

He wouldn't allow that to happen. He was too close to winning his private war with the army, and he had no intention of ending up in Leavenworth instead of paradise.

He had been considering his options, which were limited at best.

The smartest thing to do would be to escape now.

Go before Hammer figured everything out.

That was the smart thing, but not the best thing. Because if he did that, he'd be running for the rest of his life. Running was not what he had in mind for his retirement. Not even close.

While he had been here cleaning things up, he'd worked out a new plan. Not as good as the original one, but it would suffice.

Terminating Redmond and Hern now would level more weight on him over the next few days, but that couldn't be helped. It was the smart thing. Do it now. Circumstances had changed.

He'd searched for a better answer since he'd first set eyes on Hammer.

But he'd come up empty.

Hern had already dug a fire pit in a far corner of the barn. They had used the final ink and paper supplies today. The printers themselves were plastic. They had dumped everything remaining, along with as much kindling as they could salvage, into the pit, and soaked the pile with accelerant.

He glanced around the rafters and the walls. The wood on this old barn was drier than a popcorn fart. It would go up quickly enough. The trash that remained tossed about the place was flammable.

He nodded. Once the fire got going, the barn and everything in it would burn down fast.

The abandoned barn had served them well these past few months. They had no further need of it. His plan had always been to torch the place on his way out of Carter's Crossing for the final time.

Moving up the destruction sequence might be enough to get Hammer out of the way until he could leave the country.

Though he'd planned to leave the hearse here, fully loaded, until the last day, he couldn't do that now.

"Let's get this fire going so we can get out of here," Redmond said.

Hern tossed the last of the kindling on the pile. "That's the last of it."

Redmond had taken an ancient Zippo lighter off an old vet in a friendly poker game weeks ago. He flipped up the lid and rolled the striker to ignite the butane inside. Then he tossed the lighter onto the pile of debris in the pit.

The accelerant ignited and quickly flamed.

Redmond and Hern stood back from the pit, watching the fire, drinking more water.

He approached quietly from behind, weapon at his side. Neither man turned around.

He figured there was no one around within listening distance to hear the shots.

He raised the Glock 17, held it steady, and shot Redmond in the back of the head.

The noise of the gunshot was deafening inside the old barn. The bullets were full metal jackets. Cheap. Plentiful. The army had thousands of them. Easy to grab on the fly from Kelham. He'd have preferred hollow points. They'd have blasted Redmond's head apart like a cantaloupe.

As it was, the bullets he had worked just fine.

Redmond's body fell forward, into the flames.

Shocked, Hern spun around, automatically reaching for his weapon. "Hey! What the—"

Before Hern finished those words, the second round from the Glock hit him in the face.

Hern's head slammed backward and his skull and brains splattered all over the fire pit, causing the flames to hiss and spit. Half a moment later, his body crumpled to the ground.

"Sorry, guys. Had to be done," he said quietly. No need to say more.

He stood mesmerized by the fire for a few seconds. He glanced around the big, empty barn. Redmond had pulled the three trucks inside after Nina left and closed the big door, just in case she drove past. They wanted her to believe they'd already gone.

He strode to his truck and removed the three duffle bags filled with counterfeits. He tossed two into the hearse.

The fire had consumed most of the fuel in the pit already. Hern hadn't built it to take the whole building down. But he needed the fire to spread farther and faster.

He returned to the trucks. He wasn't concerned about the trucks being identified later. His was stolen, and he wanted Redmond and Hern's bodies identified quickly. The trucks would help with that.

Using a hose he'd cut into three pieces, he siphoned gasoline from the trucks onto the ground around all three of the vehicles. He left the gasoline running.

He dashed over to the fire pit where he'd left the third duffle close to the raging fire. He pulled the zipper back and dumped the counterfeits onto the flames. He trailed the paper onto the two bodies and closer to the gasoline near the trucks.

Then he pulled a book of matches from his pocket and lit the gasoline.

Soon, the two fires would meet. The remaining gasoline in the trucks might explode if he was lucky.

He ran back to the hearse, jumped into the driver's seat, and started the engine. With his foot on the brake, he pushed the transmission into drive and floored the accelerator to rev the engine.

He lifted his foot off the brake and the old hearse jumped forward toward the back wall of the barn. He could see daylight through the cracks in the old boards. When the heavy hearse slammed into the wall, the hearse broke through into the field.

He drove around the barn to the two-track and toward the road. When he was two hundred feet away, the first big explosion shook the ground under him.

"You're a lucky sonofabitch, you know that?" he grinned.

The second explosion shoved the hearse forward. He imagined he could feel the heat at his back.

He kept the pedal pushed all the way to the floor.

The third explosion blew the remains of the old barn sky high.

"Woo hoo!" he cackled and slapped his palm on the steering wheel.

Fire trucks would be on the way soon.

He turned onto the dirt road and sped away from Carter's Crossing as fast as the old beast would move.

CHAPTER THIRTY-TWO

Thursday, May 12
Carter's Crossing, Mississippi
2:45 p.m.

WHEN SHERIFF GREYSON OPENED the conference room door, Kim walked in first and Perry followed. This was what passed for a secure situation room in a small, rural county like this one. Due to budgeting issues, the room likely served multiple purposes.

She assumed it was soundproofed and monitored and had no interior or exterior windows. But it was tastefully decorated in shades of brown and green like the executive offices in any larger city.

A butler's table on one side held coffee and water and sodas. Two large flags stood in the corner. One was the Mississippi state flag, and the other the U.S. flag. A few potted plants had been placed here and there. The artwork on the walls reflected Mississippi landmarks.

Mayor Deveraux was seated at the head of a large oval table

opposite the entrance, head down, reading reports. Her wildly curly hair was still fastened at the nape of her neck, and she was wearing the heavy makeup leftover from her earlier television interview.

She glanced up over her reading glasses as they entered, her expression neutral.

"Someone want to tell me why we're here?" Major Perry asked.

Kim snagged a bottle of water and took a seat where she could see all the participants clearly. Perry and Greyson did the same and settled across the table.

Greyson said, "Mayor's got questions. Easier to bring everybody up to speed all at once. We need to get on the same page. Help us to work together more effectively."

Before he could say more, fire trucks raced past the building, distinctive sirens blaring. Deveraux's phone vibrated beside her on the table. She glanced down to read the alert.

Greyson's phone lit up, too. He opened the alert to read it.

"What's going on?" Perry asked.

"An old barn ignited ten miles west of town. The fire department's on the way," Deveraux said, without meeting Perry's gaze. To Greyson, she said, "You got a team you can send out there, just in case they need help?"

"Yeah. Let me get that going," Greyson pushed his chair from the table and left the room.

They waited in silence. This was a small town with a small department, but it seemed they'd had more problems than they could handle here lately.

Greyson returned minutes later and settled into his chair again. Kim thought he looked worn out.

"Everything okay?" Deveraux asked.

"There's nothing out there worth saving anymore. It's the old Gordon Farm. Nothing been planted out there in decades," Greyson replied.

"If there's nothing going on out there, what caused the barn to ignite?" Perry asked. "Spontaneous combustion seems unlikely, doesn't it?"

Greyson shrugged. "Kids maybe."

"Shouldn't kids still be in school?" Kim asked.

"We'll find out soon enough." Greyson ran a weary hand over his head. "Fire trucks will get out there pretty quickly, and we'll have more intel."

Deveraux exchanged a meaningful look with the sheriff before she said, "You were about to bring us all up to speed. Let's get to it. We don't know how much time you've got."

"Right. You've met Agent Otto," Greyson said, extending his right palm in Kim's direction. Then he waved to his left. "This is Major Lincoln Perry. Pentagon sent him here on the Bonnie Nightingale murder. They've seen the autopsy report. They sent another guy to Kelham. Major Eugene Hammer. Goes by Hulk Hammer. They've got the base locked down. He's interviewing everybody now, gathering facts. We should know more in a few hours."

"What's he looking for?" Deveraux asked, turning her gaze toward Perry.

Perry replied, "I haven't talked to him. I'm supposed to be undercover, eyes and ears open and liaise with the locals and all that. But I imagine he's trying to find a viable suspect."

"Sort of like looking for a needle in a haystack, isn't it?" Kim said with a smirk.

"How so?" Perry replied.

"The operating theory is that Nightingale was probably

killed by an Army Ranger, due to the manner of death. One quick slice across the neck. Swift and hard and sure. No hesitation marks. No bruising. No messing around," Kim said matter-of-factly. "Kelham is filled with Rangers. Which means, in this case, filled with viable suspects. Makes the investigation a bit tricky when everyone Hammer interviews could be the killer. Hard to separate the wheat from the chaff in a situation like that."

Major Perry offered a lazy grin. "If the job was easy, Agent Otto, the army wouldn't need high-priced talents like me and Hammer on the job, would they?"

Deveraux gave him a tight grin in response. "There was a time when I really, really loved that kind of swagger, Major Perry. When I was on active duty, every Marine in the place behaved the same way. Including me. And Sheriff Greyson here. Most of the time, it was pure theater."

She cleared her throat. "But right at the moment, I'm more interested in results than attitude."

Perry glared at her. He clearly didn't like being challenged. Kim wondered if he had a problem with authority in general or women in authority in particular.

"Either you or *Hulk Hammer* have any results to report?" Deveraux's lips twitched as if mirth at his squirming would bubble over if she didn't force it back.

Kim watched the back and forth, understanding that gallows humor was one way to handle the crimes they all dealt with every day. Besides, Hulk Hammer *was* a ridiculous nickname. Particularly for military police. He'd probably received no end of grief over it.

Kim wondered what kind of guy would allow that particular moniker to stick. If she got the chance, she'd ask him.

"Nothing to report just yet." Perry wasn't amused. He bristled at Deveraux's teasing. "And even if we did, we wouldn't be reporting to you. There's a whole chain of command for these things, Mayor. We handle our guys. You handle your citizens. Works like a charm."

"I've been deferring to Kelham my entire life, Major, as did my father before me. When it's the army's job, I'm more than happy to let you do it." Deveraux folded her hands on the table and gave him an icy stare. "But Bonnie Nightingale was a Carter's Crossing citizen. One most of us knew and liked. Most days, she helped out her cousin Libby. The same Libby who owns the diner where you had lunch."

Perry continued to glare. Deveraux kept talking.

"As far as we know, Bonnie was killed inside the city limits. If one of your guys killed her, we're not letting the army cover that up. Yes, the killer may be your responsibility. Yes, we've got plenty of things to do around here without stepping on the army's toes."

Perry said, "Glad we understand each other."

"But know this." Deveraux ignored his sarcasm. "Until we find out exactly what happened to Bonnie Nightingale, your orders are to cooperate and coordinate with Sheriff Greyson. You got a problem with that, and I'm happy to call that general at the Pentagon who sent you down here and work things out with him directly."

Perry looked like he might object. But after a moment, he shook his head. He held up both hands, palms out, in mock surrender. "No, ma'am. No problem at all."

"So what do you know about the Nightingale case so far?" Greyson asked.

"Not much that you don't already know. We're working on

it, but we're not making any real progress so far," Perry said, frowning. "We're worried. You already know that, too. Everybody still left at Kelham will be shipping out tomorrow. If we don't get this guy before then, who knows whether we ever will."

"And you want us to stay out of the way until you find him? Not a chance." Deveraux nodded once, firmly, as if she'd made up her mind and that was all that mattered. Which, of course, was nonsense.

Perry said, "While Hammer's at Kelham, I'm supposed to be nosing around town. Finding out what I can about Bonnie Nightingale."

Kim volunteered the only thing she'd really learned about Nightingale since she arrived in Carter's Crossing. "She was dating a guy named Brian Jasper. She was in Brannan's the night she died, waiting for Jasper to show up."

All three of them turned to stare at her. Deveraux and Greyson exchanged glances before she asked, "And you know this how?"

"Walt McKinney told me last night when I was at Brannan's," Kim replied.

Greyson said, "Walt told me that, too. I haven't been able to confirm she was there."

"Jasper would have known where he was supposed to meet Bonnie. There must have been witnesses in the bar that night, too," Perry said.

"Jasper might have been avoiding me. Or maybe he was just busy with duties related to the Kelham shutdown," Greyson replied. "No one else said she was in Brannan's that night. Bonnie's friends admitted they were seeing each other. Casually."

Deveraux interjected as if Greyson needed defending. "Let's remember that Bonnie died at midnight on Sunday. Her body wasn't found until Monday morning. We thought she'd committed suicide until the autopsy came back."

Kim nodded. The timing and Greyson's actions made sense in context. Believing Bonnie had committed suicide, he wouldn't have felt much urgency to follow up. Until the autopsy changed things.

Perry cocked his head and said, "Sounds like we need to talk to Jasper. Any idea where we can find him?"

Greyson replied, "He was involved in that car crash outside of town yesterday."

Kim cleared her throat. "I witnessed the crash. One woman died at the scene. Jasper was pretty banged up, but he survived."

Greyson said, "He was air-lifted in a Kelham helo to Memphis. He was in pretty bad shape. Not sure whether you can talk to him there or not."

"Well, it turns out you can't interview him," Kim replied. "When I checked this morning, I was told that he'd died during the night."

Greyson's eyes widened and he shook his head, as if the news wasn't too surprising, given the severity of Jasper's injuries.

"The intel I got was that cause of death was fentanyl overdose," Kim said quietly. "But that's all I know. Sorry."

A few long seconds of silence passed while the others considered the facts. Everybody had more questions than answers.

Deveraux turned to look at Greyson. "Tell me about Luke Price. The guy's always been a jerk and a mean drunk. But he didn't deserve to die for it. What happened there?"

"Looks like he crossed the wrong guy. Don't know who or why yet. But whatever it was got him executed." Greyson gave her the rundown from the autopsy, including the time of death, along with the gunshot evidence. He left out the part about Kim's fight with Price a few hours before he was killed. "My guys are out there searching for the murder weapon. We haven't found it yet. But we've—"

Greyson's comments were cut short when his phone vibrated, dancing on the table. He picked it up. "Greyson...Yeah...Swell...Okay..."

His frown deepened as he listened. He swiped his palm over his face and sighed. "Be there soon as I can."

"What's up?" Deveraux asked when he'd disconnected the call.

"There's a lot more to talk about. But it'll have to wait. Right now, I've got to go out to the old Gordon farm. The barn's still ablaze. Around the back, there's a gaping hole in the building. Firefighters were able to see the interior. Looks like there's two bodies inside," Greyson said, standing up and moving toward the door.

"Two bodies?" Deveraux's eyes widened. "What the hell is going on, Scott? The last murder we had here was fifteen years ago, and they were all related to Kelham. Now we've got four more. We need to get to the bottom of this and fast. We don't need everybody panicked."

Perry sat up straighter in his chair at the mention of Kelham-related homicides. He didn't ask any questions. Which meant he knew all about the old cases already.

"That's all I know at this point, Liz. We'll figure it out. It's all got to be related somehow. You know how investigations are. We need a thread we can pull to unravel the whole mess."

Greyson shook his head and squeezed his eyes shut for a moment as if considering whether to say more. "Could be a third body in that barn. They're not sure."

Deveraux gasped. "Why do they think there's another body?"

"Because there's three pickup trucks," Greyson replied. At the door, he turned and looked at Kim and Perry. "We're done with your weapons. You can pick them up at the front desk on your way out."

Kim stood and pushed her chair under the table. She looked at Deveraux. "We're still on for dinner tonight?"

"Yeah. Meet you at Libby's around seven. If you get held up, call me," Deveraux said.

Deveraux's comment about the timing of the last murders in Carter's Crossing made Kim uneasy. Fifteen years was a long time to go without a homicide in a town like this. That was the good news.

The bad news was that fifteen years ago, Jack Reacher had been involved. It seemed unlikely that he'd be back here now, running a killing spree.

But then, the Boss had sent her here. Which meant he believed there was a good chance Reacher was involved. He could have been the third man out there at that barn.

"You need some extra hands, Sheriff? You've gotta be running short-staffed," Kim said.

Greyson nodded. "If you're willing."

As if he'd been invited, Perry said, "Yeah, sure. I'll come along, too. Nothing better than a raging inferno in the already oppressive heat to get me interested."

CHAPTER THIRTY-THREE

Thursday, May 12
Carter's Crossing, Mississippi
3:15 p.m.

KIM TOOK THE PASSENGER SEAT, Perry sat in back, Greyson took the wheel. He turned on the lights and sirens after they left the parking lot, headed west of town. He drove fast and well along the twisty roads as familiar to him as the veins in the back of his hand.

"Tell us about this place where the bodies were found," Kim said, snugging her seatbelt and pulling the shoulder harness away from her neck to avoid being beheaded. She usually carried an alligator clamp in her pocket to hold some slack in the harness at the retractor, but she'd left it somewhere.

Greyson kept his gaze on the road, steering around potholes and deep ruts left by the rain. "It's an old cotton farm, abandoned years ago when textile manufacturing moved out of the county."

"What happened to the farm's owner?" Perry asked from the back seat.

"Old man Gordon was a middling prosperous farmer, but when he died, none of the kids wanted anything to do with the old place. Farming's a hard business. And there's not much money in it anymore," Greyson replied.

"So they sold the farm?" Kim asked.

"They sold the house and the land around it. But they couldn't find a buyer for the farm itself, so it's just been sitting out there, abandoned."

Perry said, "What about the barn?"

"That particular barn stands alone in the middle of a fallow field. About ten acres around it, if I had to guess. I haven't been out there in months. You have to make a point of driving past it. It's kind of back off the main roads," Greyson said, slowing to take a right turn at the intersection.

The road was narrow, twisty, and hadn't been repaved for a decade, at least. Greyson drove as fast as possible. But he was frequently forced to slow for potholes and other hazards.

At the next intersection, he turned onto a dirt road, which was rougher still. Kim bounced around on the seat like a sack of feathers.

Greyson nodded his head. "There's the fire."

There was a stand of trees off to the right that blocked Kim's line of sight to the barn itself. But the smoke rising into the sky was black and heavy.

Around the next bend, the blazing structure came into view.

As Greyson had said, the barn stood alone in the middle of the field. There were no ponds and certainly no fire hydrants out here. The fire was burning hot and fast. It would likely destroy the barn and everything in it.

Two fire trucks flanked the burning structure. The firemen attacked the fire with firehoses, but there was no way they'd be able to contain the blaze with the amount of water in those tanks. Best case, they might be able to prevent the barn from igniting the field in which it stood and spreading until it destroyed everything within a ten-mile radius.

Greyson pulled his SUV to a stop fifty yards from the blaze. He made a three-point turn and pointed the front of the vehicle toward the road. They got out and walked the rest of the way.

Kim felt the heat pulsing from the fire as she approached. She stopped well short of the firefighters, standing back out of the way. There was nothing she could do to help, and nothing to see until the fire was contained.

"Wait here. I'll talk to the crew. See what's going on," Greyson said and kept walking toward the barn.

Perry stood next to Kim. The fire itself was magnificent and hypnotic. If an arsonist was responsible, he might be nearby, admiring the results of his work.

She glanced around the vicinity, looking for any evidence that the scene had drawn spectators. But the barn was too remote. She saw only the fire crew and the sheriff.

"What do you think?" Perry asked after a while.

Kim shook her head. "Hard to say. I'm just wondering which came first."

"Which what?"

"The murders or the fire. Which came first?"

She looked around again and saw nothing but emptiness as far as her field of vision could see. "If we didn't know there were pickup trucks inside the barn, the place would have appeared to be unoccupied to anyone who might be driving past."

"Yeah. And really, who would be driving by here? That washboard road we drove in here didn't seem like it was well-traveled to me," Perry replied.

"Two bodies, maybe three inside," Greyson said.

Kim kept thinking out loud. "Did they park the trucks inside for some reason, and then something unexpected happened to cause the fire, which killed them?"

"I see what you mean," Perry said. "Or did the murders happen first, then the trucks were moved inside afterward, and then the fire was deliberately started? Depending on the cause of death, it could go either way."

"Arson destroys a lot of evidence. But not as much as arsonists often expect." Kim nodded. She walked along the two-track that led up to the barn, peering at the ground. She kicked up the dusty gravel. "They had rain here yesterday. Today, the ground is dry. If they'd driven those trucks in here yesterday, we'd see some ruts when yesterday's mud dried."

"But we're not seeing that," Perry said. "Which could mean they drove in here today after the rain stopped, and the ground was dried out and hard."

Kim kneeled to get a closer look at the gravel along the two-track. Then she stood and dusted her hands. "All three trucks could have already been inside the barn before yesterday's rain. Or, more likely, they drove in earlier today. The problem is there's an extra truck."

Perry nodded. "Three trucks, two bodies so far. Where's the third guy? And how did he get away from here?"

"All good questions, Major Perry. The third guy might be dead, too. If he is, there was a fourth guy. Either way, three guys or four guys, there's another vehicle. Greyson needs to find him and the vehicle." She looked around again.

The bad news was, unlike in most American cities these days, there were no CCTV cameras out here on the farm. No buildings or poles to mount them on, either. No electricity or running water or heating and cooling systems, either.

The good news was in an open area no trees blocked the view. Which meant the Boss could get satellite imagery. Possibly.

It was a long shot. If they'd driven the trucks into the barn, the satellite images might not show the drivers themselves, depending on the angles.

On the other hand, she could get lucky. Maybe the same trucks had been here before. Maybe the drivers had parked outside another time. Maybe they'd been caught on satellite images before.

All of which meant that if Reacher had been anywhere near this barn, he might have been recorded.

Simply because it could have been done, doesn't mean Reacher was here. She formulated the questions as she scanned the emptiness around the burning barn.

What brought Reacher back to Carter's Crossing? Who were those dead men in the barn? What did they have to do with Reacher? Was Reacher the one who killed them?

Those were just the starter questions.

She had lots more.

Because she was fairly sure Reacher wasn't one of the charred bodies inside the barn. He was way too capable to end up dead in a place like this.

CHAPTER THIRTY-FOUR

Thursday, May 12
Carter's Crossing, Mississippi
5:15 p.m.

HE'D HEARD THE FIRE TRUCKS headed toward the barn as he'd rushed away from the scene. Driving an unfamiliar hearse through town would have captured too much interest from the town folks. A witness would have remembered it when Sheriff Greyson came around asking.

So he didn't go that way. The heavy old hearse was difficult to maneuver. It bounced into the potholes. He struggled with the wobbly steering around the sinkholes, giving them a wide berth just in case. All told, the circuitous route along the back roads to his safe house had taken twice as long, but it was wiser, too.

When he arrived, he quickly moved his Jaguar out of the garage and pulled the hearse into it, out of sight. Once the hearse was safely stashed, he closed and locked the garage.

He went into the house, stripped, and dropped his clothes into the washer. He poured detergent onto the stinking pile, set the temperature, and started the extended cycle.

It would take at least two hot washings to remove the stench of sweat and fire, and whatever trace evidence of the murders remained embedded in his clothes. Then he glanced at the clock and headed for the shower to clean his body thoroughly.

When he'd finished his shower and donned fresh clothes, he hurried out again.

He'd planned to deal with Nina first before he returned to Kelham. But setting the fire and the return trip from the barn had taken too long. Hammer would be finishing his initial interviews soon.

There weren't many personnel left on the base. Almost everyone had been evacuated. The last personnel were slated to leave in the morning. Redmond and Hern should have been there, but they weren't.

When Hammer figured that out, he'd come looking for answers.

Nina had waited this long. She could wait a little longer.

He drove around to Kelham's back entrance and returned the sentry's salute on his way past. He left the Jaguar in the lot behind the barracks and headed toward the interview room, striding purposefully, like a man with nothing to hide.

His phone vibrated in his pocket. He pulled it out and looked at the caller ID. Nina Cloud. He sighed and answered the call. "Yeah."

"Have you heard?" Nina was sniffling, and her voice was thick as if she'd been crying the entire day. Which she probably had. Maybe she really was pregnant. She was certainly more emotional than usual.

"Heard what?" he replied, although he figured he already knew.

"The barn. It's burned to the ground. Everything in it is

gone. All the money. Everything," Nina said, crying softly, bewildered. "This is so horrible. First Bonnie. Then Caroline. Now the money. What's going on?"

"It'll be okay. Don't worry about it. I'll come over as soon as I'm done here. Okay?"

"Okay," she sniveled. "I need to tell you about Bonnie, too."

The mention of Bonnie raised his internal radar. What did she know? And worse, who had she told?

"You're alone?" he asked as if he was concerned about her.

"Y-yes."

"Just stay put. Take a nap. Get some rest. I'll be there as soon as I can. And don't worry," he coaxed. "It'll be okay. You trust me, don't you?"

"Y-yes."

"I've got to hang up now. I'll see you soon," he said, glancing ahead where Major Hammer waited outside the interview room door.

"I love you," she whispered.

He cringed.

"You, too," he replied before he hung up and dropped the phone into his pocket. He covered the last few feet and glanced up at the big man. "How'd it go with your interviews, Major?"

"Not as well as I'd hoped, General Murphy," Hammer replied, falling into step beside him. "To a man, everyone I've interviewed has a solid alibi. I've got a few more to question. Then I'll need to check all of the alibis out before we lift the lockdown. But so far, no gaping holes."

"How can you be sure that someone will talk?" he asked.

"Technique I learned from an old-timer. Guy named Duncan Munro. He called it his secret weapon," Hammer replied with a grin.

"What's that?"

"Confine everybody to quarters. Or the mess hall or the officer's club. MPs watching everybody, including each other," Hammer said. "Nice to still have one, by the way. Officer's club. Lots of bases don't have them anymore."

"What makes you so sure Munro's secret weapon will work?"

"It's foolproof." Hammer nodded and grinned again. "Sitting down all day. No reading, no television, no electronics of any kind. Sooner or later, someone talks from sheer boredom. Never fails."

"If you say so." He nodded, opened the door, and gestured Hammer toward the big wooden chairs. "How are you planning to confirm the alibis while you're waiting for some bored soldier to confess?"

"Leg work. No other way I know of to do it." Hammer shrugged. "Like you said, quite a few of them claim to have been at that poker tournament. Good place to start is out at the casino. I'm headed out there next."

"You got any jurisdiction on the rez?"

"No. But usually, they like to cooperate with the federal government," Hammer replied easily. "I can get a warrant for the CCTV if I need to. What's your experience out there? You think a warrant will be necessary?"

"The manager of the place is Randy Cloud. He's used to being the master of that universe. But he won't want any trouble." He cocked his head and raised his eyebrows. "Unless you think one of his employees or a member of the tribe killed Bonnie Nightingale?"

"It's not looking that way at the moment," Hammer replied.

"Make that clear to him. He'll voluntarily release the video.

If he doesn't, just go back with your warrant. You can get one quickly, can't you?" he asked.

"Might have to wait until morning. But yeah," Hammer nodded, "if it comes to that. You think it will?"

He shrugged. "Hard to tell with Randy Cloud. But if you tell him why you want to know, it'll help. He doesn't want any trouble with the locals or with the army. All he wants is to keep that steady line of gamblers leaving their paychecks at his casino."

"I've got two more guys to talk to. Redmond and Hern. Any idea where I can find them?" Hammer asked.

He shook his head. "They live off base, I think."

"Yeah, so I heard. They had a couple of days' leave, your sergeant told me. Supposed to be back tonight. Guess I'll see them when I get back from the casino," Hammer said, standing up to leave. "I'll keep you posted."

CHAPTER THIRTY-FIVE

Thursday, May 12
Carter's Crossing, Mississippi
6:35 p.m.

LONG BEFORE THE CRIME scene crews finished the grim process at the barn, Kim caught a lift to Toussaint's Hotel for a shower and fresh clothes. She had seen charred bodies before and the sight was always disturbing. The visual, once seen, was impossible to wipe from her mind's eye.

An involuntary shudder rumbled through her from head to toe.

She hurried up the front sidewalk, up the steps, and into the hotel. She didn't stop to talk with anyone in the lobby. She took the stairs to the second floor two at a time and moved toward her room.

Her phone vibrated in her pocket and she fished it out while she used her key card to open the door. As she walked inside and closed the door behind her, a glance at the caller ID reflected the one person in the world she actually wanted to talk to at the moment.

"Hey, Chico. What do you have for me?" she asked Gaspar wearily and without preamble, as if he were still her partner and the two of them were in this case together. For the thousandth time since he'd retired, she wished Gaspar was still on the job.

"Sounds like you've had a rough day," he replied, chewing on something. Which made her grin. With his eating habits, Gaspar should have weighed five hundred pounds. She had no idea what he did with all those calories.

"I'm sure you saw satellite footage of that barn. The fire was hot when we arrived and it didn't get a lot better until there wasn't much left but ashes." She talked as she peeled off her clothes. She stuffed them into the trashcan liner she found in the bathroom. She would never wear them again.

She turned on the shower and caught a glimpse of herself in the mirror. The image was horrifying. She had black soot all over her face. She must have swiped at it a few times in the heat, which left swaths around her eyes and mouth.

"Do you mind if I get a quick shower and call you back?" she asked. She didn't want to put her filthy body in the white robe hanging on the back of the door. If she did, no amount of washing would ever get it clean.

"Yeah. No problem." He clicked off.

Kim dropped the phone on the bed and stepped into the steamy hot water. Sooty rivulets ran off her and circled the drain. She quickly soaped up from head to toe. She had black marks in the crooks of her elbows and every crevice on her body. The soot was everywhere.

After three shampoos, the water from her hair finally ran clean. She lathered her body one last time and rinsed for another five minutes until she was satisfied. She turned off the water, grabbed a white towel to dry off, and then wrapped it around her head.

Only then did she slip into the white terry robe and wrap it around herself. She finished toweling the water from her hair on her way to the bedroom, where she picked up the phone and hit redial. While she waited for the connection, she found a bottle of water and opened it. She drank as if her entire body was parched.

Gaspar picked up after the first ring. "Feeling better?"

"More human, at least. Man, fires are grisly."

"And they stink."

Which made her smile and feel a little better. "So, what've you got?"

"It took some digging. But I finally found a connection between Reacher and Kelham. Something that your boss might think would draw Reacher back there," Gaspar said, chewing something like a crispy apple in her ear.

Her stomach growled. She hadn't realized how hungry she was. She glanced at the clock. Mayor Deveraux was expecting her for dinner at seven o'clock. At this rate, she'd be late.

"Can you give me the highlights and send me a report to read later?"

"Got a date or something? That Major Perry looks like a hottie in the headshots I found," Gaspar teased.

"Yeah, I've got a date with Elizabeth Deveraux. And I'm running late."

"Huh. And all this time, I thought you liked men," Gaspar deadpanned.

"Smartass. Tell me. What did you find out about Reacher?" She settled onto the bed and put her feet up. She leaned back against the headboard and closed her eyes. It had already been a very long day. And it was a long way from being over.

"You know that North Korean diplomat that died in New York last week?"

"Hana Pak?"

"Yep. Turns out he and Reacher had crossed paths before. Reacher was posted briefly to a place called Camp Stanley in South Korea. The base is closed now. Reacher was only there a few weeks. Working on a case when he was still with the 110th Special Investigations Unit."

"What kind of case?"

"Suspicious death of a woman under circumstances of interest to the army, I guess. The records are heavily redacted."

"Of course they are," she said wearily. "This is Reacher we're dealing with. It seems everything about his life that's important to my assignment is off-limits."

"Well, from what I can glean, the woman was sort of a party girl. A real looker. Her background is a little cloudy, but people called her June. She had a steady boyfriend, but she liked to mingle, if you catch my drift," Gaspar said.

Kim felt like she knew where this was going before he said the rest, but she let him continue. "Um hmm."

"Her steady guy was then Major Alec Murphy. Apparently he fell hard for June and wanted her to marry him."

"But she had other ideas?"

"Turns out that June wasn't free to marry anyone. She was already married."

"To Hana Pak," Kim said dully.

"Bingo. Pak found out about June's affair with Murphy and killed her. After an illegal dog fight. In front of the entire crowd."

"A dog fight?"

"It's a big thing over there. Lots of money changes hands. Gambling, drugs, prostitution, the whole sordid mess."

"How does any of this have anything to do with Reacher?"

"First, he was there. He was assisting with an investigation into a theft ring, I guess. It's not exactly clear why he was on the scene, but he was."

"Theft? Sounds kind of small potatoes for a guy at Reacher's level, doesn't it?" She cocked her head.

"It started out that way. Lasted years. Eventually became about twenty million dollars' worth of goods that they could prove. All stolen from the Army and Air Force Exchange Service Stores. Plenty of blame to go around. It was a joint operation between some South Koreans and some military personnel. Happened right under the noses of the brass. People went to jail," Gaspar said. "I've put all the details into a file I'll send you."

"Okay. Thanks for digging this up. Must have taken you all day," she replied.

"You owe me. I'll collect next time I see you," he teased. "But here's the thing. Reacher, Hana Pak, and Alec Murphy were all there when the woman, June, was murdered. All three of them dated the woman, too."

"What? Reacher dated June?"

"Yep. Reading between the lines, it seems like Reacher liked her. A lot. He and Murphy got into a fistfight over her the same day she died," Gaspar said. "Some speculated at the time that Reacher would have killed Murphy over June."

Kim would have liked to say that idea was absurd. But she knew it wasn't. Not where Reacher was concerned. She kneaded the headache that was starting between her eyes. "So you're thinking Reacher found out Pak was in New York and he went there and killed him?"

Gaspar replied, "Possible. But like you said before, it's not really Reacher's style to kill a guy with poison and walk away, is it?"

"Which means Pak's killer could have been this Alec Murphy?" She drank the last of the water while she thought about it. "I don't know. That's a long time to carry a grudge, isn't it?"

"I checked Murphy out. He's got a temper. And a long memory. It could have been him. Or not. I'm looking for CCTV on Pak. If there was any contact between Murphy and Pak, I'll find it." Gaspar said, sensing her impatience, "That's not the important part of this story."

He'd given her a lot to mull over. "Okay. I'll bite. And the important part is…"

"Guess who is the CO at Kelham right this very minute?"

"Alec Murphy?"

"The very same."

"The Boss knows all of this, of course. He thinks Reacher would have heard about Hana Pak because it's been all over the news for days. And Reacher has always had a knack for finding people." She sat up straighter on the bed. "The news might have prodded Reacher to solve one more murder. The Boss thinks Reacher will come here to deal with Murphy."

"Give that girl a gold star," Gaspar said with approval. "And if he's right, Reacher is already there in Carter's Crossing. Maybe he's been there for the past few days."

"Makes sense." Kim nodded, although he couldn't see her. "Because Kelham is closing. Murphy and all the other soldiers who are still here will be leaving. Reacher's window of opportunity to deal with Murphy is now."

"I'll send you the files. You can decide for yourself. It all hangs together. I haven't found a paper trail yet for Murphy traveling to New York last week. I could be wrong," Gaspar said.

"Okay."

"You don't like it?"

"It's not that. I think you're right. It all hangs together better than any other theory we've come up with." She tapped a front tooth with a knuckle, thinking it through. "We know I wouldn't be here unless the Boss believed Reacher would show up. And he always has more intel than we do. He's likely got more evidence that Reacher is here, too."

"But?" Gaspar prodded.

"But I'm just wondering what Bonnie Nightingale has to do with all of this," Kim replied as she glanced at the clock. "I've got to go. Send me the files. I'll call you later."

CHAPTER THIRTY-SIX

Thursday, May 12
Carter's Crossing, Mississippi
7:15 p.m.

KIM FINISHED HER CONVERSATION with Gaspar, dressed hurriedly, and arrived at Libby's Diner later than she'd planned. It was Thursday. A school night. People had to be at work Friday morning. Which was why most of the tables were empty. A few hadn't been bused yet. Seemed like customers ate their evening meals earlier and had cleared out already. Maybe they'd headed for the casino for a while before bed.

Mayor Deveraux was seated at a table for four in the corner. The tables nearby were all vacant. Beside her sat an open bottle of red wine and two large wine glasses.

Kim approached the table and pulled out the chair across from her. "Sorry I'm late," she said with a smile. "I didn't know Libby sold wine."

"This is my private stash." Deveraux's returning smile was like a bright light in the very grim day. She was an extraordinarily attractive woman, even now. "If you're done for the night, Libby brought you a glass."

Kim was about to decline when she glanced at the ornate label on the bottle and grinned. "Wow. That's too good to pass up. Just a splash, please. I've got work to do later."

Deveraux tipped the rich Brunello with a light hand, watching the deep red wine settle into the bowl. They raised their glasses. Kim sipped and rolled the wine around on her tongue before she swallowed it.

"That's really great. It's not often that I'm served an expensive Italian wine in a diner." She grinned again. "In fact, I'm not sure it's ever happened before."

"We do what we can out here in the wilds of mid-America," Deveraux replied cheekily.

"How'd your interview go this afternoon?" Kim asked as she settled in.

Deveraux shrugged. "It's hard to make sinkholes interesting until one of them swallows your livestock or your car in broad daylight. Then the situation gets everybody's attention."

Kim grinned. "I'll bet it does. What are you going to do about it?"

"The experts tell me it's all about the train. Jurisdiction is murky. The feds control transportation, generally speaking. These tracks were laid decades ago, and the feds handed the responsibility for maintenance to the railroad company. It feels like they've been taking liberties with the foundations to save money," Deveraux explained while she perused the menu, just as a matter of form. "The trick now is to get the railroad company to solve the problem before something more serious happens."

Kim could think of nothing to offer in response, nor any good reason to say it. She nodded.

Deveraux changed the subject. "How did things go out at the old Gordon barn? Did they find a third body?"

"No," Kim replied. "No positive IDs yet, but Sheriff Greyson is running the plates on all three trucks. We may know more soon."

"Makes sense that the dead men owned the trucks. Maybe he'll get lucky." Deveraux nodded. "Any solid guesses?"

"About the identity of the victims?" Kim cocked her head while she scanned the menu, just in case Libby had added a special or something. No such luck. "I saw the bodies briefly. Both men were average-sized. That's about all anyone can tell at this point. Best guess is neither one is Reacher, which is what I needed to know. Maybe you wanted to know that, too."

The tension Deveraux held in her shoulders visibly relaxed. The tense lines around the corners of her mouth slackened. She raised her wine with a steady hand and took another sip. "Was I that obvious?"

Kim held the stem of the glass, pondering the question. "I take it you still have feelings for Reacher?"

"I hadn't thought about him in years." Deveraux's smile was a little weaker. She seemed to be remembering something that both pleased and perplexed her.

"Reacher was the one who got away?" Kim asked, slightly surprised, and genuinely curious. She found the idea hard to fathom.

"Not exactly." Deveraux shrugged. She drained her glass and refilled it. "I haven't been pining for him or anything like that. I didn't even realize he had made such a lasting impression on me. There was never any question that we were just having a bit of fun back then."

"Fifteen years is a long time to carry a torch for a guy you only knew for a few days, such a very long time ago," Kim said, swirling the wine and watching it cling to the side of the glass. "Did you learn anything important about him back then?"

"Not much. Hell, maybe that was part of the appeal. When you don't know anything about a guy, he's kind of a blank slate. In your head, you can write him any way you want after he goes, you know?" Deveraux replied.

Kim could see that. Maybe she was feeling some of the same things. Maybe the Boss had been right about the subtext in her recent reports. *Was* she going soft on Reacher?

She shook the idea off and put some firmness into her tone. "He was still in the army back then. Here on assignment. You were the sheriff. Were you working together?"

"Not officially, of course. He wasn't even here officially. There was another guy out at Kelham taking the lead in the case. His name was…Munroe? No…" Deveraux frowned as she concentrated on locating the missing gray cells. Her face cleared when she found the intel. "Yes. That's right. Duncan Munro."

"Were you investigating the murders back then? Three women killed. Happened here in your town, right?" Kim asked.

"We thought it was only one woman at first. Reacher was the one who figured out there were two more," Deveraux replied. "And the death of the one we knew about before Reacher arrived didn't make much sense. It seemed like she was a party girl who crossed the wrong man and paid the price for it."

"You didn't like that theory?"

"Her steady boyfriend was deployed, off and on. Some top-secret assignment out of the country." Deveraux shook her head. "If she was just a party girl, why didn't she have more than one guy hanging around? At least when her steady wasn't here?"

Kim said quietly, "Turned out she wasn't a party girl at all, I take it."

"Like Bonnie Nightingale wasn't a party girl, you mean?" Before Deveraux had a chance to say more, Libby rushed up to take their dinner orders.

They chose the cheeseburger and fries because they knew from experience that it was fast and easy and good. Libby dashed back to the kitchen.

"Poor woman has to be dead on her feet every night," Kim said as she watched Libby rush away. "Doesn't she have any help at all?"

"Besides Bonnie Nightingale, you mean?" Deveraux replied.

Kim arched her eyebrows and said nothing.

"She'll replace Bonnie, but not right away. They were friends for a good long time. Libby is having trouble dealing with the loss," Deveraux replied.

"Does she know Bonnie was murdered?" Kim asked.

"No reason to put that out there until we find the killer." Deveraux shook her head. "Libby is grieving enough as it is. Hell, everybody who knew Bonnie is grieving."

"And you don't have any theories about what happened to her?" Kim asked.

"Everybody's got theories." Deveraux shrugged.

"Do you know Alec Murphy?" Kim asked.

"General Alec Murphy? The CO out at Kelham?"

"That's the guy."

"I've met him once or twice. That's all. Why? You think he had something to do with Bonnie's murder?" Deveraux asked.

Kim shook her head. "I don't know. His name came up. I don't know him. What's he like?"

Deveraux said, "From all accounts, he's a mean son of a bitch. But like I said, I don't know the guy. And don't want to. He'll be the last one out at Kelham. Which is just fine with me. I'm looking forward to having the army off my turf."

After a few moments of silence when she realized Deveraux wouldn't say more, Kim cleared her throat. "Before you drink too much wine and can't think straight, let's get the Reacher interview out of the way, okay?"

"Ask away."

CHAPTER THIRTY-SEVEN

Thursday, May 12
Carter's Crossing, Mississippi
8:15 p.m.

"AS YOU KNOW, Reacher's being considered for a special classified assignment. I take it you felt he was a reasonable guy, back then. Could he be counted on to follow orders? Or at least follow the law?" Kim asked.

This question was the core of what she'd come to think of as the Reacher paradox.

On paper, he seemed both skilled and deadly. He had medals and commendations enough to paper a room. Which was good.

But he was also uncontrollable. He did whatever he wanted when he wanted to do it without regard to personal consequences. He could be heroic at times. But he also seemed to have only a passing regard for the law.

Given that he was a military policeman and an army officer back then, disregard for the law wasn't a positive character trait in Kim's view.

This trait made him seem simultaneously competent and unhinged. She didn't want to believe Reacher had gone rogue.

A guy who might be better left unfound than picked up dusted off and sent back into battle.

Deveraux cocked her head and seemed to consider the question for a good long time. Finally, she said, "I'm not really sure how to answer that. Reacher didn't work for me. I wasn't responsible for him, and he didn't impact my job security."

"Right." Kim nodded, waiting for Deveraux to work things out.

"You read the file. The situation back then was untenable. People at the top of the ladder with absolute power did what people like that too often do. Reacher didn't like it. He handled it." Deveraux said, draining her glass. She folded her hands on the table. "Hard to take issue with the results. Those guys got what they deserved."

"You were a cop, too. You knew, then and now, that the cops catch the bad guys, and the judges put them away. That's the system. It's not up to the cops to deliver justice," Kim said quietly.

"So I guess some might say that he was a rogue cop. And they'd be right. But I appreciated what he was trying to do. As I mentioned this morning, I certainly understood it." Deveraux nodded and refilled her glass. "You know what we were dealing with. Young women murdered, probably because they were pregnant, and the boyfriend didn't want to deal with the consequences of his actions."

"Indefensible. So Reacher killed them." Kim said flatly.

"He paid the price."

"How's that?" Kim arched her eyebrows.

Deveraux said, "He lost his job over the way he behaved.

His last case was the one we worked together here in Carter's Crossing. He loved the army. He made no secret of it. Given everything that happened, it was a pretty stiff price to pay."

"Not everyone would agree that losing a job, even one you're good at is the moral equivalent of losing lives," Kim replied. Nor did she believe Reacher lost his job because of what had happened here. His file was full of similar incidents, and the brass never showed him the door before.

"Tell me." Deveraux cocked her head. "What would you have done?"

Before she was required to answer, Libby arrived with the cheeseburgers. A few moments were spent with delivering the food and refilling water glasses before Libby dashed away again.

The aroma made Kim's stomach growl. While the burgers were hot and fresh, they dug in.

Which allowed Kim to pretend Deveraux's last question was never asked.

Deveraux didn't push it. Some questions were best left unanswered.

But if the Boss was right and Kim had begun to romanticize Reacher, then Deveraux was several miles ahead along that road. She seemed to be holding something back, but Kim didn't expect her to spill whatever it was after a single bottle of wine.

Kim changed the subject. "How long were you and Sheriff Greyson married?

Deveraux laughed. "We're still married."

Kim blinked. Twice. "He called you his ex."

"We don't live together anymore. But there was no need to get divorced. It's not like either one of us is going to find someone else as long as we live in this town."

After a pause, Kim said, "Why'd you split up?"

Deveraux shrugged and took another bite of her cheeseburger. Kim waited, but the answer never came.

"What about you, Agent Otto? I'll bet the FBI is your whole life now. But you were married once." She grinned when Kim blinked again. "Yeah, I checked."

Kim shook her head slowly as she wiped the burger juice off her fingers. "My divorce seems like such a long time ago that I almost said I'd never been married without even thinking about it."

"What happened?"

"It's complicated."

"I don't have anywhere else to go tonight," Deveraux said, leaning back.

"We were incompatible," Kim eventually replied before turning her attention to finishing her meal, but the conversation had dulled her appetite.

Deveraux swirled the deep red wine in her glass and waited as if she had all the time in the world.

Kim finally grinned and held out her glass. "If we're going to talk about my ex, I'll need more wine."

Deveraux refilled the glasses and pushed her empty plate to the side. "Was it true love?"

"I thought so at the time. We were in college together. Then law school. We were living in DC. At first, Van was the guy I thought would be my soul mate forever." She laughed uncomfortably because talking about Van seemed surreal.

She rarely even thought about Van, let alone discussed him. She hadn't seen him in years. She wasn't certain she could pick him out of a lineup.

Kim quipped, "Of course, I also thought I was going to be a tax attorney and work in Chicago. We can see how that went."

"So what happened?" Deveraux asked.

"He decided he wanted to be a politician. Back in California. Having a mixed-race wife didn't fit into his election plans." Kim shrugged.

Deveraux's eyes widened with surprise. "You're not Asian? I'd never have guessed. Not that I'm an expert, but I spent some time in Asia when I was in the Marines."

"My mother was a Vietnamese war bride. My dad's family has lived in the Midwest for about a hundred years. He served in Vietnam. They met and fell in love there." Kim explained her history briefly, which was more than she normally told anyone. "I have three older brothers who look like my dad, all born in Michigan. I've always felt tall and blond and German on the inside. But my younger sister and I look like my mom."

"Well, your mother must be very beautiful," Deveraux said.

Kim blushed slightly before she shrugged again. She wasn't used to compliments. It had been a while since anyone had commented on her appearance at all.

She nodded and sipped the wine, which really was excellent. "So you can see how Van would think my family might cause a problem for his ambitions."

Deveraux frowned. "I don't actually. Sounds like he was simply looking for an excuse, doesn't it?"

"Maybe so. Maybe he'd found someone else and he was too big a coward to admit it," Kim offered, simply to change the conversation. She didn't plan to pour her heart out to Elizabeth Deveraux even if she did offer a great bottle of wine to ply her with.

"What happened with his election?"

"I have no idea. I never checked," Kim said flatly.

Deveraux let the subject drop. She poured the last of the wine into the two glasses. "Shall we have coffee and pie?"

Before Kim had a chance to agree, the door opened and Perry came inside. He'd changed out of his smoky clothes, too.

He strode over to their table with his hands jammed into his front pockets. He nodded toward Deveraux and then turned his attention to Kim. "Good to see you Mayor. Otto, I'm headed out to the casino. Greyson's already on his way. Do you want to come along?"

"What's going on?" Deveraux asked.

Perry replied, "Greyson found charred money in the barn after they put the fire out. His hunch is that it might have been stolen from the casino."

"Yeah. Let's go." Kim pulled two twenties out of her pocket and tossed them on the table. "Thanks for the wine," she said to Deveraux.

Perry followed behind Kim as they walked out to his rented SUV. She opened the door and climbed into the passenger seat. When he was settled behind the wheel, backing out into Main Street, she said, "Why does Greyson think the fire and the cash are tied to the casino?"

"The registrations came back on all three trucks. One was stolen. The other two belonged to a pair of guys from Kelham. Greyson says they're regulars at the casino," Perry said.

"He thinks the third guy, the one who was driving the stolen truck, is likely to be at the casino now?" Kim asked. "Makes more sense that he'd have left town after he killed those two and torched the barn, doesn't it?"

Perry shrugged. "Greyson says he's just playing the odds."

"Yeah, well, maybe Greyson should keep his day job," Kim replied. "The odds are that he's wasting his time and ours, too."

Perry glanced across the cabin. "You got a better idea?"

"Yes. We need to see Major Hammer," she replied. "Can you call him? Get him to meet us somewhere?"

Perry grinned. "Already done. He's at the casino, too."

Kim nodded. "We need to make a quick stop first."

CHAPTER THIRTY-EIGHT

Thursday, May 12
Carter's Crossing, Mississippi
8:30 p.m.

IT HAD TAKEN LONGER than Murphy had expected to get off the base. There'd been no time to leave his Jaguar and find another vehicle. Tomorrow was the final closing walk-through at Kelham. He would be the last man out. He was looking forward to turning the lights off on his old life and moving forward.

Most of the personnel and usable equipment had already been packed up and shipped out. There was nothing much left. The army would move the last bits off-site at some point. Even later, the property would be repurposed like all the other military bases that had closed over the years. But none of that was his problem.

He'd been a soldier more than half his life. He didn't expect to miss the army. Not for one minute. By this time tomorrow, he'd be a free man once again.

Truth was, Murphy didn't remember what it felt like to be master of his own destiny.

He imagined he'd feel freer, able to come and go as he pleased. No orders to follow. No senior officers to please. Because of the counterfeiting operation he'd been running here, he had more money stashed away than he'd ever spend in the rest of his lifetime. He didn't have any heirs and didn't expect to have any in the future. All of which meant his fortune would be more than enough.

All he had to do was finish up, deal with Nina, and bug out tomorrow at dawn. Which filled him with pleasurable anticipation. Not that the army cared how he felt or what he wanted. Not that he gave a crap what the army cared about, either.

Nina lived southeast of Carter's Crossing. When the tribe had moved onto the reservation and built the casino, her brother had moved into a suite in the casino hotel. But Nina had stayed in the home she'd always loved.

Her house was set back from the road on a few acres of land. Her grandfather had built it himself, as Nina had proudly told him when they first met. The trees had been cleared and the lumber was used to build the simple rectangular dwelling. The exterior siding had never been painted and the wood had weathered to a silvery sheen that fairly glowed in the moonlight.

When Murphy turned the last curve along the winding driveway, no lights were burning inside the front rooms of the house. Maybe Nina had taken his advice. She might be sleeping in her bedroom in the back, which would make what he'd come to do so much easier.

He parked and walked up to the front door. Nina never locked her doors. She said the chances of anyone coming out this far to rob her were slim, and she didn't have anything inside worth stealing anyway. Everyone who knew her was already aware of that.

Murphy turned the knob, pushed the door open, and went inside. He didn't turn the lights on. He walked softly across the hardwood floor toward Nina's bedroom. The door was open. Soft light from the bedside lamp washed through the dark hallway.

He pulled the silver flask from his back pocket and moved into the room.

The bed was unoccupied.

On the bedside table was a note held in place by a gold poker chip. Her big scrawl was easy to read without touching the paper. *Casino. See you there. Love, Nina and Junior xoxo*

He shoved the flask into his pocket, swore under his breath, turned around, and stomped out. He slammed the door behind him.

Tilting his head to the moon, he bellowed every ounce of frustration he felt. "Damn you, Nina. Why can't you ever, even once, just do what the hell you're told!"

The shouting didn't improve his mood or change his situation. Nina had to die tonight. Even if he had to hunt her down first.

Murphy restarted the Jaguar and turned around and drove along the winding driveway back the way he'd come. Big River Casino was fifteen minutes away if he traveled by the main roads. But he didn't want to take the chance that he might be seen.

He drove the back roads instead.

Which gave him plenty of time to think about what he'd say to Major Hammer if he ran into him.

Murphy flipped on the radio and caught the top of the local news. The fire out at Gordon's farm was the lead story.

Firefighters had found two bodies inside. Their names hadn't been released pending notification of next of kin.

His luck was holding. So far.

He pushed the accelerator and sped up as much as he dared on the dark gravel road.

"Maybe the bodies won't be identified soon enough," he said aloud, even as he realized what a thin hope that was.

Everything that had gone wrong right up until this very minute was all Nina's fault. She should have kept her mouth shut. But she didn't.

She'd told Bonnie Nightingale, of all people.

Nina's blabbing had cost him. Tonight, he'd make sure she paid for her mistakes.

CHAPTER THIRTY-NINE

Thursday, May 12
Carter's Crossing, Mississippi
8:45 p.m.

"WHY IS HAMMER AT THE CASINO?" Kim asked as Perry navigated around a sinkhole near the railroad crossing large enough to swallow a pickup truck. The broken pavement was marked with orange cones and a flashing danger sign.

This particular hole must have appeared sometime today because Kim hadn't seen it last night when she was investigating the train.

"He's looking to confirm some alibis for the night of Bonnie Nightingale's murder, he said. And hoping to find the two guys who should have been at Kelham this afternoon, but weren't," Perry replied, peering through the windshield, watching for pedestrians or something. "I'd really like to get a look at the train tonight. If we get separated, I'm planning to be back here before midnight."

She nodded, pointing, "Brannan's is about halfway down the block."

He steered onto the one-sided street and rolled slowly along until he found a parking place close to the front door. He angle parked, nose in, and snugged up close to the curb.

Kim unlatched her seat belt and reached for the door handle. Before she stepped out, she said, "Let me take the lead. I've already met the bartender. I think he knows something about Bonnie Nightingale, and my feeling last night was that he wanted to tell me more about it."

"If he had more to say, why didn't he just tell the sheriff?" Perry asked.

Kim shrugged. "Maybe he did. But Greyson didn't share that with me. Did he tell you?"

"Nope," Perry said with a grin.

She looked in the window, where she saw a crowd similar to last night. "The McKinneys are inside. Keep an eye on them. I don't think they'll try anything in front of all these witnesses, but they're not all that bright."

"No kidding," Perry replied.

Kim opened the door and stepped out into the warm and humid evening. She glanced across at the train tracks. A big man was walking alone near the crossing. A few cars passed by, on the way to Kelham, probably. A young couple, arms linked, walked northward on the broken sidewalk in front of the bars and boarded up shops.

She imagined that the traffic was pretty much the same as any Thursday night. Maybe the same as any weeknight. Perhaps people were walking around the night Bonnie Nightingale died. Kim wondered if Greyson had made any effort to find witnesses. She made a mental note to ask him.

Kim walked on. She avoided three large holes in the pavement and made her way onto the cracked sidewalk.

She glanced inside. Walt McKinney was tending bar. The three McKinney cousins were playing pool. A few other customers were sitting at one end of the bar, talking quietly together. Some of the tables were also occupied.

Nothing noteworthy was on the television tonight.

Walt looked up and met her gaze when she pulled the heavy door open and walked inside. Perry followed along behind her.

The McKinneys saw her come in, too. The same three that had been here with Luke Price last night. The same three Kim and Perry had argued with on Main Street this morning.

All three of them gave her an aggravated scowl. They were like cookies cut from the same dough. If they weren't so dangerously stupid, they'd have been comical.

Laughing at them would be a swift ticket to another fight. So she didn't.

But she wanted to.

She walked up to the bar and leaned forward. "Hi, Walt," she said.

Perry stood next to her, back to the bar, looking out into the room.

"What can I get for you and your friend?" the bartender asked.

"What do you recommend?" Perry said, which was a smart question.

Kim didn't want another stale can of beer.

"We're St. Louis fans here, as she can tell you. We've got Bud and Bud Light on draft," Walt replied, grabbing mugs before Perry had a chance to agree.

Walt tilted the mugs under the red draft handle, expertly allowing the golden liquid to slide down the side of the mugs until they were filled with just the right amount of foamy head resting on the top.

Kim took the beer and sipped. It was wet and cold, which was a big improvement over the night before. But it was no Labatt. She and August Busch might have shared a common ethnicity, but she didn't love his beer.

"Walt, I came back because I need to know about Bonnie Nightingale. You told me she was in here the night she died. Who was she with?" Kim asked.

Kim sensed movement behind her. The little hairs stood up on the back of her neck. She glanced at Perry, who was watching the room casually.

She looked over her shoulder just in time to see one of the McKinneys sink the last ball into the corner pocket. The win was followed by whooping and high fives, and then all three McKinneys ambled out of the bar. Which made her nervous. She'd have preferred them to stay inside where Perry could keep an eye on them.

Once the McKinneys left, Walt said, "Hell of a thing about Luke Price, wasn't it?"

Kim looked him straight in the eye. "Yes it was. Any idea who killed him?"

"I sort of thought it was you." Walt raised his eyebrows. He tilted his head toward the front door. "That's what my cousins think, too. You might want to be careful out there. Price wasn't much of a man, but my cousins liked him."

"Thanks for the heads-up," Perry said. "We'll take the matter under advisement."

Walt's nostrils flared and his grip on the bar towel tightened. Nothing would be gained by another fight. Kim glared at Perry and moved to de-escalate hostilities.

"I didn't kill Price. Last time I saw him, he was lying flat on his ass on your floor." She nodded in the general direction.

"Right over there."

"Well, somebody killed him after he left here last night. And you're the only one he'd had a beef with that night. So my cousins assume that you're the one who killed him. That's reasonable, wouldn't you say?" Walt's conversation was easy, but the subtext was that Kim should watch her back.

"Thanks for the warning," Kim replied. "Now, about Bonnie Nightingale. Who was she in here with the night she died?"

Walt shrugged. "She was dating Jasper. I told you that. She came in to wait for him."

"Did he show up?"

"After a while. She waited with his friends until he got here."

"What friends?"

"Three guys from Kelham. Redmond, Hern, and Murphy, I think. That's the usual posse Jasper ran with," Walt said, cleaning up the glasses and the napkins and organizing this and that behind the bar. He seemed like he needed something to do with his energy all of a sudden.

"Come on, Walt. Bonnie's dead. Jasper's dead. Price, too. All of them were your customers and your friends if I had to guess. If this keeps up, you're not going to have many customers left except your cousins." Kim paused for a deep breath and to let what she'd said sink in. "There's something going on here. Don't you want me to figure it out before someone else gets killed?"

Walt seemed to think about the question for a while. He served beers to the guys at the other end of the bar. Then he came back and did more fiddling around the sink.

Perry dropped a ten on the bar and said, "Come on, Otto. Let's go. We're wasting our time here."

He walked toward the front door and waited for her to follow.

"Tell me what happened, Walt. Please," Kim said.

"I don't know what happened. Bonnie was drunk. I told you. She was upset."

"Upset about what?"

"About Nina. Her friend, Nina Cloud."

"Nina Cloud, one of the managers of Big River Casino?" Kim asked.

"You think there would be more than one Nina Cloud in a town this size?" Walt grinned.

"What was Bonnie saying about Nina?"

Walt replied, "Bonnie had an argument with one of those guys. Like I said, she was drunk. The argument went on for a few minutes. The Cardinals were on and I was busy. There were a few people here at the bar. I didn't hear the whole thing."

"What *did* you hear, then?"

"Right at the end, Bonnie said something about Nina and Murphy going to New York City. She said Nina was upset about it, didn't deserve to be treated that way. Bonnie called Murphy a lying bastard," he paused, looked down, cleared his throat, and looked up again.

"And then what happened?"

"Murphy backhanded her. Knocked her a good six feet. She landed hard on her butt, crying. She got up, holding her cheek, and ran out." He stopped for a breath. "And that was it. Next thing I heard, Bonnie had thrown herself in front of the midnight train."

"Did she say why Nina was so upset about the trip to New York with Murphy? Seems like a crazy thing to start a fight over. It doesn't make much sense, does it?" Kim said, thinking aloud.

"Unless something happened while they were gone. Was that it?"

Walt shook his head. "I don't know. That's all she said."

Kim nodded and backed away from the bar. "Did you tell Sheriff Greyson about all this?"

Walt looked her straight in the eye. "Not all of it. He was busy the night he came in here. Didn't have a lot of time. He seemed like he wanted to confirm that Bonnie had been here, and I said she was. I told him she was waiting for Jasper."

"What about the rest of it?"

Walt shook his head. "He got called away and had to cut the conversation short. I just figured he'd found out everything he needed to know some other way. Or maybe he hasn't had the time. He's been pretty busy, as I'm sure you've noticed. Kelham closing has put a lot of extra stress on everything around here."

"Okay. Thanks. I'll follow up." Kim turned to leave, but then she remembered something else. "Was Price in here that night? The night Bonnie died?"

Walt cocked his head and squinted toward the ceiling, as if he had to think about it. "Yeah. I guess he was."

CHAPTER FORTY

Thursday, May 12
Carter's Crossing, Mississippi
9:05 p.m.

PERRY DROVE DIRECTLY TO Big River Casino and Resort. He didn't need the GPS in his rental. The route was clearly marked with signs along the roadway. The casino itself was visible in the distance across the flat farmland.

When they reached the long driveway, Perry turned right. A flashing sign announced the weekly poker tournament. Which was probably why Libby's Diner had emptied early and the casino's parking lot was about half full tonight.

Perry drove toward an open parking lot that was bigger than a baseball field.

The front of the casino itself resembled a fancy lodge constructed of massive logs, like the great lodges Kim had visited as a child in National Parks like Yellowstone and the Grand Canyon. The logs of the facade were flanked on both sides by two-story rectangular buildings designed to blend into the landscape.

Kim had quickly perused the casino's website on her phone. The resort boasted hotel rooms, a spa, the hottest table games and slots, as well as high-end and relaxed dining options.

The lot was almost full. A wide variety of vehicles ranging from sports cars to travel coaches, and everything in between was parked in an orderly fashion. A disproportionate number of pickup trucks filled the rows.

"This place is as busy as a shopping mall at Christmas," Perry said as if surprised.

The valet was hopping tonight, taking keys and moving vehicles as fast as the runners on duty could hustle.

Perry drove past the valet stand and found an open parking slot about halfway down the center aisle from the front entrance.

"I'm leaving this here," he said, looking toward Kim as he put the key fob on the floor under the mat. "In case we get separated and you need to leave without me. All you have to do is push the start button. Let me know where you've left the vehicle and I'll come pick it up."

"Okay," Kim replied as she opened the door and stepped outside.

The muggy warm evening was worse than when they'd left Brannan's. It engulfed her from head to toe in a wet blanket of moisture. She could only imagine what it must be like here in mid-August when the air would be so saturated. It would be difficult simply to breathe.

They left the SUV, walked side by side toward the front entrance and up the stairs to the big doors, which were propped open without concern for the escaping air-conditioning. Kim threaded her way through hordes of people moving in and out like bees to a hive as Perry followed.

Inside, Kim glanced around the cavernous open space filled with clanging, beeping, chiming, and chirping slot machines. The visual noise was as deafening as the cacophony of sounds.

The cashier windows were off to one side in the back. A small line of people waited to buy credits or cash them in, she assumed.

"Looking for someone in particular?" Perry asked, glancing around.

"Not really," she replied. But as she said the words, she realized they weren't true. She was looking for Reacher. Always. Was he here?

The local gamblers looked like gamblers everywhere. No fancy cars in the parking lot or sparkling diamonds on beauties in evening gowns. The glitz and glamor images she'd seen on billboards along the roadway were pure fiction. Gamblers didn't dress like that, not even in Las Vegas.

At these Native American casinos in mostly rural communities, the patrons were mostly ordinary people looking for a few hours of entertainment. More than a few gamblers seemed to be desperately seeking grocery money, which sadly, she'd seen in casinos before. Too many people who couldn't afford the losses gambled away their paychecks in places like this.

As the crowd grew, the noise became overwhelming. So was the hanging wall of cigarette smoke. Perry tapped her on the shoulder and pointed toward the bar on the other side of the gaming floor. "I'm meeting Hammer in there."

She nodded and walked alongside him. "What does Hammer look like?"

Perry grinned. "Like three hundred pounds of ferocious meanness. But looks are deceptive."

Kim nodded, saving her voice for a conversation that mattered. She'd see Hammer for herself soon enough.

Once they passed through the gambling floor and moved into the bar, the noise abated slightly. This Western-themed décor flowed into this room, which was also more than half full of customers. The tables were occupied, but there were a few empty stools left at the bar.

She looked down its length and spied a huge man dwarfing everyone else around him. He was focused intently, talking with a smaller man.

Kim smirked and poked Perry in the shoulder. "I take it that's our guy?"

"Yep. The one and only. Major Eugene Hulk Hammer." Perry met the man's gaze and nodded, threading through the crowd in that direction with Kim following close behind.

By the time they reached Hammer, the smaller man had moved on. Hammer bent down to hear when Perry said, "Major Hammer, this is FBI Special Agent Kim Otto."

"Good to meet you, Hammer," Kim extended her small hand and he engulfed it in one big paw. She felt like David shaking hands with Goliath. The mental image made her grin. "Who was that guy you were talking to just now?"

"Randy Cloud. One of the managers here. The other manager is his sister, Nina. She's around here somewhere, too. I met her earlier," Hammer replied. His voice was low and rumbly and hard to hear over the crowd. "They both knew Bonnie Nightingale well. They're pretty upset about her death. Especially the sister."

"Did he give you the CCTV footage for the night Bonnie Nightingale died?" Kim asked. "Was she here at a poker tournament?"

Hammer frowned. "Not sure why you're asking. But yes."

"Anything interesting on the video?" Perry wanted to know.

"Whaddaya, writin' a book?" Hammer grumped as he yanked his cell phone out of his pocket and pulled up the CCTV footage. He pushed the play button and handed the phone to Perry.

Kim watched the clips Hammer had transferred to his phone. Each was only a few seconds long. Maybe twenty seconds, total.

The first batch showed four men and two women entering and leaving the casino from the CCTV at the valet stand. There was a time stamp on each clip. Kim recognized one of the women as Bonnie Nightingale. She didn't know the others.

All six were inside the casino from just after eight o'clock that night until just before eleven o'clock.

Hammer had also copied clips of all six inside the casino at various times during the evening. The four men had played poker. The women had waited in the bar. Every frame showed a martini in the women's hands. The men were drinking brown liquor straight out of crystal glasses.

Perry moved to return Hammer's phone. Kim reached out to grab it first. Quickly, she sent the video clips to herself and Gaspar. Then she backed up to the first set of clips and moved closer to Hammer.

"Who are these people?" she asked.

He pointed, naming them one at a time. "Redmond, Hern, Jasper, Nightingale." He indicated a set of two males and then a man and woman together, all entering the casino. The next clip was a single image of the last two, a man and a woman. "Murphy and Cloud."

"Thanks." Kim looked at them each closely and then returned his phone. She thought she recognized the woman he identified as Nina Cloud.

She looked different. She must have been wearing a wig, and her makeup was heavier.

But Kim's gut said it was the same woman.

She'd seen her on video before. Several times. On television news clips of that North Korean diplomat who was poisoned in New York.

Nina Cloud looked like the woman standing next to Hana Pak at the dog fight.

She asked, "What did you conclude from these clips?"

"Just because I'm big doesn't make me stupid." Hammer rolled his big shoulders in what might have been a shrug for a reasonably-sized man.

"And vice versa for us little people," Kim said cheekily. "So what'd you learn here?"

"Same thing you did, I imagine." Hammer finally cracked a grin and seemed to ease up a bit on the attitude. "The six of them were all together here for a while, earlier in the evening. But none had a solid alibi for the midnight train."

Kim wrapped it up. "Which means they don't have solid alibis. Any one of them could have lured Nightingale out there. And, I suppose, killed her. Just in time to dump her on the tracks so the train could dispose of the body."

Perry looked down at the floor as if he might find all the answers in the swirling pattern on the carpet. "So everybody else out at Kelham has a solid alibi for Nightingale's time of death, I take it? Meaning you've narrowed it down to four soldiers and one female civilian."

Hammer pushed away from the bar. "Pretty much. But it's not just any four soldiers."

"What do you mean?" Kim asked.

"The big guy with the brown hair in those clips? That's

General Alec Murphy. Kelham's CO," Hammer said. "And he led me to believe he didn't even know who Bonnie Nightingale was."

"Sounds like your work's not quite done out at Kelham, then," Perry said.

"And I don't have a lot of time left to wrap this thing up. I need to find Redmond and Hern tonight." Hammer flexed his arms absently, like a wrestler preparing to enter a big match. "Whoever is left out there is shoving off at dawn tomorrow. Murphy is the guy who'll certify that the base is officially closed. They'll all be gone. And I, for one, don't feel like chasing them around the globe when they're dispersed."

"Can I help?" Perry asked as Hammer turned to leave.

"I'll let you know," he said, a brief moment before his eyes widened. "Looks like my job just got a little easier."

"What do you mean?" Kim asked.

Hammer nodded his head toward the other end of the bar. "General Murphy just walked in."

CHAPTER FORTY-ONE

Thursday, May 12
Carter's Crossing, Mississippi
9:10 p.m.

HE'D PARKED IN THE back of the casino lot and hustled inside to find Nina. The last place to look was the management office. He didn't want to waste time. She rarely hid out in there when the casino was busy.

Methodically, he'd combed through the crowds on the gambling floor and stopped to check the cashier's cage. He'd hung around outside the women's restroom, just in case. No luck.

He finally made his way to the bar.

Nina didn't often drink when she was working, but he'd known it to happen. She didn't seem to limit her exposure to the smoky casino or her alcohol intake lately, either. Which was another thing that made him question this alleged pregnancy. If she was pregnant, wouldn't she want to be more careful, for the baby's sake?

Customers were lined up three deep at the bar to get a drink during a break in the poker tournament. His gaze scanned the crowd but didn't locate Nina.

He moved along the length of the bar until he found a less crowded opening near the center.

"Hey, Joe," he called out to the bartender on duty. "Have you seen Nina?"

Joe looked up briefly from the cash register and shook his head. "About half an hour ago, maybe."

He waved his open hand by way of thanks and turned to scan the busy room more closely. Nina was a striking woman. She stood out in a crowd. If she'd been here, he'd have spied her.

He didn't notice Major Hammer standing at the far end of the bar with two others until it was too late to take evasive measures.

"Crap," he whispered under his breath. He'd been confined to base like everyone else. Hammer would be pissed to see him wandering around.

And Hammer wasn't alone.

He didn't recognize Hammer's companions. A tiny Asian-looking woman. And an average guy who carried himself like a soldier. But if the man had been on active duty at Kelham, he would have known him. So maybe this guy was a veteran.

The place was full of vets most nights. Guys who had been posted at Kelham once upon a time and for various reasons had become attached to Carter's Crossing. He could spot them instinctively. They had a certain way about them. The army had made sure of it. Training like that was impossible to shed, even if they'd tried. Most of them didn't.

He'd seen several veterans like that while he was looking throughout the casino for Nina. A couple of guys on the main floor were almost as big as Hammer, but older.

He did a double-take when he glimpsed a guy leaning against the wall near the poker tables. Something about the man reminded him of Reacher, his long-ago nemesis. When he blinked and looked back, the guy wasn't standing there anymore.

He shook it off and kept going.

The idea was preposterous anyway.

He inhaled deeply. Now, to deal with Hammer.

He was a solid poker player. And this was the right time for a bluff. He widened his eyes and nodded toward Hammer and strode purposefully forward toward the group.

"Major," he said as he approached, "I'm glad I finally found you."

Hammer frowned. "I don't have any calls showing on my phone from you, General."

He ignored the rebuke. He outranked Hammer, and he wasn't taking any guff on his last night, regardless. "Redmond and Hern have returned to base. I ordered them to stay put until you could interview them. They're handling last-minute details now."

The statement was a lie, but Hammer wouldn't know that.

Before Hammer had a chance to reply, Nina Cloud walked up behind him. She put her arm around his waist and rose up on her toes to kiss his cheek.

"I hear you've been looking for me," she said and then flashed a bright smile toward the three others. "I'm Nina Cloud."

He scowled and pushed her arm away. "Nina, this is Major Hammer. And...I didn't catch your names."

The guy said, "Sir, I'm Major Lincoln Perry. And this is FBI Special Agent Kim Otto."

Murphy cringed when Nina's years of experience in the hospitality industry overwhelmed whatever good sense she'd once possessed. She smiled and shook hands all around like she was hosting a cocktail party. Then she jumped into chatting about the casino and how she hoped they were enjoying themselves until he itched to backhand her across the room.

He pursed his lips and barely held back his anger. "Nina! These people are working."

"Pleased to meet you, General Murphy. Ms. Cloud," Agent Otto seemed to sense the volatile situation and stepped forward to take Nina's hand.

Otto held on just a bit too long while gazing intently at Nina's face. "I think we've met before, haven't we?"

Murphy's anger clicked up about ten notches. He could feel the heat rising from his chest to his face.

Nina cocked her head. She seemed puzzled. "I don't think so."

"In New York. Weren't you in the city a few days ago?" Otto asked casually.

What did the bitch know? And how did she know it?

Nina's eyes widened, and she shook her head. "No. No. No, you're mistaken. It wasn't me. I wasn't there."

Otto adopted a puzzled expression he knew in his gut was totally fake. She said, "Well, anyway, I understand you were friends with Bonnie Nightingale. I'd like to ask you a few questions about her. Is there somewhere we can talk?"

Nina's composure faltered. She crumpled like a used cigarette pack.

"Bonnie?" she whimpered as her eyes filled with tears. She covered her face with both palms.

Murphy couldn't allow Nina to answer anything more. She was already on the verge of collapse. If she talked, she'd say too much. He wouldn't let her take them both down. He'd come too far.

He inhaled sharply. Murphy had been commanding men and women more than half his life. He would not allow his plans to be derailed by a tiny little firecracker with a gun and a badge.

"Now is not the time, Agent Otto," Murphy said more sharply than he'd intended.

"Is that so, General?" she said, standing her ground, which only served to infuriate him. She didn't seem to care.

"It is. We're leaving. I've got work to do, and I assume you can make more productive use of your time as well." He put his arm around Nina's shoulders, looked at Major Hammer and replied, "I'll see Ms. Cloud home and meet you back at Kelham."

Before they could attempt to stop him, Murphy turned and led Nina stumbling forward.

"Straighten up," he snarled under his breath into her ear, squeezing her cruelly. "You want to go to prison? Walk out of here like you've got nothing to hide."

Nina sniveled and gasped, but she managed to pull herself together after half a dozen steps.

Now, if they could just make it past the crowds to the exit. He kept his arm around her waist and dragged her forward.

CHAPTER FORTY-TWO

Thursday, May 12
Carter's Crossing, Mississippi
9:45 p.m.

KIM WATCHED MURPHY and Nina wend through the crowd toward the gaming room floor while Perry filled Hammer in on what he'd learned about Bonnie Nightingale, and they formulated a quick plan.

Hammer would return to Kelham to interview Redmond and Hern. Then he'd catch up with Murphy and try to get the truth out of him.

Perry would go back to Brannan's, and then follow up with Sheriff Greyson and Mayor Deveraux.

Kim pulled her phone out of her pocket and reviewed the video clip of the woman standing beside Hana Pak at the dog fight in New York. The video was grainy, and the image wasn't sharp, either. But still.

"Perry. Hammer. Look at this. Is the woman Nina Cloud?"

She handed the phone to Perry, and the two men watched the clip twice.

"Send it to your office," Hammer replied. "The FBI has all sorts of software that should answer the question pretty quickly."

"Already sent. I should be getting an answer here shortly," she said, squinting up to see the big man's face. "But I'm not crazy, right? Ignore the hair and the makeup. Look at the eyes."

Perry squinted through both the New York video and the clips from the casino's CCTV a few times before he said, "Could be her."

"Walt McKinney said Bonnie argued with Murphy the night she died. Something about a trip to New York. Remember that?" she asked Perry. "Walt said Murphy was angry and knocked Bonnie to the floor when she mentioned it."

Perry handed back her phone. "So you think what, exactly?"

"I think Nina Cloud might have murdered Hana Pak. And General Murphy helped her do it. Or maybe she did it for him. She seemed pretty clingy to me," Kim said. "Hammer, are there any bioweapons stored or developed at Kelham? Poisons? Things like that?"

Hammer frowned down at her. "That would be classified intel. But since there were two companies of Rangers there who regularly deployed out of the country, I'd guess it's possible. Depending on what the poison was, and why the army had possession of it."

"Any way either of you can find out?"

Perry said, "I can make a call. See if I can get some answers."

Kim nodded. "I need to make a call, too. But I don't want to do it here. I'm going outside where it's a bit quieter, and I'll get a better signal."

She glanced toward the exit. The bottleneck at the archway between the gambling floor and the bar was still mobbed while the tournament's break continued. She swiveled her neck to look behind her, seeking another way out. She noticed Sheriff Greyson talking with Randy Cloud.

"I'll be right back," Kim told Perry and Hammer. She threaded through the crowd toward Greyson.

When she walked up, Greyson noticed her and nodded, but kept his attention on Randy Cloud. Kim didn't interrupt.

Greyson handed a piece of burned paper to Cloud as he said, "We found partially destroyed bills like this in the fire out at the Gordon farm. It looks like a fifty-dollar bill. Since people don't generally go around burning up money, I'm thinking it might be counterfeit. We'll test it to be sure. Has anybody reported any counterfeit fifties in the casino lately?"

Cloud examined the charred paper, front and back, and returned it to Greyson. "Maybe. I don't handle the cash. You'd need to ask Nina."

"She hasn't mentioned any problem with people trying to pass counterfeit bills in the past, oh, six weeks or so?" Greyson pushed.

Cloud shook his head, but his expression grew troubled.

"Is that the sort of thing she'd tell you if it was happening?" Greyson asked.

"We get a lot of cash coming through here, Scott. Some of it is counterfeit. It's really easy to print money these days and a lot of desperate people will try to pass the bills in a casino. You know that. Sometimes, the people don't even know the bill is fake. Someone else gave it to them and they just assume it's real," Cloud said. "But we make a note of it. If the person tries to pass off fake money more than once, we kick them out for a while.

We usually just figure handling fake bills is a part of running a casino business."

Kim said, "So you're saying what? Nina would have told you if she'd seen a significant number of counterfeits, but if it was just a few here and there, she wouldn't have mentioned it?"

Randy Cloud turned to look at her. "I didn't catch your name."

"FBI Special Agent Kim Otto," she replied evenly, reaching into her pocket to pull out a business card and hand it to him. "We're working with Sheriff Greyson on this."

"I thought counterfeit money was handled by the Secret Service," Cloud replied as he read the card, frowning.

"I'm just helping out here," Kim said.

"I see. Well, federal agents have been in here from time to time, following up on counterfeits. But we've never had any serious issues," Cloud said, and the troubled expression on his face deepened. "Are you involved in this because of Bonnie Nightingale?"

Kim arched her eyebrows. "Why would Bonnie Nightingale be connected with counterfeit money?"

"I don't know that she would. And I hope she wasn't." Cloud shook his head sorrowfully. "But she worked here part-time as a cashier. She and Nina were close friends, too. I just wondered if she'd been taking counterfeits and that's why she killed herself. You know. Feeling like she'd let Nina down or something."

Greyson said, "Where is Nina now, Randy? I'd like to talk to her and get this cleared up."

"I haven't seen her for a while. I've been busy with the tournament. I'm not sure exactly where she is." Cloud shrugged as he glanced around the crowd, and the bartender caught his attention. "I need to get back to work. Come by tomorrow and we can talk more. When we're not so busy."

Cloud rushed off, and when he was out of earshot, Kim said, "Nina Cloud left a little while ago with General Murphy. They probably haven't made it out of the parking lot yet, if you want to go after them."

"I'll catch up with her later. I know where she lives. First, I need to bring you three up to speed." Greyson looked up, caught Perry's gaze, and waved him over. Greyson led them all to a quieter corner.

"What's up, Sheriff?" Perry asked after he introduced Hammer.

"We're still working the Gordon farm fire. There's enough evidence out there to keep a big city crime scene team busy for days. And we're a small department," Greyson said. "We've called in the Mississippi Bureau of Investigation to help us out. We'll know more after the autopsy reports come back."

Kim asked, "Did you find another body?"

"Just the two." He shook his head. "We ran the VINs and plates on the three trucks. One of the trucks had been reported stolen a few days ago. The plate on that one was also stolen. Off a hearse that went missing in Memphis last week."

"A hearse?" Hammer asked. "Why would anyone steal a hearse?"

"Dunno. But we think the third man killed the two and used the hearse to get away. Could have something to do with the burned counterfeit bills we found. Still working on that." Greyson shrugged. "But for now, working theory is it's most likely that the two dead men are Anthony Redland and Eddie Hern."

Kim stared at him. "Redland and Hern?"

"Yeah. Registered owners of the other two trucks. We connected them to the plates and VINs. Vitals on the public records loosely match up with them, too," Greyson said. "So it's a guess, but it makes sense at the moment. Unless something better comes up."

Kim shook her head. "Except that Murphy said Redland and Hern were alive and well and back at Kelham tonight, didn't he?"

Hammer swiped one of his big mitts over his head. "Yeah. That's what he said. I was headed back to Kelham to interview them both."

Perry said, "Can you call out there? Find out if Redland and Hern are waiting, or not?"

Hammer nodded, reaching into his pocket for his phone. He walked a few steps away for privacy. Or maybe to hear the conversation, given the rising noise levels.

The pack of people between the gaming room and the bar was now at least six deep and all the way across the archway. All of them seemed to be yelling at each other at the same time, raising the decibel levels to the point of pain for Kim's ears.

"So we need to go find Murphy," Kim looked at Perry. "Nina's with him, too. If we hurry, we might catch them in the parking lot." She turned toward Greyson. "Maybe you want to come along."

Greyson sighed. Deep lines had etched into his face since the morning. He had to be exhausted. "Yeah, guess I'd better. We'll never make it through that mob. The back exit is this way. Follow me."

CHAPTER FORTY-THREE

Thursday, May 12
Carter's Crossing, Mississippi
9:55 p.m.

THE CROWD WAS SO THICK, he could barely move.
Grasping Nina tightly around the waist, Murphy glanced over his
shoulder. Hammer was still standing at the far end of the room
with Perry and Otto.

He spied Sheriff Greyson talking with Randy Cloud, and his
stomach clenched. Greyson had plenty of time to work out that
Redmond and Hern were the bodies in the barn.

Murphy had to get out of here before Greyson told Hammer
what he knew.

He needed to get Nina outside to the Jaguar and get away.

Before Hammer came looking for him.

Murphy turned his attention to forging a path ahead. The
archway between the bar and the gaming room was effectively
blocked by a mob of customers waiting to be served.

There was a back exit, but to get there, he'd have to walk past Hammer and his posse again. Unwise.

He needed a better way. So he did the first thing that came to mind.

He reached down and swiftly gathered Nina into his arms like an old-fashioned husband sweeping his wife across the threshold of their first home as if she'd fainted. People in the immediate vicinity gasped.

"Can I get through here? She needs some air," Murphy said, pushing forward with Nina's head resting on his shoulder. She was too heavy to carry like this for a long distance. But maybe he could get through the crowd.

Patrons moved aside, separating as much as possible, given they were packed into the archway like bullets in a box. The thought would have made him grin under different circumstances. As it was, he didn't have the luxury.

"Coming through. Please step aside." Murphy pushed and twisted and forged ahead, making slow progress between bodies pressed too close together, but moving in the right direction.

After a solid five minutes, at least, he broke through to the gaming room floor, staggering under Nina's full body weight. He set her down but kept a tight arm around her waist.

"Come on. Let's get outside," he said, leading the way.

Nina resisted. "I need to get my purse. I can't leave without it."

"Where is it?"

"In the cashier's office. I can run over there and come right back. Only take a minute," she said, squirming against his restraining arm.

He relaxed his hold and grasped her hand instead. "I'll come with you."

She shook her head. "You don't need to. It'll be faster if I go alone."

He ignored her pleading. "I'm coming with you. Or we can leave without your damn purse. Your choice."

Nina seemed to deflate a little, but she said, "Okay."

Murphy glanced toward the cashier cages. They were on the opposite side of the gaming floor from the exit. He estimated a full minute to walk over there, another minute to walk back. Maybe she could grab her purse in another minute. Three-minute delay. Tops.

"Let's go." He'd seen an open pathway between the slot machines and set off at a brisk pace, practically dragging Nina along with him. She stumbled and then stepped quickly to match his long strides, like a child being towed behind by an angry father.

Murphy moved as quickly as he could without drawing undue attention. Walking between the slot machines shielded him from Hammer's gaze, should Hammer try to come after him.

They reached the locked entrance to the cashier's cages without difficulty. He rapped hard on the door. One of the cashiers Murphy didn't know called from inside, "I'm coming! Keep your shirt on!"

He glanced swiftly in all directions, tapping an impatient foot on the carpet, while he waited.

Nina said, "Mellie! It's Nina. Open up."

"I'm not allowed to let you in here, Nina. You gave me orders. Nobody comes in while we're handling the money during a tournament," the woman said.

"Oh for crap's sake," Murphy said under his breath, running a palm over his face in frustration. He gave Nina's arm a jerk

328 | DIANE CAPRI

and shot a sharp frown toward her. "Get the damn purse now or we're leaving without it."

Nina said, "I forgot my purse, Mellie. Can you just hand it out to me?"

A few seconds later, Mellie slid the deadbolt, opened the door slightly, and peered through the crack. When she saw Nina, she thrust an arm through the opening, holding out Nina's purse.

"Thanks, Mellie," she said as she grabbed her bag and Mellie pulled the door closed.

Murphy heard Mellie slam the deadbolt home again. "Let's go. We've got to hurry."

He grabbed her hand and hurried back through the slot machines on the gaming floor.

Nina held the purse close to her body and stumbled along behind him.

He strode quickly toward the exit, Nina in tow, while scanning the room to be sure Hammer was not close by.

They reached the front exit just as a busload of tourists stumbled through. He stood to one side, still grasping Nina's hand until the throng thinned. Then he pushed his way past the stragglers, dragging Nina with him.

When he reached the outside, he kept going. The quiet was almost deafening outside the overwhelming noise of the casino.

Nina was breathing hard, struggling to keep pace.

"I can't do it. I can't go now. Go without me. Pick me up in the morning, like we planned," she whined, pulling him back.

"Come on, Nina. Hurry up. I can't carry you. We've got to make it to the car before Hammer sees us," Murphy said, yanking her forward.

She stumbled and fell forward down the stairs. She landed face-first on Murphy's back, pushing him off-balance.

To right himself, he was forced to release her hand.

She snatched her arm back, regained her balance, and ran wildly into the night, still clutching that damn purse.

Which was the first time he wondered what the hell she had inside the purse that was so damned important.

CHAPTER FORTY-FOUR

Thursday, May 12
Carter's Crossing, Mississippi
10:05 p.m.

GREYSON LED THE WAY, around the end of the bar, toward
the restrooms into a narrow hallway in the very back of the
building. Opposite the restrooms was an emergency exit door.
Signs posted around it warned that the door would lock
automatically when it closed behind them.

Kim pushed the bar across the door, causing it to unlatch and
open into the night air. On the other side were a small platform
and three steps that led to a stained and cracked sidewalk nestled
deep in the mud. A surprising number of weeds struggled to
grow up through the cracks.

She turned her head for a quick scan in all directions. The
area around the back exit was brightly lit by floodlights on tall
poles. On the left side of the platform, the sidewalk led to a row
of dumpsters across the back of the property. On the right, the
broken concrete pavers led around the building.

Kim hustled down the steps and headed toward the parking lot.

The others caught up quickly. They were halfway to the corner of the building when she heard the heavy door close solidly behind Greyson, the last man out.

"Where are we going?" Hammer asked, striding beside Perry, and already puffing hard. It took a lot of energy to move such a bulky man at a swift pace. Kim marveled at his lung capacity.

Briefly, she wondered how much surface he'd need to stop his momentum.

"There's only one big parking lot that runs all the way across the front," Greyson said, trotting up from behind to catch them. He gestured as he explained. "Employees have reserved spots on the other end of the building. If Murphy and Nina are still here, we'll find them out there."

Kim came around the corner of the building first. The massive expanse of black pavement stretched ahead in all directions, greater than a football field. She paused until all four men caught up with her, sweeping her gaze across the rows and rows of vehicles in all shapes and sizes.

A wide driveway ran along the front of the building. The ribbon of asphalt flowed beneath a broad portico that covered the valet stand and the steps leading to the front entrance. Vehicles drove through, stopping briefly to collect or drop off passengers.

More vehicles were arriving from the road out front, driving along the rows, stopping at the valet stand, or simply moving through.

People who had parked in the lot were walking along the drive lanes between vehicles, headed into or out of the casino.

Here and there, she caught a quick glimpse of a golf cart, running guests to and from their vehicles.

Kim twisted her head and, finally, her body, to scan the entire lot. She didn't see Murphy and Nina from this vantage point. Her view was obstructed by pedestrians, the portico, and the rows of parked vehicles.

She was tall enough to see over the tops of the small sedans, but SUVs, trucks, campers, and buses blocked her view. Looking across the lot from here was a waste of time.

"I'll run over to the valet stand and ask if anyone saw Murphy and Nina leave. If not, I'll search the center lanes," Kim said. "You guys want to split up and take the rest of the lot?"

"Be careful," Hammer said. "Everybody's armed, right? Situations like this can get real ugly, real fast."

Perry was the youngest and fittest of the three men. "I'll take the far right end, and check out the employee section, too. It's possible they're headed for Nina's vehicle instead of Murphy's," he said and ran off in that direction before the others could argue.

Hammer said, "I'll take the middle left quadrant and then move on to help Perry. Greyson, if you'll take the far left."

While they sorted themselves out, Kim ran toward the valet stand. Following two dozen steps behind Perry, she watched for Murphy and Nina, peering down the parking lanes as she crossed.

She was barely winded when she reached the valet stand. She slid in between groups waiting to drop off and pick up vehicles. A woman was collecting claim checks and money and punching tickets to give the runners. Kim waited for a break in her line of customers before she approached.

The woman looked up, smiled, and reached out an empty palm. "Do you have your claim ticket?"

Kim shook her head and replied, "I'm looking for Nina Cloud. Have you seen her in the last few minutes?"

"Nina?" The woman frowned, crinkling her brown eyes as if she wasn't sure how she should reply.

"Randy sent me to find her," Kim said, making it up as she went along because the last thing she needed to do was start a panic by flashing her badge. "She was headed this way. Did you see her?"

The mention of Randy Cloud's name seemed to solve the woman's problem. "Oh, sure. Well, I think I saw Nina leaving with General Murphy."

"Which way did they go?" Kim asked, glancing around the lot again. She had no idea what kind of vehicle Nina drove, so she said, "Did they head for Nina's car?"

The guy Kim had stepped in front of had lost his patience. "Lady. For cripe's sake. We need to get home. Can't you just call your friend on her cell phone, like a normal person?"

"I'll be right with you, sir," the cashier said before she looked at Kim again and pointed two aisles over. "I think I saw General Murphy walking up aisle four when he came in. You might try that one."

"Thank you," Kim said, turning toward the scowling impatient patron. "She's all yours."

She trotted toward aisle four while fishing her cell phone out of her pocket. She pressed the redial button on her last call to Greyson. He picked up right away. "The valet says Nina and Murphy might be headed down aisle four. I'm on my way there now. Tell the others," Kim said. "I'll call you back if I find them."

"Same here," he said and disconnected.

Kim dropped her cell phone into her pocket and picked up

her pace, dodging people and weaving between vehicles as they came and went.

The parking lot was well lit except for the shadows cast by the vehicles and the people. Visibility was good enough to identify her prey from about a hundred feet.

Kim jogged past two more aisles, turning her head to look down them quickly. She didn't see Murphy or Nina immediately, so she kept going.

When she reached aisle four, she turned to jog toward the opposite end, looking at each vehicle as she passed. Parked SUVs and trucks were pulling in and out on each side of the aisle. A few times, she'd seen couples in the front seats, but none were Murphy and Nina.

The farther she moved from the casino entrance, the quieter the night became while the noises dissipated on the open air.

Kim heard snippets of conversation now and then from all sides. A few arguments and angry tones, but mostly people were laughing about their wins and losses as they made their way along.

The roar of vehicle engines as they started up and rolled past in both directions became more distinct to her ears.

She'd trotted halfway down aisle four when she heard a woman somewhere ahead scream, "Leave me alone!"

Kim had spoken only briefly to Nina inside the crowded casino, but the pitch and timbre of the screamer's voice seemed familiar.

Several vans and large pickup trucks were parked between the screamer and Kim. She couldn't see what was happening on the other side.

"Leave me alone, I said!" the woman screamed again. This time, the command was followed by a gunshot.

Kim broke out into a full run, weaving between vehicles for cover, headed toward the voice, drawing her own weapon as she went.

She didn't slow down to contact Greyson or the others. She figured they'd have heard the gunshot and be on the way.

Up ahead on the right, a full-sized RV camper was parked, it's nose protruding into the aisle. Kim slowed as she moved up closer to the engine block.

Over her own heartbeat pounding in her ears, she heard the woman arguing with a man somewhere on the other side of the RV.

"I said, get in the car!" he growled angrily.

"And I said no," she replied.

From this short distance, Kim recognized the voices. Murphy and Nina.

But she couldn't see them. Not yet.

Kim placed her back to the RV's front quarter panel and looked around the parking lot. She didn't see Perry, Hammer, or Greyson coming to back her up.

"I'm not going with you. I'm going home. I'll be ready in the morning. Like we planned," Nina said at a more normal volume. She was angry, but she was also crying.

Nothing worse than a domestic dispute with guns in a parking lot.

As Hammer had said, this could end badly. Very badly. Domestic disputes too often did.

Kim crouched low and poked her head out to look around the nose of the RV. Murphy and Nina were standing near the Jaguar.

Nina was crying. She'd dropped her purse on the ground. In one hand, she held a small pistol.

Murphy stood nearby, maybe ten feet away. He had both

hands up, palms out as if to show he took her threats seriously. And maybe he was.

"Nina, come on," he said, calmly, trying to settle her emotions, too. "What are you doing here? Please just get in the car. We'll go to your place, get your stuff, and then go."

"What about Redland and Hern, huh? Are we just going to leave them behind? That's not what we planned. We're all leaving tomorrow. At dawn. In the helo. That's what we planned. That's what we're doing," Nina said, still crying, snot running down her nose and tears streaming from her eyes.

The pistol hung loosely in her limp hand. She waved it around when she talked.

"I told you. We can't do that now. We have to go tonight. Redland and Hern will catch up. Don't worry about them. They've survived plenty of missions more dangerous than this. They'll be okay," Murphy continued to coax her, edging closer.

"No. I'm not going until tomorrow. That's the end of it." Nina raised the gun and pointed it directly at his chest as if she might shoot him where he stood.

Kim stepped out into the lamplight, weapon ready. "Put the gun down, Nina. I don't want to shoot you. But I will. And from this distance, I won't miss."

Murphy saw her first.

Nina faltered. She swiveled her head to glance over her shoulder toward Kim's voice.

Seeing his chance, Murphy rushed Nina and knocked the pistol out of her hand. It fell onto the pavement and skidded under the Jaguar.

He grabbed Nina around the torso, pinning her arms to her sides. Then he spun on his heel and shoved her into the passenger seat of his Jaguar and slammed the door.

"Murphy! Stop! FBI!" Kim yelled, holding her weapon, prepared to shoot.

He ran around the back of his vehicle, crouching low behind the Jaguar.

Before she had the chance, he raised his own weapon and fired toward her.

Two quick shots, both went wide. Maybe he'd aimed wide, or maybe he was a bad shot. It didn't matter. She returned fire and took cover.

While she was out of range, he opened his door and jumped behind the wheel. He fired up the engine and threw the transmission into reverse.

She ran toward the Jaguar. She was ten feet away when he slammed the accelerator and the Jaguar bucked backward out of the parking space.

He slapped the transmission into drive and sped forward.

Shooting the driver at this point wasn't safe. Too much potential for collateral damage.

Kim pulled her cell phone out and hit the redial for Perry. She stood watching the Jaguar's retreating bumper for a few seconds.

"On my way. Coming in behind you," he said before she had a chance to say anything at all. "Hammer and Greyson should already be there."

She swiveled her body quickly to check the aisles in the immediate area. Which was when she saw Hammer seated on the ground.

Greyson stooped down next to him with a first aid kit. Greyson's vehicle was parked in the next aisle, lights flashing, and the door was open.

A small crowd of onlookers had already gathered to gawk.

Kim kept her eye on the retreating Jaguar and jogged over to help. "What happened?"

"Murphy shot me." Hammer's left bicep was bleeding profusely, even as he covered it with his right palm and applied pressure. He was breathing rapidly and he looked pale. Probably shock. Maybe too much blood loss.

Greyson tore open a big gauge bandage and handed it to Hammer, as he opened a roll of tape. "Put this on the wound."

Perry drove up beside them and pushed the passenger door open. "Jump in!"

Greyson said, "I've called an ambulance and backup. Go ahead. I'll catch up as soon as I have Hammer under control."

"Copy that." Kim dove into the passenger seat.

Pedestrians in aisle four noticed the flashing lights and meandered through the parked vehicles, heading to see whatever was happening.

Perry was forced to slow enough to avoid the pedestrians. He weaved around them, moving forward slowly, giving Kim enough time to fasten her seatbelt.

"What happened?" Perry asked.

She gave him the quick facts. "I thought his two shots were aimed at me and went wide. But maybe he was trying to hit Hammer."

Perry said, "Did you hit Murphy?"

Kim replied, "He moved pretty quickly, both before and after my shot. I didn't have a visual the whole time."

Perry glanced quickly across the cabin. "Which means what? You hit him or you didn't?"

"Odds are heavily in my favor. But I can't definitively confirm."

When he cleared the last of the pedestrians in the row, he

340 | Diane Capri

raced as fast as he dared across the bottom of the parking lot toward the exit.

He turned onto the long driveway and accelerated toward the road.

At the intersection, he said, "Which way?"

They both peered through the windows, looking for Murphy's retreating taillights.

Kim pointed. "There! Turn left. He's heading north, away from Carter's Crossing."

While Perry drove across the bumpy pavement in hot pursuit, she hung onto the handle overhead and stared, sweeping her gaze across the landscape. The last thing they needed was another vehicle coming across the road at a high rate of speed.

But she kept the Jaguar's taillights in her line of sight at all times.

CHAPTER FORTY-FIVE

Thursday, May 12
Carter's Crossing, Mississippi
10:35 p.m.

MURPHY KEPT HIS FOOT on the accelerator, putting as much distance between him and the SUV as possible while he navigated through the casino's busy parking lot.

He floored the accelerator when he made it to the long driveway. At the road, he turned left, away from Carter's Crossing. He planned to take the backroads to his safe house.

Once he turned off the main road, five miles ahead, he'd reach the cover of the trees. Night shadows and unfamiliar terrain would slow his pursuers down.

The main road was one of the worst in Carter County. With all the money the damn casino was making, they could have paid to fix the road. It was old and dotted with the kind of small sinkholes that the locals had been pressuring the mayor to fix.

The Jaguar bounced in and out of one pothole after another, slowing progress and jarring his body all the way to his teeth.

His left leg throbbed with every hard bounce. He'd taken a grazing bullet from Otto's gun along the outside of his left thigh. No big arteries along there, so the wound was not fatal. But it hurt like hell and distracted his focus.

"What are you doing? Where are we going?" Nina kept sniveling and shouting out from the passenger seat.

He'd told her to be quiet several times. She'd ignored him. He'd tried to tune her out. But she kept breaking his concentration.

"Let me out of this car! I don't want to go with you!" she screamed at deafening decibels.

"Nina, I'm warning you," he said in the stern tone that had sent many soldiers ducking for cover.

"I want out!" Nina screamed.

He couldn't take another moment of her nonsense.

He lifted his right hand off the steering wheel.

Briefly.

Just long enough to backhand her a solid blow across the mouth. Hard enough to loosen a few of her teeth to prove he was serious.

"Shut. Up," he demanded, grabbing the steering wheel again. "I need to think. I can't do it with your hysteria filling the entire cabin."

Whether he'd startled her into submission or she'd finally managed to control herself, he didn't know.

He didn't care much, either.

Her silence was exactly what he needed. If she started that crap up again, he'd be justified in delivering a more permanent solution.

While he'd had his right hand off the wheel, the Jaguar had drifted slightly and bounced through another deep pothole.

"Dammit," he said, gritting his teeth.

Blood oozed from his leg. He felt it soaking his pants, running down to his socks and into his shoes.

He ignored the pain. He'd suffered worse in combat and street fights. He'd lived a long and violent life. He had the scars to prove it.

This wasn't the first time he'd been shot and it wouldn't be the last.

The more distance he put between the casino and the Jaguar, the less traffic he met on the main road. There were few streetlights out this far from town.

He stole a glance at the odometer. He was close. He peered into the darkness, looking for the dirt road where he could turn west and make his way through the backroads to his safe house.

The turnoff was on the left side of the road. There were tall weeds on both sides. You'd have to know it was there, or you'd miss it driving past at a reasonable speed.

He could lose them back in the woods. Failing that, at least he'd have the cover and the advantage of familiar surroundings.

He slowed and turned on the high beams, watching through the dirty windshield for the narrow turnoff.

"If you're looking for Moab Road, you've got another couple of miles to go," Nina said, more reasonably than she'd said anything in the past hour. "There's a sharp curve and then a big oak tree on the right, about twenty feet before the turnoff."

Murphy remembered both the curve and the oak tree after she mentioned it. He'd seen the oak several times in daylight. It had been hit by lightning years ago and the big old trunk was split straight down the middle.

He sped up again, watching for the curve and the oak tree.

He saw it illuminated in the high beams about half a mile

ahead. He turned off the headlights and hurried around the curve to get out of sight of the SUV.

He waited until the very last minute to slow down.

Murphy slammed the brakes hard and turned, running across the grates over the culvert and then deeper into the cover of the woods onto Moab Road.

The old gravel roadway hadn't been graded in years. It had washed out in several places. Driving over it was like riding off-road across rocky terrain.

The Jaguar didn't have the suspension for such conditions.

Nina held onto the overhead handle. She whimpered off and on as if in pain. He didn't care.

He'd slowed to barely moving, using the headlights to his best advantage, but it was rough going. Ten miles of this and he'd turn onto better travel conditions for the remaining miles.

For now, he winced with every bounce and kept moving.

CHAPTER FORTY-SIX

Thursday, May 12
Carter's Crossing, Mississippi
10:50 p.m.

KIM CONTINUED TO WATCH Murphy's Jaguar while she pulled out her cell phone and called Gaspar. After three rings, he hadn't picked up, which was unusual. She let the call keep ringing another dozen times before she admitted defeat and disconnected.

Perry's full attention was on the road and the vehicle ahead. He'd increased his speed as much as he'd dared, given the road conditions. But Murphy had a significant head start and knew the roads. Perry didn't.

The distance between them widened.

"Check the GPS. See if you can figure out where we are and where he might be going," he said when she hung up the phone.

She flipped the GPS on and while it scanned for a signal, she tried Gaspar again. Once more, he didn't answer.

The GPS finally located itself. A map came on the screen

showing the county road they were driving. There was no name or number on the map. The road ran parallel to Carter's Crossing's Main Street and the railroad tracks, toward Tennessee to the north and deeper into Mississippi on the southbound side. No crossroads showed up nearby.

Kim hit the redial on her phone to call Sheriff Greyson. When he picked up, she put the call on speaker.

"Where are you?" he asked.

"Looks like we're traveling on one of your worst county roads. We're moving about forty miles an hour between one big pothole and the next. GPS says we're north of the casino. East of Carter's Crossing," Kim replied. "Any clue where Murphy might be headed?"

Greyson said, "There's nothing out that way to interest him that I can think of. He must be planning to double back toward town at some point. He could be headed to Kelham. Maybe planning to enter from the north side. There's an old, unused gate over there."

"Unless he has a breakdown of some kind, we're never going to catch him on this road. He had too much of a head start. Where's the next road that crosses this one and comes back west?" Perry asked.

"About fifty miles or so north. You might ask Deveraux. She knows this county like the back of her hand. Could be a backroad of some kind that I'm not aware of," Greyson replied. "Meanwhile, I'll send someone out to Kelham to watch for him. And I'll get somebody out to Nina's place, too. Just in case they head over there."

"How's Hammer?" Perry asked, keeping his attention focused on Murphy's bouncing taillights in the distance.

"He's on his way to the hospital. Tough SOB thinks he's a

Marine or something. He refused to ride in the ambulance. Insisted on driving himself," Greyson said.

"Did he make it over to the hospital?" Kim asked.

"He'll be okay. Too pig-headed to be anything else," Greyson said. "One thing you need to know. Redland and Hern are not on base. Hammer called the MPs. They checked. Redland and Hern are still AWOL."

Kim nodded. "Which means they're actually in the morgue like we thought. Had to be them we found dead out at the barn."

Greyson sounded tired and weary. "That's a solid bet. The coroner has sent off the dental records to the army, with Hammer's name to expedite the request. We should get something back soon."

"The army never does anything soon, Greyson," Perry said, swerving to miss a big pothole in the roadway.

The SUV caught the edge of it and bounced like a basketball. Perry's head hit the roof. Kim was tossed up as far as her seatbelt would stretch and slammed back down into the seat.

When they'd both landed on their seats again, Murphy's vehicle had disappeared.

"What the hell?" Perry said, speeding up while he scanned the road and both shoulders, looking for the Jaguar.

Greyson said, "What's going on?"

"We lost Murphy," Kim said. "Big curve in the road ahead. He's on the other side. Or he might have turned his lights off. It's damn dark out here."

"Could be an ambush," Greyson warned. "Hammer says Murphy thinks fast on his feet, so expect him to do something crazy if he feels cornered. If he killed Redland and Hern, he won't care about adding two more notches in his gun."

Kim said, "In the parking lot back there at the casino. When he and Nina were arguing about leaving. She wanted to wait until tomorrow. Murphy said they were going tonight. Can you ask Hammer if he has any idea where Murphy was supposed to go tomorrow at dawn when Kelham is slated to close up?"

Perry said, eyes straight ahead, straining to see Murphy's vehicle, "Find out how he was planning to get out of there, too. Kelham has an airstrip. The CO should have bug-out plans in place. It's the army. There will be records."

"Yeah. I'll ask him and call you back," Greyson said before he rang off.

Perry found a stretch of good pavement and sped up to close the gap behind Murphy.

When they rounded the curve, the road ahead was empty as far as the eye could see.

No taillights of any kind.

No oncoming headlights, either.

Nothing but acres of land and a few trees on either side of the road and a big old oak tree on the right side of the tree, its trunk split down the middle.

Kim checked the GPS. "According to this map, the road goes straight for another five miles before it turns back to the left. But I don't see a crossing road at all."

Perry slowed down, peering into the night through the windshield. He flipped on the high beams. "Keep your eyes open and your weapon ready. If Murphy pulled off somewhere intending to ambush us, we'll know shortly."

They drove miles beyond the big curve in the road. Murphy's Jaguar had disappeared. Perry turned around and drove over the same stretch of pavement twice more.

No Murphy.

No evidence of where he'd gone, either.

Kim said, "He must have turned off onto a side road somewhere. We're not going to find it out here in the dark. Let's head back to Carter's Crossing and follow through from there."

Perry turned the SUV around once more. "Let's just take one more pass. He's turned off somewhere. That's the only answer. We should be able to find it."

Kim's phone rang. It was Gaspar.

"Sorry. I didn't hear your call. What's up, Suzy Wong?"

"Can you ping this phone?"

"Yep. Got you on the screen already. You're in a vehicle, headed south. Looks like a county road," he said.

"Exactly. We're chasing a guy and we lost him. He was driving a Jaguar. Can you see it on your systems?"

"Eh, I'm not some sort of super geek, Otto. I've got equipment and skills. But I'm not psychic," he said.

"Right. There's nothing much out here as far as the naked eye can see. Just look for the second signal. That model Jaguar should have a GPS. You should be able to ping it," she said, listening to Gaspar's keys clacking on his keyboard.

After a few moments, he came back. "Okay. Maybe. Looks like he could be on a dirt two-track or something like that. Extrapolating from his position now, I'd say the entrance is about a hundred yards in front of you, on your right."

Perry slowed down even more and Kim rolled down the window to peer into the darkness. All she saw were tall weeds along the shoulder.

Until Perry was right up on the turnoff.

"Wait. Stop. It looks like the weeds are tamped down right there. Could have been done by Murphy's vehicle, I guess," she said.

"You want to try driving through there?" Perry asked, with dubious enthusiasm.

"Waste of time," Gaspar said. "He's moving slow, but he's got a solid head start. I'll watch. You go back toward Carter's Crossing. I can lead you to him along better roads."

"Sounds like a plan," Kim replied, as Perry steered the SUV southward toward the casino and then west into town. "Leave the line open and talk to me, Chico. Tell me what you see."

"Copy that," he said, as was his habit. "Any Reacher sightings down there I need to be aware of?"

"No such luck." Kim paused to consider the question.

Had she seen Reacher? Maybe. A few times, she'd thought so. Then again, she couldn't say for sure.

She shook her head inside the darkened SUV.

Perhaps not.

CHAPTER FORTY-SEVEN

Thursday, May 12
Carter's Crossing, Mississippi
11:05 p.m.

MURPHY AND NINA BUMPED along the abandoned Moab
Road for a while before he turned the headlights on again.
Progress was slow.

Nina had stopped blubbering. She sat in total silence, belted
into her seat for a while. Eventually, she said, "Where are we
going?"

"First, to my safe house. Then, to Memphis. We'll catch a
private flight from there to Mexico, as we planned," he replied.

"I don't have my clothes. Or any of my things," Nina
whined. Everything that came out of her mouth made him itch to
slap her again.

He clenched his teeth and kept his hands on the wheel, partly
to control the urge. "We have plenty of money. You can buy new
things."

"What about my keepsakes? My heirlooms? I have artifacts

from the tribe that I've loved all my life," she said, continuing to grate on his last nerve.

The muscles in his jaw worked as he inhaled deeply. He could kill her now. Leave her out here in this field. No one would find her until he was long gone.

Two things stopped him. The extra time it would cost to kill her and dump the body was a minor issue.

The bigger problem was the baby. If she was pregnant, the fetus would share his DNA. Right now, he might still get away without detection. The child's DNA would paint a bulls-eye on his back. Randy Cloud would never give up until Murphy was hunted down like a dog.

Which wasn't the way he'd planned to spend his golden years. Not even close.

"Nina, please. For the love of all things holy, just be quiet," he said with all the menace he felt toward her. "Otherwise, I'll shut you up myself."

Something about his tone or the situation finally soaked through to her. She moved as far away from him as she could get inside the cabin.

But she stopped sniveling.

And she didn't say another word.

The GPS unit in the Jaguar had been blinking on and off for the last two miles. When it came back on again, the signal strength was strong enough to keep the screen awake. He saw the county road he was looking for two miles ahead.

This one ran east and west, skirting the south side of Kelham, north of Carter's Crossing and east of the train tracks.

As he approached the intersection, he turned the Jaguar's headlights off again. He slowed to walking speed and crept toward the road.

Tall weeds concealed the connection here, too. He craned his neck to look hard in both directions.

He saw no oncoming headlights or vehicles of any kind. Country folks and military folks had long ago tucked in for the night. This wasn't a route to the casino. There was no reason to be out here on the road at all. And no one was.

He pushed the accelerator to increase speed and crossed the culvert onto the seldom traveled county road. He turned west and headed toward Carter's Crossing.

This road was better than the other one and it was used by more traffic. On the north side of Carter's Crossing, it ran parallel to US 72 almost all the way to Memphis.

They consumed the miles in silence until he reached the turnoff for the back way toward his safe house.

Murphy drove carefully, watching for anything out of the ordinary.

Running into Hammer at the casino had been bad luck. Hammer would discover that Redmond and Hern were not on base if he hadn't already.

Then Greyson would connect the missing soldiers to the bodies in the barn.

Not much solid police work later, Greyson and Hammer would connect Murphy to the dead soldiers.

All of which was a shame. He'd hoped to disappear after completing the closure at Kelham, his final assignment for the army he'd served more than half his life.

He couldn't do that now.

He needed to be out of the country before dawn. At dawn, he'd be missed at Kelham. He had to be gone before then.

Murphy never spent time thinking about what might have happened if things were different. If Jasper had died in the crash.

If Nina hadn't told Bonnie about Pak. If Price hadn't confronted him in that alley.

If this, then that.

Speculating was a total waste of time and resources.

Soldiers had died engaging in such foolishness.

Murphy always played the hand he'd been dealt. Smarter that way.

Right now, that meant reaching the hearse and then completing the drive to Memphis. After that, the flight to Mexico.

He turned onto the dirt road that ran parallel to the railroad tracks, across from the one-sided street. He could see the lights on inside at Brennan's. He glanced at the clock on the dashboard. It was well after eleven. The train would be passing soon.

Murphy turned into his driveway.

A new structural crack had appeared on the approach in the short time he'd been gone. Not surprising. They were all over this area. They seemed to get worse every time the train went past. One of the reasons the safe house was so cheap.

This one was larger than usual.

He'd heard about sinkholes opening up and swallowing whole neighborhoods. Something like that could happen here. In twenty minutes, he wouldn't even care. Solve some remaining issues he couldn't get done now, if it happened. But he'd never been that lucky in his life.

He drove the Jaguar over the wide, uneven gravel and around behind the garage and parked.

Some of the tension drained from his body. They'd made it this far.

So far, so good.

He shut off the engine and sat for a moment in silence.

"Come on, Nina. I'm sorry. I didn't mean to be so harsh. You know I love you. I was stressed. That's all." Then he inhaled deeply and said more gently as he touched her arm, "Let's get inside. We've got twenty minutes, tops. Then, we're on the road to Memphis."

"I know. I love you, too." Nina's posture softened, and she wiped her eyes and unlatched her seatbelt. "I bought some things for the baby. They're back at my place. I wanted to take them with us."

Murphy leaned across to plant a quick kiss on her cheek. "I promise you can buy more stuff for the baby. As much stuff as you want. But we have to go. Now."

"I didn't think you cared about the baby," Nina said, glassy tears welling in her eyes.

"Of course, I care," he replied, holding his anger at bay.

"It's just…I was pregnant once before. I never told you. It was fifteen years ago. The father was the CO at Kelham back then. And he…died. I lost the baby—" she was crying now, silently. "I-I never really got over it."

"I'm so sorry," he said, reaching out to hug her awkwardly across the console. "I didn't know. Everything will work out better this time. I promise."

He gave her one last squeeze and then opened her door. "Let's go now, okay?"

She nodded, climbing out of the seat, and then stood near the Jaguar in the darkness while he came around from his side.

He draped his arms over her shoulders and led her into the house. "Watch your step here," he said, gripping her arm to make sure she didn't fall.

Once inside, he gave her a little pat on the butt and said,

356 | D<small>IANE</small> C<small>APRI</small>

"You go grab a shower while I put a few things together. Ten minutes. No more."

He hurried into the study to open the safe. He pulled the remaining contents, including the forged passports and three currencies, as well as the flask containing the poison. He planned to administer it to Nina when they reached Mexico. Like Pak, it wouldn't kill her right away. But the Rohypnol would keep her docile long enough for him to ditch her and board the plane to Fiji.

Murphy dumped the last of the cash into a black leather duffle and zipped it closed.

He found the second duffle, a brown canvas one, in the closet where he'd left it last week.

He glanced at the clock on his desk and compared the time to the digital readout on the timer.

Scheduling the explosion to match the midnight train was pure genius. He grinned. The blast might damage the train. It would definitely bring everyone running. They'd all be busy.

Guaranteed cover for his escape in the lumbering old hearse.

Showered and dressed, Nina came into the den. She looked and smelled amazing. What a shame.

"I'm excited about Fiji. The baby's going to love it there." She sidled up in front of him and gave him a long, slow kiss. "Ready?"

"Yep," he replied. "Meet me in the kitchen. I'll be right there."

She gave him a seductive glance from the doorway. He smiled as if overwhelmed with lust.

After she'd gone, he pushed the start button on the timer.

He picked up the black duffle and hurried to join her in the kitchen.

Murphy grabbed Nina's hand and led her through the back door into the muggy night.

At the garage, he punched in the code. The big door rolled up, revealing the hearse parked inside.

Nina turned for one last look at the little house. Wistfully, she said, "We spent so many happy hours here."

Murphy heard the midnight train in the distance, coming up the tracks. "Come on, Nina. We've got to go. Jump in."

CHAPTER FORTY-EIGHT

Thursday, May 12
Carter's Crossing, Mississippi
11:35 p.m.

PERRY RETRACED THEIR ROUTE, which led them back to
the casino and then on toward Carter's Crossing.

While they relocated, Kim kept Gaspar on the line. "Still
have Murphy's GPS signal?"

"It comes and goes. The good news is there's two cell
phones in the Jaguar. They're not all winking out
simultaneously," Gaspar replied.

"How long before you can triangulate a solid interception
point?" Kim asked once she could see the outskirts of Carter's
Crossing ahead.

"He's driving along the dirt road on the other side of the
tracks from Brannan's," Gaspar said. "Possible he's headed
home. There's a few small frame houses in that area."

"Yeah. I saw the houses myself. I know where that is," Kim
replied.

Gaspar's tone was preoccupied while he worked. "Satellite images show about six homes widely spaced. Hundred years ago, there may have been more. The area has been gentrified somewhat since then."

Immediately before the railroad crossing, Perry turned right onto the dirt road that ran parallel to the train tracks and the one-sided street. Kim spotted Brannan's in the distance. The lights were on inside and McKinney's red pickup was parked out front.

The street and the neighborhood were quiet. There were no lights on in any of the houses that she could see from the road. Kim glanced at the digital clock on the dashboard. 11:46 p.m.

"Looks like you won't have to go far to check out the midnight train," she said to Perry. "It'll be coming through here shortly. You don't want to be anywhere near those tracks when it thunders past."

Gaspar said, "Murphy's GPS signal just stopped. I've got stronger signals on the two cell phones now. Looks like the Jaguar has parked behind a garage. Murphy and Nina have left the vehicle and moved into the house. You're almost there."

He rattled off the address, which wasn't very helpful because Kim couldn't read any of the addresses in the dark.

Illumination along the wrong side of the tracks was poor. Streetlights were widely spaced at each end of the road. There was no moonlight.

Kim said to Gaspar, "Call Greyson. Tell him where we are and why we're here."

"Copy that," he replied with a grin in his voice. "Be right back."

Nothing seemed to faze the guy. Why should it?

He was sitting in front of a computer screen with a cup of java instead of waiting to ambush a killer. At times like this, she was sharply reminded how much she needed a new partner at the scene in addition to the one on the phone.

Perry drove slowly along the street. He turned off the headlights and lowered all four windows as they approached the house where Gaspar believed Murphy and Nina were inside.

"Pull over. We'll go the rest of the way on foot," Kim said.

Perry parked on the shoulder and they left the SUV as quietly as possible.

Weapons ready, Kim crouched low and stayed in the shadows. She hurried toward the house. On the way, she saw lights on in several rooms.

The shades were drawn and she saw no silhouettes inside.

From this vantage point, it was impossible to locate Murphy and Nina precisely. The air was warm and muggy, which made it difficult to breathe. Dewy perspiration formed above her lips and across her forehead.

Kim heard a door close around the back of the house. She paused to listen.

She heard voices, probably Murphy and Nina, but she couldn't make out the words. Then, she heard the unmistakable sound of an electric door opener lifting a heavy garage door. At the top, the door clicked into place.

Silently, Perry came up next to her. "You heard that?"

"Yeah. We've got to catch them now or they'll be gone again." Kim whispered back.

She felt the ground shake. Just a mild, constant tremor at first. Like a distant earthquake.

She looked southward down the train tracks. She saw a tiny pinpoint of light in the distance. The midnight train's single headlight was coming on fast.

The tremors deepened as the train approached.

Kim stood well away from the tracks, but she knew that the distance wasn't enough. She'd feel the ground tremble, and the wind wash over her when the train sped past. The rumbling would continue for what felt like a long time after the train was already gone.

"Come on," she said, leading the way.

Carefully and as fast as possible, they hurried around the house, eyes scanning the area, but focused on reaching the garage before Murphy and Nina escaped again.

Kim noticed the wide crevice in the driveway a brief instant before Perry tripped, stumbled, and fell forward. He landed hard on his left side and grunted.

Murphy was standing at the open garage door, preparing to toss two duffles into the hearse.

He heard the noise Perry made when he fell. Perhaps he felt the oncoming train, too.

He flipped around to spy Perry sprawled across the gaping ditch in the gravel.

Murphy shoved Nina farther into the open maw of the garage.

Nina lost her footing and slammed hard against the hearse. She screamed with shock and pain.

"Get in the car!" Murphy called out a moment before he raised his weapon and fired toward Perry.

Kim stopped to help Perry climb out of the trench. When he was upright, she returned fire while Perry scrambled along the ground for cover.

She heard Murphy yell out when one of her shots hit him in the belly.

He went down. But he didn't stop.

From the garage floor, Murphy fired again and again.

He couldn't see his targets, but he wasted his ammo firing in their general direction anyway.

The midnight train rumbled ever closer. The whistle blew loud and long in the distance. The lights and bells at the crossing began to clang.

The ground shook harder and longer than ever before. The train kept coming, louder, and harder.

Suddenly, the train was right on top of the tracks behind them. The noise and the wind and the shaking consumed and battered everything around them.

Just as the train's engine rumbled past, the ground shook so hard that Kim bounced up and down whole inches, almost knocking them both over this time.

On the last bounce, the earth gave way.

The trench separated into a wide maw of gaping darkness. Two feet. Five feet. Ten.

As it gaped, the land on the other side, where Murphy and Nina were inside the garage, began to sink.

Murphy continued to fire as the garage and the land on which it sat sunk lower and lower into the massive pit.

Both Kim and Perry shot back, running backward, seeking safety from the disappearing earth.

After the locomotive, the endless sequence of rail cars hammered past, squealing metal hurtling north with speed and momentum and massive weight.

The train scarred the very air as well as the earth and everything remotely close to it. The crevice that Perry had tripped over opened wider and wider.

The domino effect. One thing after another.

The hole widened and deepened.

The front of the garage fell into the hole.

Murphy and the hearse, and whatever was inside it, sank into the hole with the garage.

The hearse rolled backward and landed on Murphy. His screams could barely be heard over the deafening noise.

Then the back of the garage came down.

As the hole grew bigger and bigger, the garage continued falling, crumbling, and breaking apart from the surrounding earth.

The cement sidewalk crumbled into the hole.

Kim reached out to grab Perry. He tossed his arm over her shoulder and they scrambled away from the widening sinkhole as the train cars continued to thunder past.

Just as they cleared the edges of the hole, running toward the SUV, the train's caboose thundered past.

Kim's breath came in quick, short bursts. Perry limped badly, moving as fast as he could.

The SUV was ten feet ahead.

They were almost there.

"Come on, Perry. You can do this," Kim shouted over the monstrous noise. They kept going.

A moment later, Murphy's house exploded.

The house burst into a million tiny pieces, launching like missiles through the air.

The first blast was quickly followed by smaller explosions when the gas line broke and parts of the house ignited.

Flames shot up, illuminating the night, shining a big spotlight on the length and breadth of the giant sinkhole into which the entire garage had disappeared, taking everything inside along with it.

Bits and pieces of the house and dirt and gravel rained down on them all the way to the SUV as they ran.

Kim hurried to settle herself behind the wheel and pushed the button to start the engine.

Perry limped quickly and arranged himself in the passenger seat. He was hurting, but she had no time to help with that now.

Before he'd closed the door, Kim accelerated backward and sped south to the crossroads while debris of various kinds pelted the SUV.

She executed a three-point turn and floored the accelerator to move east of the train tracks, the explosions, and the sinkhole as fast as possible.

When the SUV was far enough away, she stopped.

The flying debris stopped, too. But everything flammable in the house and the garage was burning.

She and Perry got out of the SUV and stared at the destruction.

The train was long gone. She saw the flashing lights on the caboose in the distance.

Within moments, the fire sirens sounded in Carter's Crossing.

For the second time in less than twenty-four hours, the fire trucks rushed to the scene of a massive fire.

From her vantage point, now that the train was gone, Kim looked across the one-sided street on her left. The McKinneys, all four of them, stood on the cracked sidewalk outside Brannan's. They stared at Murphy's destroyed house and the sinkhole that swallowed his garage and the land around it, mouths agape.

As the fire department arrived, Greyson, lights flashing and sirens blaring, drove in. He parked alongside the road near where Kim and Perry stood.

When he got out and walked over to join them, Kim glanced his way.

She noticed a life-sized lump on the ground nearby, off the shoulder of the road. She trotted over and knelt down.

Nina Cloud was huddled into a tiny ball, face blackened with soot, hair and eyes wild. Obvious signs of shock. Clammy, chills, rapid heart rate. But still alive.

CHAPTER FORTY-NINE

Friday, May 13
Carter's Crossing, Mississippi
9:35 a.m.

THE NEXT MORNING, Kim awakened like a drunk after a
three-day bender. Her phone had pinged with a message from the
Boss at five o'clock. She was booked on a flight out of
Memphis. *No objections entertained.*

She'd slept another hour, then dragged herself out of bed and
into the shower.

Her secure hot spot connected with a strong signal, and she
had no idea what conditions would be like later in the day.
She'd taken the time to complete her reports and upload them
to her server. Paying her insurance premium, once again. She'd
mainlined two pots of strong, black coffee in the process.

Downstairs, she'd checked out and said goodbye to the
Toussaint's desk clerk, who was filling in for Janine Wood
this morning. Janine was over at the hospital with Nina Cloud,

the woman said. Nina and Janine had been friends from birth. Their mothers were sisters.

Kim smiled and said, "Small towns."

The desk clerk agreed. "Everybody around here knows each other somehow."

She had phone calls to make, but she could do that on the long drive back to the Memphis airport.

Checked out and packed up, she stowed her bags in the SUV.

She tried calling Sheriff Greyson. The calls went straight to voicemail. He was still working the crime scene. Or he'd gone to bed and dropped into immediate oblivion. He had to be exhausted.

She drove along Main Street one last time, resisting the urge to return to the scene of last night's disaster. The best way to help Greyson now was to stay out of the way. If he needed anything from her, he knew to call.

Libby's Diner was open for breakfast. She'd agreed to meet Mayor Deveraux, so she parked out front and went inside.

Deveraux was seated at the same table where Kim had last seen her. But this time, she wasn't alone.

Libby was perched in the seat next to her like a bird expecting to fly at any moment. Kim joined them and filled the waiting plastic mug with Libby's good coffee.

"I really didn't know what to think about you when you came in that first time," Libby said, glancing at Kim briefly. "Everything about Bonnie was still so raw then, you know?"

Kim nodded. She had pieced several things together after last night. Some of which she should have realized sooner. "Bonnie was involved in passing the counterfeits out at the casino. You knew that, didn't you?"

"Bonnie never could keep any kind of secret." Libby stared

down at the table and fidgeted with the sugar packets. "She didn't deserve to die for that. Nina was involved and she's one of the managers. Bonnie figured it was okay because Nina participated, too."

"Makes sense, I guess."

"Bonnie didn't do much. She switched some of the fake bills for real ones, now and then. She only worked part-time, after all," Libby said, still staring at the table, shaking her head miserably. "She made a big mistake. She crossed the wrong guy at the wrong time. No way she would've seen that coming. Bonnie always led with her heart. And everybody liked that about her. Just never thought she'd get killed for it."

Deveraux patted Libby's hand. "Bonnie was a good person. Everyone will miss her."

Libby cleared her throat and stood up. "What can I get you both for breakfast? Belgian waffles and fruit are good today."

"I'll have that," Deveraux said.

"Make it two," Kim added.

"Coming right up." Libby trudged toward the kitchen, moving slower than she had a couple of days ago. They watched until she pushed the swinging door open and disappeared into the kitchen.

"Is she okay?" Kim asked.

Deveraux replied, "She will be. It'll take a while, but she'll get there."

"Have you talked to Greyson?"

"All the time. I went out to the site this morning. I've never seen so much destruction from a sinkhole around here before," Deveraux said, shaking her head like the issue weighed heaviest on the mayor's shoulders.

"What do you think caused it?"

"Like I said before, we've had a lot of little sinkholes around here for the past few years. Then we had that larger one show up near the train. Now this. I've been talking to experts about the problem for weeks. Truth is, they don't always know. In a few days, they'll come in and check everything out. Take soil samples and the like." She paused for a deep breath and shrugged. "We really don't know. Might never know. It was probably a combination of unstable underground caves in the area and two hundred years of that train pounding along the tracks like it does. That'd be my guess."

"I've heard about sinkholes that swallowed buildings and killed people before. But I'd never seen it with my own eyes," Kim said quietly, still marveling at the power of crumbling earth. "For a while there, I thought Perry and I might end up at the bottom of that hole along with Murphy and Nina."

Deveraux nodded. "Nina was lucky. I stopped off to see her at the hospital this morning."

"How is she feeling?" Kim asked.

"Guilty."

Kim raised her eyebrows. "She feels responsible for Bonnie's death?"

"She *is* responsible for Bonnie's death. And a lot more besides. Nina has always been unflinchingly honest in her self-assessments."

"You like her, then?"

"The casino is a big part of the business community here. I'm the mayor. Not only have I known Nina personally for years, but I also work with her quite a bit. Randy, too. So does Greyson." Deveraux shook her head and seemed to have more on her mind. "It's hard to wrap my head around all of this, you know?"

Kim nodded. "It's a lot to take in."

"Trusting people is hard, isn't it? They so often let us down," Deveraux said, cocking her head.

"Yeah," Kim nodded. She knew all about breaches of trust. She'd suffered plenty of betrayals in her lifetime. What had happened with her ex-husband was only one of many soul- crushing experiences in her personal life and her professional life, too.

Libby brought the waffles piled high with fruit and whipped cream. She set them on the table and retreated once again.

Kim ate a few bites of the waffle, watching as Deveraux attacked hers with gusto. She looked up and smiled with whipped cream all over her mouth like a kid. The woman certainly knew how to eat.

Deveraux took a break after a few bites. She had more to say. "Greyson interviewed Nina at the scene last night."

"I figured he might have. What did she say?"

"She was pretty messed up. But she confessed that she was in New York with Murphy at the dog fight."

"That's not much of a confession. It's obviously her on the videos, once you see it."

"Everything is obvious once you know it," Deveraux nodded. "Nina says she gave Pak the drink from the flask, but she claims she didn't know it was poisoned."

"You believe that?" Kim asked.

Deveraux shrugged. "Nina said that when Pak died, she freaked out. She admits she told Bonnie about it all. Bonnie threatened to tell Greyson. Murphy found out."

"So Murphy is the one who killed Bonnie," Kim said slowly, putting the timeline together in her head. "Murphy is probably the one who killed Redmond and Hern. Jasper, too. Did Nina admit all of that?"

Deveraux nodded. "Easy enough to blame a man who is already dead. But Greyson says he thinks she's telling the truth."

While Deveraux continued eating, Kim considered the facts with Nina's confessions added in.

Everything made sense. Nina closed it all up and put a neat bow around it all for Greyson. With the army now gone from Kelham, the community would accept that answer gratefully.

Things could go back to what passed for normal in Carter's Crossing.

No reason to keep beating this particular dead horse.

"I'm glad Nina is going to be okay. I didn't know her at all, but she seemed rather fragile to me," Kim finally said.

"Nina's very fragile." Deveraux shook her head, lifting her coffee cup to her lips. "She won't be okay. She has not been okay since Reacher was here the last time."

"What do you mean?" Kim leaned in, feeling like her ears had literally perked up.

Before Deveraux could respond, Perry limped in. He'd been to the hospital. They'd examined him and fitted him up with a surgical boot on his left leg. Cracked ribs had him taking short, shallow breaths, but there was nothing more the doctors could do about those.

"You were talking about Nina Cloud when I came in, weren't you?" He sat, poured coffee. "Far as I'm concerned, Nina is one lucky woman."

"How's that?" Deveraux asked.

"She got out of that sinkhole alive, for starters. I'd say that's pretty damned lucky. Wouldn't you?" Perry said.

"She's not feeling very lucky right at the moment," Deveraux said slowly.

Perry arched his eyebrows and widened his eyes. "Because?"

Deveraux gave Kim a meaningful look before she said, "Nina was pregnant, but she lost the baby last night. Murphy was the father. The last time she was pregnant was fifteen years ago. The CEO at Kelham was the father of that child, and Nina lost her baby then, too."

The little hairs on the back of Kim's neck raised to attention and the butterflies in her stomach jumped around like crazy. "Fifteen years ago? When Reacher was here, you mean?"

Perry's eyes widened even further. "Jack Reacher? He was here back then, and he's here, now, too? He saved Nina twice?"

CHAPTER FIFTY

Friday, May 13
Carter's Crossing, Mississippi
10:05 a.m.

KIM CLEARED HER THROAT. "Hold on there, cowboy. What do you mean Reacher is here now?"

"Nina said a big guy pulled her out of the sinkhole just in time and left her on the side of the road last night. Nobody else around there at the time besides you and me," Perry said. "Who could have done that besides Reacher?"

"She was incoherent when we found her. Babbling all kinds of crazy things." Kim's eyes widened. "She said a big guy, and I assumed she meant Hammer had found her at the last possible minute. Greyson said Hammer drove his own car to the hospital. He could have detoured to Murphy's place. Plucked her literally from the gaping earth and moved on. Right?"

"Are you going to eat that waffle? I'm starving." He grinned, and Kim pushed the plate toward him. He dug in like a man who hadn't eaten in years.

With his mouth full, he said, "I did think it was Hammer at first. Until I asked him about it."

"What did he say?" Kim asked.

"Said he'd like to take credit for rescuing a damsel in distress but remember he got shot in the casino parking lot. So he was at the hospital when it all happened. Not at the sinkhole site at all," Perry said between bites. The waffle was almost gone already. "So I hobbled down the hall to Nina's room and asked her directly. She told me it was Reacher. She knew Reacher from before. He'd helped her that other time somehow, too."

Kim turned to Deveraux. "Did you know about this?"

"Reacher didn't mention it to me." Deveraux nodded, a slight grin lifting her mouth at the corner. "Nina told me this morning."

Kim narrowed her eyes and stared at Deveraux. "So you're saying he's been here in town this whole time? And you knew that and didn't tell me?"

"He asked me to tell you, and I quote, *Mother Nature sure is a bitch, isn't she?*" Deveraux said, with an amused smile. "I think he admires you."

"Where is he now?" Kim demanded, scowling fiercely. When was she going to learn to trust her gut where Reacher was concerned? She *knew* the Boss was expecting Reacher to show up. When she thought she'd seen him, she should have marched right toward him.

Next time, I will. Come hell or high water.

Deveraux shrugged. "The sheriff has been trying to find him. No luck, I'm afraid."

"What was he doing out at Murphy's place last night?"

"I've been thinking about that." Perry cocked his head, "He must have already been there waiting when Murphy and Nina drove back from the casino. We'd have seen him otherwise. Everything happened too fast for him to come after the sinkhole started. Murphy dying was bad luck, as far as Reacher was concerned."

Kim nodded. She knew what Perry meant. Public service homicide, Reacher would have called it.

Either way, Murphy was dead and Reacher was gone. Again. She'd failed to find him.

She wasn't used to failing and she didn't like it. Not even a little bit.

And she wasn't sure how she felt about all that. She'd have plenty of time to think about it on the plane.

She glanced at the clock. It was later than she'd meant to stay. She stood up and tossed two twenties on the table.

"Sorry. Say goodbye to Libby for me, will you? I've got a plane to catch."

"Drop by any time you're in the area," Deveraux said.

Kim said she would.

Deveraux and Perry turned back to breakfast.

As she walked out of the diner, she noticed again that the sky was clear and blue, and there was no wind to speak of. Both the driving and the flying should be easy. Kim made her way out to the SUV and drove toward US 72.

The sun's glare on the asphalt was almost blinding, even with her aviators covering her eyes. Traffic was heavier than she'd expected. There were a lot of long-haul truckers on the road, which was nerve-wracking.

She kept her grip on the steering wheel and paused the cruise control to slow her speed. The trip to the airport would take longer than planned. Nothing she could do to speed things up.

About thirty miles west of Carter's Crossing, she caught a

glimpse of a hitchhiker ahead in the distance. Something about his size, his stance, tickled her instincts.

She hadn't slept well or long enough. Maybe she was being too fanciful. But he'd been in Carter's Crossing, and he was on his way somewhere else. For sure.

A pickup truck had pulled over onto the shoulder ahead of the man, and he'd climbed into the passenger seat and the vehicle was already rolling again.

She'd only seen him for a minute. Two at the most.

Could it be Reacher?

She pushed the accelerator to the floor. The truck wasn't that far ahead. She might catch him if she tried.

Her phone rang. She considered ignoring it, but she'd been trying to call the Boss all morning. So she picked up.

"Today's your lucky day," he said by way of greeting.

"How's that?" she asked.

The truck increased speed and passed another eighteen-wheeler up ahead. She closed the gap between her SUV and the eighteen-wheeler, planning to do the same.

But traffic made it impossible for her to pass.

She dropped back to give herself more stopping distance, should she need it.

The Boss was talking. "You have a new partner. His name is William Burke. He'll meet you at the airport in Rapid City, South Dakota, tonight."

"What? Why am I going to Rapid City, anyway?" She craned her neck and checked her mirrors, anxious for a chance to pass the big rig.

"Closest major airport," the Boss said. "Details in the files I sent you. Download them before you get to Memphis. Read on the plane."

He hung up.

The traffic cleared.

She pressed the accelerator and passed the eighteen-wheeler, fighting the wind like a housefly passing a jetliner.

When her visibility cleared ahead, she saw miles of empty pavement.

The pickup truck and its passenger must have turned off on one of the side roads.

For a moment, she considered going back to search.

But reason prevailed.

She wasn't sure the hitchhiker had been Reacher. And she had no idea where the truck had turned. By the time she found the truck, she'd miss the only flight from Memphis to Rapid City today.

If the Boss was sending her to Rapid City, it was because he thought Reacher was headed there, too. She'd have another chance.

Her phone rang. Gaspar. She picked up the call.

When there's only one choice, it's the right choice.

She continued heading west.

"How can I be of service to you this fine Friday the 13th, Suzy Wong?" he asked with a smile in his voice.

"I hope that's not a bad omen," she replied.

"You haven't walked under any ladders or kicked a black cat, have you?" Gaspar teased.

"No. But it looks like I'm finally getting a new partner tonight. Name's William Burke."

"Seriously?" He snorted and choked on his coffee.

"What's so shocking about that?"

Gaspar controlled his coughing jag and said, "*William Burke*? Same as the infamous serial killer?"

Kim's brain hadn't made the connection until Gaspar mentioned it. Burke's case had been required learning when she was training at Quantico. Burke hadn't been a classic serial killer. He'd had no sexual motive. He was more like a volunteer assassin. The sixteen murders he'd committed were done for profit. He'd sold the corpses to medical research. Right up until the time he was hanged, he'd insisted his actions supported the common good.

"Doubtful. Not unless the old Scot's a ghost. He's been dead almost two hundred years."

Kim nodded, although Gaspar couldn't see her. "Can you check him out for me?"

"Will do."

"Thanks, Chico."

After a brief pause, he said, "Cooper's a snake, Kim. Watch your back."

Kim said nothing and kept her eyes on the road.

She whispered, "Hope for the best. Plan for the worst."

The other big news is Diane Capri—a friend of mine—wrote a book revisiting the events of KILLING FLOOR in Margrave, Georgia. She imagines an FBI team tasked to trace Reacher's current-day whereabouts. They begin by interviewing people who knew him—starting out with Roscoe and Finlay. Check out this review: "Oh heck yes! I am in love with this book. I'm a huge Jack Reacher fan. If you don't know Jack (pun intended!) then get thee to the bookstore/wherever you buy your fix and pick up one of the many Jack Reacher books by Lee Child. Heck, pick up all of them. In particular, read Killing Floor. Then come back and read Don't Know Jack. This story picks up the other from the point of view of Kim and Gaspar, FBI agents assigned to build a file on Jack Reacher. The problem is, as anyone who knows Reacher can attest, he lives completely off the grid. No cell phone, no house, no car...he's not tied down. A pretty daunting task, then, wouldn't you say?

First lines: "Just the facts. And not many of them, either. Jack Reacher's file was too stale and too thin to be credible. No human could be as invisible as Reacher appeared to be, whether he was currently above the ground or under it. Either the file had been sanitized, or Reacher was the most off-the-grid paranoid Kim Otto had ever heard of." Right away, I'm sensing who Kim Otto is and I'm delighted that I know something she doesn't. You see, I DO know Jack. And I know he's not paranoid. Not really. I know why he lives as he does, and I know what kind of man he is. I loved having that over Kim and Gaspar. If you haven't read any Reacher novels, then this will feel like a good, solid story in its own right. If you have…oh if you have, then you, too, will feel like you have a one-up on the FBI. It's a fun feeling!

"Kim and Gaspar are sent to Margrave by a mysterious boss who reminds me of Charlie, in Charlie's Angels. You never see him…you hear him. He never gives them all the facts. So they are left with a big pile of nothing. They end up embroiled in a murder case that seems connected to Reacher somehow, but they can't see how. Suffice to say the efforts to find the murderer and Reacher, and not lose their own heads in the process, makes for an entertaining read.

"I love the way the author handled the entire story. The pacing is dead on (ok another pun intended), the story is full of twists and turns like a Reacher novel would be, but it's another viewpoint of a Reacher story. It's an outside-in approach to Reacher.

"You might be asking, do they find him? Do they finally meet the infamous Jack Reacher?

"Go…read…now…find out!"

Sounds great, right? Check out "Don't Know Jack," and let me know what you think.

So that's it for now…again, thanks for reading THE AFFAIR, and I hope you'll like A WANTED MAN just as much in September.

Lee Child

ABOUT THE AUTHOR

Diane Capri is an award-winning *New York Times, USA Today,* and worldwide bestselling author. She's a recovering lawyer and snowbird who divides her time between Florida and Michigan. An active member of Mystery Writers of America, Author's Guild, International Thriller Writers, Alliance of Independent Authors, and Sisters in Crime, she loves to hear from readers and is hard at work on her next novel.

Please connect with her online:

http://www.DianeCapri.com

Twitter: http://twitter.com/@DianeCapri

Facebook: http://www.facebook.com/Diane.Capri1

http://www.facebook.com/DianeCapriBooks